WELLS AND WANDERERS

- AMORITES -

LIGHT OF NATIONS
BOOK ONE

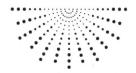

CHRISTINE DILLON

LINKS IN THE CHAIN PRESS

www.storytellerchristine.com

Plagues and Papyrus - Egyptians (Light of Nations #2)

Cover Design: Lankshear Design

Cover Photo: Amanda Silva/Unsplash.

ISBN: 9780645354799

*A **FRIEND** LOVES AT ALL TIMES, AND A (SISTER) IS BORN FOR A TIME OF ADVERSITY.*
PROVERBS 17:17

With grateful thanks to friends who have been like sisters to me. You've taught me so much as you've walked alongside me. Sometimes you've needed to rebuke me but you've also prayed for me, and cheered me on. Naomi, the two Lisa's, Joy, Carey, Elizabeth, Julie, Jenny - thank you to all of you. You have been some of God's many gifts to me.

I will make you as a light for the nations,
that my salvation may reach to the ends of the earth.

Isaiah 49:6b (ESV)

I will make you into a great nation, and I will bless you ... and
all peoples on earth will be blessed through you.

Genesis 12:2-3 (NIV)

LIST OF CHARACTER AND PLACE NAMES

Fictional Characters

Inanna - Amorite girl, the younger twin sister of Utu. Children of Mamre and Attar.

Utu - twin brother of Inanna.

Mamre - Chieftain of Kiriath Arba (Hebron). Father of Utu and Inanna.

Attar - mother of Utu and Inanna.

Job - close friend of Utu's.

Biblical Characters (found in Genesis 12-25)

I have chosen to use more Hebraic-anglicised versions of the familiar names. This helps us approach the story with different eyes and hopefully makes the biblical parts, feel less familiar.

Avram/Avraham - (more familiar in English as Abram/Abraham) from Ur, via Harran. Married to Sarai and a wanderer in Babylon, Mesopotamia, among the tribes of Canaan, and even as far as Egypt.

Sarai/Sara - Avraham's wife.

Lot - Avraham's nephew. Married with two daughters. He moved to live in Sodom.

Hagar - Egyptian slave of Sara. She becomes Avraham's second wife.

Yishmael (Ishmael) - son born to Avraham and Hagar.

Yitzchak (Isaac) - Avraham and Sara's son.

Rivka (Rebekah) - Yitzchak's wife.

Eliezer - head steward for Avraham. Initially from Damascus and the father of Jemimah (fictional) in this story.

Abimelech - a Philistine chieftain in the region of Beersheba. He becomes a friend of Avraham.

Place Names:

* **Oaks of Mamre** - a planting of oak trees outside the walls of Kiriath Arba (Hebron). Probably named after Mamre, the chieftain of the town.

* **Ur** - Avraham and Sara's original home. A city in Mesopotamia between the Tigris and Euphrates rivers. Modern day Iraq.

* **Beer Lahai Roi** - named by Hagar when an angel of the Lord speaks to her. Yitzchak later moves to live in this area around the time of his marriage.

* **Cave of Machpelah** in the field of Ephron - the place that Avraham and Sara are buried and the first piece of land that Avraham owns in Canaan. It is outside Kiriath Arba where he spent many years.

PROLOGUE

Kiriath Arba (Hebron), Canaan

About 1900 B.C.E.

Inanna could still hear her mother exhale with deep disappointment as she said for the umpteenth time, "It isn't seemly for a girl."

A great number of things weren't seemly for girls. Running, whistling, being too noisy, ruffled clothing, a head covering that slipped. Mama sighed over her every day.

Inanna envied Utu, her twin brother. He was not bound by these restrictions. Utu's life could have been one vast round of climbing trees and exploring, but he preferred to help with their father's herds and talk to the older men. Inanna couldn't understand why he wasted his freedom.

Mama repeatedly told her not to climb trees and play with the boys, which was exactly what Inanna most wanted to do. All she wanted was to be free. Free of the restrictions put on girls. Free of the restrictions she saw her mother and her friends laboring under. Free like the eagles she spent hours watching as they cruised in the skies far above their home.

"Utu, I think we got mixed up in the womb. I'd make a better boy and you'd make a better girl."

"Perhaps." He looked at her with that irritating way of his.

Sometimes she wanted to shake him. But not today. Today she wanted to climb the oak trees outside the town gates.

"Don't go outside the gates," he said. "You know Mama wanted you to help her with the washing, down at the river."

Inanna rolled her eyes. "Washing isn't how I want to spend the day."

She ran toward the trees. As she ran, she heard Utu's exasperated groan as he battled with whether to let her face their mother's wrath alone or to keep her in his sight. After only the briefest pause, his footsteps pounded after her.

Reaching the bottom of her favorite tree, she looked back towards him. "Help me."

"When are you ever going to accept who you are?" he muttered as he made a cradle with his hands.

"Maybe never," she said, putting her bare foot in his hands and stretching for the lowest branch. Utu boosted her into the tree, and she scrambled up.

Utu shook his head at her, then shrugged and jumped for the lowest branch. She winked at him. No matter how many times he admonished her, he always followed her, never wanting to leave her on her own in case she got into worse trouble. Trouble was something she naturally seemed to land in, but Utu was always there for her. He said he had an internal warning system when she needed him.

Inanna climbed higher up in the tree, reveling in the rough bark underfoot and the way the sunlight danced on the leaves and dappled the ground below with shadows.

She'd just begun to imagine herself standing on the prow of a ship, something she'd never seen but planned to one day, when the frantic thumping of a drum pulsed through the air.

"Raiders!" Utu said, scrambling upright from the branch he'd been sitting on.

The women at the river were already running up the hill, having abandoned their baskets in their haste. They didn't scream. They just ran. This was the fourth raid this year.

Utu almost fell in his haste to descend the tree.

"There's no time, Utu." Inanna's words tumbled over each other. "We'll have to stay here."

Utu looked up at her, eyes wide. There were too many branches to negotiate below him, and a long sprint to the town gate.

The raiders would be on camels. Swift and silent. Able to get close before they were spotted by the watchmen on the city walls.

Inanna frantically looked around for the densest foliage of the tree and inched her way forwards, trying not to shake the branches and give away their position.

"Ammuru, protect us," she whispered under her breath.

She found a branch she could straddle, which was more hidden than other parts of the tree. Then she bent over, trying to make herself as small and comfortable as possible. Who knew how long they'd have to be up here?

A wail rent the air. Through a chink in the branches, she saw the first in the line of raiders scoop up a child who'd not been able to keep up. *Ammuru, curse them.* These raiders were becoming a summer menace worse than locusts or famine.

The beating of the drum stopped abruptly, and the familiar creak of their town's main gate being slammed shut cut off any other options. By now, Mama would be scouring the frantic crowd inside the gate, wondering if she and Utu had gone out. Not knowing if they'd made it back inside the safety of the city walls.

Inanna squeezed her eyes shut. If they got out of this, she'd stick closer to home. At least, until she grew tired of the restrictions and had to stretch her wings again.

A rough voice yelled something to the raiders, and two of them came towards their grove of trees. The men didn't bother to keep quiet.

3

The crunch of leaves and twigs came nearer and nearer. Inanna concentrated on breathing silent, shallow breaths. *Don't move a muscle.*

The pungent smell of camel filled her nostrils, but she didn't open her eyes even a crack. If she couldn't see him, perhaps he wouldn't notice her.

A camel let out a waterfall of urine. The raiders were close. Too close. With a loud belch, the camel moved on, and Inanna released a shaky breath.

They were safe. The raiders were moving off and leaving a tense silence behind them.

Achoo.

Utu's sneeze erupted into the newly quiet glade and determined their future.

The raider turned around with a curse and soon came to glare up at them. "You up there," he said in a heavy accent. "Come down, and it will be easier for you."

Inanna never was one to make things easy.

CHAPTER ONE

Egypt
Three years later

"*P* sst."

Inanna nearly dropped the heavy basket of washing that she'd come to spread out on sun-warmed stones. She looked around. Utu was half hidden behind a bigger rock. They seldom saw each other because Utu attended to Pharaoh's animals, while Inanna was indoors doing the household duties she'd always despised.

Checking over her shoulder, Inanna drifted towards Utu while still spreading out the clothes. Her supervisor was strict and seemed to have a godlike ability to sense when any of the slaves stopped working.

"Have you heard?" Utu whispered.

"Heard what?"

"Pharaoh's taking another concubine."

"So? That's hardly news." Inanna continued with the laundry, laying out another item of clothing and making sure it was flat. Pharaoh had so many women in his household that he probably didn't know most of their names.

"Yes, but I've been given to the woman's brother as part of the deal," Utu said.

Inanna dropped a tunic on the ground. "No!" she said, her throat tight. She might not see Utu much, and sometimes he annoyed her, but knowing he was nearby made captivity easier.

He hadn't talked to her for days after they were captured. Too angry, she'd guessed, but the long journey with the slavers had allowed him time to get over it.

"I don't think I'm leaving immediately. They've come from Canaan because of famine."

Her breath caught in her throat. Famine? What if Mama and Papa were struggling? "How serious?"

"Serious enough for the master to come here. They've been here a while. Not here, but somewhere out there." He waved his hand vaguely towards the north, then glanced around to check that they still hadn't been spotted. "Someone saw his sister and told Pharaoh about her."

Inanna shuddered. "Poor girl."

"She's no youngster." He backed away. "Someone's coming."

Fear tingled through her. Inanna immediately turned her back on her brother, picked up her now-empty basket, and headed towards the warren of buildings behind the palace. She and Utu had long ago mastered the skill of brief conversation.

* * *

"*Y*ou've taken a long time. I've been looking for you everywhere," Inanna's supervisor said. "No one can understand Pharaoh's new concubine. Maybe you speak her language." She thrust a clean tunic into Inanna's arms. "Wash up, change, and come with me."

Inanna's stomach fluttered. She'd never been anywhere of importance in the palace complex. She hurried towards the large water jars and dipped a ladle in to fill a smaller basin.

Within minutes, she was dressed in the rough linen shift. Being one of Pharaoh's slaves had two main benefits—better food, and clothing. Slaves of poorer masters often worked without any clothes at all.

Inanna followed her supervisor along the corridor, turning right, then left, and then up a flight of stairs. After another long corridor, she was ushered into a much brighter room full of women. In the center of the room, a woman was immersed up to her chin in a bath. The cloying scent of some sort of flower came from the bath. She was probably in the beautifying process readying her to spend the night with Pharaoh. Not that the woman needed much beautifying.

The woman could have been thirty but the eyes that looked back at Inanna were much older. Older and sadder and more afraid. When would men like Pharaoh ever learn that women didn't necessarily dance with delight to be chosen? Some women just wanted to be left alone. Alone to be themselves. Alone to be at peace. Not having to run at someone's beck and call all day. Maybe this woman only wanted freedom. Inanna's heart clenched with pity.

"Well, speak to her, girl," her supervisor said harshly. "We haven't got all day. Use one of your Canaanite tongues and see if she understands."

Inanna spoke a few words of Jebusite. There was no flicker of recognition in the woman's eyes. Inanna switched to Hittite, but that didn't work either. Maybe this new concubine wasn't from Canaan after all. Inanna switched to one of the common trade languages in their region. "Are you a Canaanite?"

"I'm no Canaanite," the woman in the bath said, her tongue slow with the words. "I'm originally from Ur, between the Rivers."

Inanna blinked. Perhaps this woman's language was closer to Amorite then. Her ancestors claimed they were originally from between the mighty Tigris and Euphrates.

"I'm Inanna," she said in her mother tongue.

The woman's eyes focused. "The goddess of heaven, love, and war. That's a grand name for a slave."

7

Inanna gave a wry smile. "I wasn't always a slave." A wave of home-sickness for her mother and her old life as a tribal chieftain's daughter washed over her. She might have been one of many children, but her father had often bounced her on his knee and said she was the one most like him.

"I'm Sarai."

Inanna's supervisor tugged her arm. "What is she saying?"

Inanna reported the woman's name and where she was from.

"Can you tell me what will happen to me?" Sarai interrupted.

Inanna hesitated. Who was she to say anything? Yet, for some reason, this woman's plight already tugged at Inanna's heart. Maybe it was just because she was someone with whom Inanna could speak her own language. When she'd arrived in Egypt, she'd been miserable with no one to communicate with. She'd been beaten regularly and called "stupid." Stupid was the first Egyptian word she'd learned, but she'd made sure it wasn't the last.

"There's usually a week of beauty treatments. Then you go to Pharaoh."

"Not long then," Sarai muttered.

Some women would have been delighted to be chosen by Pharaoh. An occasional night of duty in exchange for a life of privilege. Several of the slaves in the household had caught Pharaoh's wandering eye and been happy to leave slavery behind. Inanna shivered. Thank goodness she was plain enough to escape notice. She had no intention of exchanging one form of slavery for another. She might seem settled to her fellow slaves, but somehow she was going to get home. Home to Mama and Papa. Home to all that was familiar.

She'd failed on her two escape attempts while she and Utu were still in Canaan. Once they'd reached the desert, she'd had to give up. Even she could see there was no point in escaping only to die of thirst within a few days.

"Is your brother intending to go back to Canaan?" Inanna asked Sarai, a dull pain in her stomach. She'd lost too much. She didn't want to lose Utu as well.

Sarai swallowed and a tear leaked out of her eye. "He'll go back whenever he hears the famine is over ..."

Then both of them would be separated from their brothers. Well, not if Inanna could help it. She had to get close to this group of people. Somehow. Close enough to be able to leave with them and not be discovered. Inanna didn't have the faintest hint of a plan, but she'd be alert to opportunities.

"I'll leave you here as you're the only one who can speak this woman's outlandish language," Inanna's supervisor said, then nodded to the perfumer. "Make yourself useful while I find someone else to do the washing and cleaning."

Inanna wasn't sure if she was happy or not. She hated inside duties and lived for any moments outside in the fresh air. Assisting in making Sarai more beautiful wouldn't be much fun, but maybe she could find out something useful.

Once the room was empty apart from themselves, the perfumer motioned for Sarai to get out of the bath.

Sarai stood to her feet, the water cascading off her body.

"Here, girl," the perfumer said, throwing Inanna a cloth.

Inanna tentatively rubbed Sarai's back.

"Don't rub, pat," the perfumer said with a snort.

Inanna apologized and followed the instructions. Once she'd dried Sarai off, the perfumer made Sarai lie down. She spread out a selection of containers, presumably each containing some sort of lotion or other.

The perfumer looked up at Inanna. "Now watch what I do and try to do the same."

The woman emphasized the word "try," implying that Inanna was unlikely to succeed. Inanna clenched her teeth and watched how the woman held her hands and smoothed the lotion on with long strokes.

Inanna took some of the lotion and spread it on Sarai's skin.

"Not so much at once," the perfumer said, her voice harsh. "That ointment costs more than you are worth."

Inanna bit her lip to keep in the words she wanted to say. She spread the lotion, striving to follow the perfumer's technique, and kept her eyes down. This was too close to Sarai. Too intimate with someone she'd only just met.

"Her skin certainly needed this," the perfumer said.

"Well, she's crossed a desert to get here."

The same desert Utu and Inanna had had to walk across, tied on a rope behind a camel. The raiders had said it was her own fault for attempting to run away. She'd made her first escape attempt only a day after their capture. She hadn't even made it to the outskirts of the camp before turning back, because she couldn't bear to leave her brother behind, whether he was angry or not. The second time she'd been smarter and told Utu she was going. Utu had predicted the escape would fail, but he wouldn't let her go on her own. They'd actually managed a brief time of freedom before the raiders had recaptured them. They'd beaten her that time but not enough to mark her, just enough to ensure she didn't try again. She'd been thankful she and Utu had been sold to the same household once they'd arrived in Egypt —not that they'd seen much of each other.

"Ask her why she's crying," the perfumer said, nudging Inanna with her toe.

Inanna had been too busy with her own memories to hear the subdued sobs. She asked Sarai the question but softened it. The poor woman obviously wasn't thrilled to be here.

"We thought we were far enough away from the capital to be safe," Sarai said, with a hiccup.

Inanna translated the answer.

The perfumer snorted. "No one is safe from Pharaoh. He has spies in the farthest reaches of his kingdom." She smoothed on more lotion. "Pharaoh would have been concerned about the influx of refugees fleeing Canaan's famine."

And pharaohs had to be constantly alert to protect their throne. Would Inanna's own family be among the refugees? Probably not. Leaving an area almost guaranteed someone else moving in. Her father, Mamre, and the other clan heads would try everything they could to survive, but they'd have to be even more alert for the desert raiders taking advantage of the situation.

The two women continued the task in front of them. Once it was finished, the perfumer packed up her containers and placed them in a basket. "Go to the kitchen and find Hagar and ask her for a meal for myself and Sarai."

Inanna scrambled to her feet. She'd have to grab something along the way. Even though she'd spent half the day here, she was still considered far too lowly to eat with the perfumer.

CHAPTER TWO

*U*tu emptied the animal skin of water into the stone trough at his feet, then went back to the well and dropped the water bag on its long rope down the well. Once it was filled with water, he began to haul it to the surface. Twice a day, five of them hauled water for Avram's vast flocks and herds.

He'd been part of Avram's camp for six sunsets already. After tomorrow, he'd be rotated on to another duty. Eliezer, his master's steward, had told all the new slaves that they'd keep changing duties until he decided where each person was best fitted.

In Pharaoh's household, he'd simply done what he was told. As one of the younger slaves, he'd worked at the jobs no one else wanted. He wrinkled his nose. Far too much dealing with human excrement and filth. He much preferred working with animals.

A week earlier, Eliezer had met all the slaves being transferred from Pharaoh's household, told them what was expected, and sent them off to start work.

The water drawers settled into the rhythm of dropping the skins in the water with a plop, allowing them to fill, then hauling them to the surface, before pouring the water into the troughs angled out from the center point of the well. Each shepherd brought their part of the flock in, then departed towards that day's pastures.

Even after a week here, it was obvious Eliezer managed the camp and the five hundred people who lived there like an army. Everyone had their place and knew precisely what was expected of them.

Three summers of slavery had made Utu tough, but his back and hands were on fire before this job was even half finished. As his water bag reached the surface, he snatched a handful of water. It flowed down his parched throat, and he took another few mouthfuls. In Pharaoh's household, he would have already been scolded for even such a short break, but here the men were encouraged to take breaks. It was enough to make someone sing, and sometimes the men did. Songs of praise to a creator god. Not a god he was familiar with. There'd been no mention of Baal or Ammuru or Asherah.

Utu dropped the water bag down the well. Was Inanna alright? Utu hadn't seen her in a week. Oh, he missed her. They'd been inseparable the first nine years of their life. She always led him into scrapes, but he always scrambled after her and tried to protect her from the worst of her impulsiveness. He'd been angry with her after their capture, but he hadn't been angry for long. What was the point? It wasn't as if she'd intended for them to be captured. If he'd held on to his anger, he'd have harmed himself as much as her.

How many beatings had she endured in Pharaoh's household? She'd never mentioned any. Maybe she'd learned to curb her tongue and wandering feet. Maybe, but he doubted it. Stormy winds were not easily tamed.

Once the flocks were finally watered, one of the shepherds came over. Together, they checked each animal's feet and general condition before releasing them into the pastures. Pharaoh had given them many new animals and access to precious pastures along the Nile. Beyond the watered plains near the Nile, it was desert. Utu shivered. He still remembered the desert crossings with the raiders. The vastness of the sands and rocks had been terrifying. The worst had been the two sandstorms they'd endured. Both had been blinding, choking, howling masses of sand that blasted every bit of exposed skin and left them breathless. The raiders had scoffed at his fears and told him those were small sandstorms. Inanna might dream of returning to Canaan, but the thought of crossing the desert again was enough to deter him. How ironic and devastating it would be if he returned to Canaan with Avram and Inanna was left behind.

Utu's stomach rumbled.

"Sounds like time to eat," the shepherd said with a grin.

The shepherd, Utu, and Job, another boy his age, found a spot under the shade of a sycamore fig tree. The shepherd unwrapped a cloth containing three barley loaves. There was olive oil to dip the bread in, and curds and dried raisins. The first figs would be ripe enough to harvest within a few weeks, and they'd dry as many as possible and store them ready for future use.

As Utu munched, he looked up into the tree. Would Inanna still want to climb any tree she saw? Probably, although there was no opportunity in Egypt and their last tree-climbing experience might make her think twice.

"Who are you thinking of?" the shepherd asked.

"How do you know I'm thinking of someone?" Utu asked.

"I often see that look on people's faces as we remember those left behind."

The man was perceptive. "My twin sister is a slave in the palace." He'd been surprised how little he missed the rest of their family. Of course he missed his mother, but his father had never taken much notice of him. There were too many older half-brothers clamoring for Papa's attention.

The shepherd raised an eyebrow. "So you weren't too happy to be given to Avram?"

Utu shook his head. "Not at first. I prefer working for Avram, but not if it means leaving my sister. I've always prayed for us to stay together."

"Well, make sure you're praying to the right god," the shepherd chuckled. "I wasted a lot of time praying to the wrong ones."

"What do you mean?" Utu asked.

"I worshiped the gods of Ur, especially the moon god. I thought they were real, but in the end, everything was taken from me, and they did nothing."

Utu said nothing even though his mind churned with questions. Could he probe more deeply with someone he'd just met? Questions hadn't been welcomed in Pharaoh's household.

"My mother died, then my two sisters," the shepherd continued. "No matter how many sacrifices we made, they made no difference. Eventually I decided I wouldn't serve the gods of my ancestors any longer."

The shepherd stared at the ants carrying the crumbs from their lunch. He sighed. "I was angry for a long time." He drank a mouthful of water from their shared waterskin, the sound of his swallow loud in the somnolent heat. "Angry enough to leave Ur with Avram and Sarai and their father. There was nothing to stay for. Once I abandoned my gods, it was easier to leave."

"Where did you go from there?"

"We meandered northwest at the pace of the sheep, sticking to the edges of the Euphrates River until we arrived in Harran. We stayed there for a good long time. That slow trip helped me somehow, in here." He tapped his chest. "I find looking after sheep relaxing. All they need is water and food and protection."

Utu couldn't see the attraction, but maybe quietness meant something to a grieving man.

Job had been listening intently but saying nothing. Now he asked, "When did you come south to Canaan?"

"Well, it's a story you might well describe as crazy." The man looked across at Utu and Job and raised an eyebrow.

Who didn't love stories? "Go ahead, tell us." Utu leaned back and crossed his hands behind his head. Overhead, puffy clouds moved like sheep across the sky.

The shepherd stretched out his legs. "The major move came when Avram was already seventy-five."

"He doesn't look anywhere near that age." Utu might have guessed fifty, but the master seemed ageless.

"He's over eighty now." The shepherd swatted at a fly. "Let me see if I can remember the story. Avram used to tell us often, whenever we complained about leaving Harran." He closed his eyes. "His god came and said to him, 'Leave your country, your people, and your father's household, and go to the land I will show you.'"

"Did this god tell him where to go?" Utu asked.

The shepherd opened his eyes. "Do you want to hear this story or not?"

Utu nodded.

"Avram's god told him, 'I will make you into a great nation and I will bless you.'" The words came out as a sort of chant. "'I will make your name great, and you will be a blessing. I will bless those who bless you and whoever curses you, I will curse, and all peoples on earth will be blessed through you.'" The shepherd paused and looked across at Utu and Job.

"And?" Job asked.

"And that was it. We packed up and left."

Utu looked at the shepherd, a frown furrowing his brow. "He just left his father behind?"

"Yes, he left everyone behind except Sarai and his nephew, Lot."

"And what was this god's name?" Job asked.

"I don't know. He certainly was not one of the gods of Ur. Avram did say their family had stories from their ancestors about the god who created the whole earth and everything in it, but when I first knew Avram, he still worshiped the gods of Ur."

"And how did this god appear to Avram?" Utu battled to keep the doubt out of his voice. Only priests claimed to communicate with the gods, and even they never claimed they'd actually seen one.

The shepherd shrugged. "I don't know. I think it was just a voice, but the words were clear."

"He wasn't ... you know?" Utu said, imitating drinking.

"Drunk, you mean?" The shepherd shook his head. "And Avram isn't the fanciful type."

From what Utu had seen, Avram seemed well in control of everything in the camp. He even knew most of their names. Utu had never been called by name in Pharaoh's household.

"Then where did you go?" Job asked.

"Slowly south, at a sheep's pace." The shepherd glanced around the flock with a practiced eye. All was peaceful. "We eventually reached the great tree of Moreh at Shechem. Avram said his god appeared to him, but he hasn't ever told us what his god said." He shrugged. "Seems reluctant."

"Maybe it wasn't good news."

"I don't think so. This god has always seemed to make good promises to Avram. Avram made an altar at Moreh and praised his god. Later, when we moved near Bethel, he made another altar." The shepherd swept his arm around to indicate all the flocks. "We have too many animals to stay anywhere for more than a few weeks. Once the grass gets scarce, we move on."

"What happened to his wife?" Utu asked. There had been no sign of a wife or children, only his nephew, Lot, whom Utu had mistakenly thought was Avram's son until one of the other shepherds had put him right.

The shepherd surged to his feet without answering and flapped his arms as an eagle soared too close. There were still a few smaller lambs that would make a nice meal for a hungry eagle.

What had happened to Avram's wife? It would have to be a question for another day.

CHAPTER THREE

"*I*nanna, the perfumer wants to see you in her room," a messenger called as she scurried past, already intent on her next task.

Inanna had been sitting outside Sarai's door, wondering why the usually punctual perfumer hadn't arrived.

Inanna searched the corridors, having to ask directions several times, until she reached the perfumer's area, a combined living quarters and workshop. She hesitated at the doorway and then called out a greeting. Inside, the woman groaned, which Inanna took as an invitation to enter.

The workshop was a mass of shelves lined with clay jars. The air was pungent with a multitude of scents, scents Inanna was beginning to recognize after a week of this new work. Bunches of dried herbs hung from every possible place.

Another groan from the back room propelled Inanna forward. Pushing aside the curtain, she peered into the room behind. The perfumer lay on the sleeping platform clutching her stomach.

"You'll have to finish the treatment," the woman muttered from between clenched teeth. "I can't possibly work today."

Odd. She was the third person Inanna had seen this morning with the same symptoms. Maybe they'd eaten something that disagreed with them.

"I put all the ingredients in the basket on the bench." The perfumer broke off with a groan. Her skin was pale with red blotches, and a film of sweat stretched across her forehead. Inanna took a step back. She didn't want to catch whatever had struck the woman down.

Another groan. "You know what to do."

And Inanna did. They'd been doing the same thing for five days already. First, a warm scented bath, then a whole-body massage with beautifying lotions. She could do the lotion application, but she didn't know anything about the contents of the lotions. That sort of information was secret, handed down from mother to daughter. And no Egyptian was going to share their secrets with a foreigner.

* * *

Sarai looked up as Inanna entered her room. Once again, she was up to her neck in a warm bath. Despite the warmth, she was pale and serious.

"Are you feeling well?" Inanna said, putting down the heavily laden basket.

"As well as can be expected in the circumstances," Sarai said.

"Lucky you. Lots of people are sick," the water carrier said.

So it wasn't just the perfumer and the few Inanna had seen. "How many?"

The water carrier pursed her lips. "Some of the cooks and most of the water carriers. A few of the men who work the fans to keep Pharaoh cool, half the counselors, a good number of the priests …"

"And all with the same symptoms?" Inanna asked.

"Vomiting, fevers, sweats, and boils in painful places." The water carrier dropped her voice to a whisper. "People are asking if it's a curse."

Sarai moved so abruptly that the bath water slopped over onto the floor. "Curse? What kind of curse?"

"They're saying someone must have done something to anger the

19

gods." The water carrier whispered again, as though to avoid further angering any listening gods.

Inanna wasn't going to bother to whisper. She no longer believed the gods even existed. They certainly had not answered any of Inanna's prayers for rescue or returning home, so she'd stopped praying and decided to rely on her wits from now on.

"Pharaoh has demanded answers from the priests."

If Pharaoh was demanding answers Sarai might have a reprieve for another night or two. Although Sarai could be in danger herself as the superstitious Egyptians were just as likely to blame Sarai for the plague. Most of the problems in the kingdom were conveniently blamed on foreigners, the people least able to protect themselves. Inanna had lost count of the number who'd lost their lives because of some false charge or other.

The water carrier left. Inanna held up the towel and helped Sarai out of the bath and dried her as she'd been taught.

Once Sarai had settled on the couch, Inanna massaged in the first of the lotions and they chatted. Whatever ingredients the lotions contained, they had made a huge difference to Sarai's desert-roughened skin. She now glowed with health and somehow looked even younger than she had a week ago.

* * *

No one turned up with a meal. After waiting until her stomach ached, Inanna said, "I'll go and see what's happening."

The outside passage was deserted. As she walked towards the kitchen, she almost gagged on the smell of vomit coming from room after room. Inanna pinched her nostrils and continued to walk forwards.

Only Hagar, the cook she'd met last time who'd been unusually friendly and helpful, was still in the vast area. Hagar looked up as Inanna entered and smiled a smile of such warmth that it made Inanna blink. The palace was a place of frowns and commands.

"You're not sick then?" Hagar asked.

Inanna shook her head. "Only faint with hunger."

"We must be the only ones still standing. You may as well take what you want. No one else will need it." Hagar gestured towards the cool areas where food was stored.

Another first. Inanna's mouth watered in anticipation.

"Is the foreign princess well?" Hagar asked.

"I don't think she's a princess, but she's fine."

"If Pharaoh likes her then she'll be a princess." Hagar smiled grimly. "Princesses can have long memories once they get a little power."

A lesson Inanna might be wise to remember. She'd almost forgotten that Sarai might soon be so far above her that they'd not be able to talk as they had been.

Inanna first slung the water bag across her body, leaving her hands free for other items. Then she gathered a selection of cheese, raw onions, leeks, and bread together. She even dared to take some meat, something she was never permitted to eat. A smile twitched the corner of her mouth. No point in letting such food go to waste.

Hagar pointed towards the cool room. "There are fresh cucumbers and pomegranates under that damp cloth." Hagar even insisted she take some sweet seed cakes.

"If I'm not here later, just come and get what you need. Pharaoh isn't sick and will expect the foreign princess to be ready for him."

Inanna swallowed. Was she going to have to make all the final preparations herself? She had no idea what the final process involved, and the cosmetic expert was no doubt ill as well.

Once back at Sarai's room, Sarai insisted that Inanna eat with her. It was the best meal that Inanna had eaten in a long time. Pharaoh didn't starve his slaves, as a dead slave wasn't any use to him, but he also didn't give them many extras.

Sarai pushed some of her cake towards Inanna. "Help me finish this."

Inanna didn't hesitate, just in case Sarai changed her mind. She hadn't eaten anything sweet since she'd left Canaan, where she used to sneak treats from the cook. Yet another thing that had often earned her mother's reprimand. Inanna licked her fingers.

Now that the perfumer wasn't here, perhaps Sarai would answer some questions. "Why did you leave Ur?"

Sarai was quiet for a long moment. "Well, at first I thought it was because one of our brothers died. He was only young. Although we spent much silver at the temple, he did not get well." She sighed. "So maybe my father was disappointed in the gods he'd served all his life."

Disappointment and disillusionment with the gods was something Inanna knew well.

"It took many moons to reach Harran and we lived there for a long time before coming south."

"But why move to Canaan? Surely it didn't offer anything new to you."

"Along the way, my b-brother …".

Sarai had been reticent to say anything about this brother of hers. Maybe he ruled with an iron fist, and she was scared of him. Tension gripped Inanna's shoulders. Was Utu's life worse than it had been under Pharaoh? *Please no*, rose in her heart, although she knew not to whom she prayed.

"My brother met a new god who gave us many promises, which he has not kept." Misery tinged Sarai's voice and she twisted her hands in her lap.

What kind of promises would make a woman look so unhappy?

"The new god told us to follow him."

"To Canaan?" Inanna asked.

Sarai shook her head. "He never told us where we were going. Just to follow."

Inanna raised her eyebrows. Just follow. Strange. Most gods wanted sacrifices as proof of loyalty.

"So we followed and were led to Canaan and then here. Sometimes this god speaks to my … my b-brother directly and sometimes it seems as though we just respond to the circumstances, like the famine."

Had the god meant for Sarai to end up here, in Pharaoh's household? Or had a beautiful woman just been too close to the center of Pharaoh's spy network?

Inanna hated to break off their conversation, but it was time for Sarai to be dressed in her finery. Together they worked to clothe her in the finest of linens. Halfway through the process, Sarai blinked back tears.

"What's the matter?"

"The clothes." Sarai gulped. " I have never worn clothes that revealed so much."

The linen was translucent. Inanna agreed with her but what could they do? It wasn't like Sarai was dressing to go to the market. As they were finishing, a voice called out from outside and Inanna invited the woman in. It was a mere girl, not the cosmetics expert she was expecting. The assistant? Or the assistant to the assistant?

The girl flushed. "Everyone else is sick."

Hopefully the girl had at least watched the process many times, even if she'd never actually applied the cosmetics.

With a few false starts the girl managed to paint on the kohl which made Sarai's eyes look even more doe-like. Then she added greenish malachite eye shadow. Then red ochre was mixed with animal fat for Sarai's lips.

Once they were finished, the girl leaned down and took out a flat case from her basket. She opened it and Inanna gasped at the gleam of the pectoral necklace. She'd never seen silver, but that was what it must be. Silver, rarer and more expensive than gold. Precious stones of turquoise and dark red made the pattern. They fastened it around Sarai's neck and Sarai reached up her hand and stroked its surface. Jewelry fit for a princess. How many others had worn it before her?

The girl packed her cosmetics together and bowed herself backwards out of the room.

Sarai clutched Inanna's hand. "Don't leave me."

"You do know I'll have to leave eventually, don't you?" Inanna said.

"Yes, but can you wait in this room?"

Poor, fearful Sarai. Beautiful and youthful as she looked, Sarai was actually a woman of seventy, mature in years and used to not having unwanted attentions. Maybe Pharaoh would be hit by the plague or change his mind. Not that it would do much good. Eventually he'd demand to spend the night with Sarai.

"I'll take you to the door and stay out here," Inanna promised. The promise was only possible because Pharaoh had his own entrance to the next room.

Sarai's lips moved as they walked towards the entrance to the inner rooms.

"Are you praying?" Inanna asked.

Sarai nodded. "To Avram's god."

Hopefully he was more powerful than Inanna's own gods had proved to be. "May the god you serve be with you."

"Amen," Sarai murmured as she went through the doorway in front of her to wait for Pharaoh.

* * *

*I*nanna jerked awake. The window was a dark square through which a few stars shone. There. There was the sound again. A violent retching and a splash onto the floor. Sarai? No, it sounded like a man. It had to be Pharaoh. Pharaoh being violently ill.

Tension straightened Inanna's spine. She longed to get Sarai out of there, but there was absolutely nothing she could do. If it was Pharaoh, then entering the room would mean death. For a man who claimed to be a god, he'd never forgive someone who knew he vomited like a slave.

"Sarai's god. Help her. Protect her," Inanna murmured into the darkness. "Not that I believe you exist, but just in case you do, keep her safe."

Inanna stayed awake until the first cockcrow of the morning. Pharaoh—if that was who was sick, and who else could it be?—vomited repeatedly during the long hours of darkness. Sometimes Inanna could hear the murmur of voices. Was Sarai talking to

Pharaoh? That must be a first. Inanna doubted Pharaoh usually talked to his women.

* * *

"*I*nanna," came the whisper, accompanied by a prod of a sandalled foot.

Inanna blinked sleepy eyes and focused on Sarai. A Sarai still completely clothed and with cosmetics unspoiled.

"Sorry," Inanna mumbled. "I didn't mean to fall asleep."

"I didn't get much sleep either, but he answered."

"Who answered?" Inanna said, shaking her head to clear it.

"Avram's god." Sarai pulled Inanna to her feet. "The plague hit Pharaoh hard soon after he arrived." She giggled and covered her mouth with her hand. "Sorry. I shouldn't laugh at anyone's misery, but the timing couldn't have been better. And now he knows."

Inanna must be befuddled this morning, because she didn't have a clue what Sarai meant. "What does he know?"

"That he shouldn't have taken me into his household."

"What do you mean?" Sarai was talking in riddles this morning.

"Help me get out of these clothes first," Sarai said, reaching up to unfasten the pectoral necklace. "Then stick close to me and you'll see."

CHAPTER FOUR

"What have you done to me?" Pharaoh said, the words slow and drawn out like a sleeping snake stretched out on desert sand.

Inanna shivered. Snakes could wake up.

She and Sarai were hidden behind a woven papyrus screen. Somehow, during the long night two nights earlier, Sarai had proved herself a friend to a man who probably had no friends. Sarai had told Inanna that after the first round of vomiting, Pharaoh had been so miserable he hadn't minded when she'd gone over and laid a damp cloth on his forehead.

Pharaoh had threatened Inanna and Sarai, saying they'd regret it if they ever said anything about his night of weakness. Inanna grimaced. She'd had to clean up all the vomit.

"Sovereign ruler, I feared for my life." A voice Inanna didn't recognize but was presumably Avram's, answered.

"Indeed?" Pharaoh said.

His tone sent chills down Inanna's spine.

"You should have told me she was your wife."

Wife! Inanna looked over at Sarai, wide-eyed.

"Sorry," Sarai mouthed.

"Now take your wife and go. Go back to where you came from, and don't return. Perhaps then your god will heal this household."

Pharaoh obviously believed the plague was caused by Avram's god. The kitchen had been functioning properly this morning when Inanna had gone to collect Sarai's food. Maybe it was just a coincidence. A convenient coincidence, but the plague seemed to be over. People looked pale and shaky but devoured their food hungrily.

"Thank you, your excellency," Avram said.

Footsteps sounded, leading away from them. Pharaoh's private door creaked as it opened, then closed.

A head peered around the screen, and an older man with a black beard streaked with white reached his hand towards Sarai. "Come on. Let's leave before he changes his mind."

So that was that. Inanna walked towards the doorway which would lead her back to the slave quarters. She blinked back the tears that sprang into her eyes. Utu would be going with Avram and Sarai, and she'd never see him again. She clenched her fists. She'd begun to think that life might be changing, but no. She was stuck here.

"You too, Inanna," Sarai said.

What? Inanna spun around.

"Pharaoh isn't going to allow you to stay, not with what you've seen and heard. You're part of the deal."

Joy surged in her heart. Utu. She'd see him again. Maybe, if Avram's god smiled on her, she might make it back to Canaan. Once there, nothing would stop her heading home. She'd wait and use her head this time. No rushing into ill-prepared escape plans. This time she'd be careful. This time she'd succeed.

"Don't go and collect anything. We'll give you what you need," Sarai said, handing her a veil.

Inanna had only the clothes she stood up in anyway. Even when she'd found a pretty rock or two to keep, they'd been stolen by someone else.

She put on the veil and scurried after Avram and Sarai, heart singing. So what if she was still a slave. Being a slave in Sarai's household had to be better than being a slave in Pharaoh's palace.

Outside, a group of Pharaoh's palace guard stood straight and ready for action. They escorted Sarai and Inanna back to Avram's camp. It was bedlam, with clouds of dust everywhere. The bleating of sheep and goats was almost drowned out by the bellowing of camels. Ahead of them tents were being taken down and placed on camels. Orders were shouted, but everyone seemed to know what they were doing.

"Stick close to me," Sarai said.

Inanna stuck. She had no task to do in this situation, and she knew no one except Sarai, Avram, and Utu. She kept her eyes open, scanning the workers for Utu. Not that he'd have any time to talk to her, but even to see him would be good.

What would he be feeling as they packed up? That he'd never see her again? He'd been protective of her for as long as she could remember, fighting other children who taunted her and making sure she didn't get into too much trouble. Not that he'd always succeeded, but he'd tried. For that, she was grateful. He'd paid a high price for her impulses.

Avram headed off somewhere, but Sarai took her to a relatively quiet corner in a tent larger than most. "You can help roll the carpets."

It would be good to do something. Inanna found the end of a carpet and another veiled figure to help her. Together they rolled the main carpet and left it ready to be put in a cart, as it was too big for a camel. Had Sarai made the multi-colored design herself?

It was hot in a veil and Inanna wasn't used to wearing one. Sarai had suggested they covered their faces until they were out of Egypt, but few of the other women were covered to such an extent. Inanna pushed hers aside and mopped her face with her arm.

"Oh, it's you," a familiar voice said.

"Hagar!" The one person from the palace Inanna had regretted leaving. "How did you end up here?"

"I too was part of Pharaoh's gift when Sarai was returned to her brother."

Hagar would soon discover the truth about Avram and Sarai's relationship, but Sarai might keep up the charade until they were out of the country. Inanna didn't know Hagar well, but she'd been kind. Kindness among slaves was rare as water in a desert.

How many Egyptian slaves had joined the household? Poor things. Gifted to someone they knew nothing about and having to learn a new language and how to serve an unknown master and mistress. Pity tightened her belly. It was heart-wrenching to have to leave the only country they'd ever known.

* * *

*U*tu sneezed as a large cloud of dust and leaves swirled past. Already, vast herds of animals had left and were headed north along the papyrus-lined Nile river.

He'd been assigned to help take down the array of tents. Each tent had to be beaten to remove the dust that had accumulated during the long months since the last rain. Utu took a cloth from around his neck and wrapped it around his nose and mouth, then swung the beater to connect with the nearest section of the tent in front of him. Thwack, thwack, thwack. Sweat trickled in a rivulet between his shoulder blades. When he finished the first side of the tent, he moved on to the next section. Behind him, two others worked to pull out the tent pegs and coil the cords. Goat's hair tents were wonderful in the rain, as the fibers swelled to prevent leakage, but the fibers also collected dust. He sneezed again.

Thwack, thwack, thwack. Utu settled into the rhythm of his work. Their team of men would clean the tents, fold them, and then pack them on carts, making sure that the tent remained together with its own poles and ropes. Each tent was marked with a different colored thread to differentiate it from its neighbors.

He'd be aching tonight after yet another kind of unfamiliar work. When his muscles started screaming at him, he gladly passed the beater on to another man in the team and switched to pulling up pegs and coiling ropes. He also made sure to take a drink of water from the skin lying in the tent's shade. He'd seen one of the water carriers neglect to drink. The man ended up with a splitting headache and vomiting. Eliezer had called them together and insisted on them drinking enough.

Mid-morning, Utu spotted Avram's return, accompanied by a group of veiled women. Why had he been at the palace, and did it have something to do with their abrupt departure? Earlier this morning a group of new slaves had arrived, accompanied by even more flocks and herds and a long line of camels. Eliezer would be busy providing food, clothing, and accommodation for all the new arrivals.

Utu mopped his head with his forearm as the beater who'd replaced him passed the beater to the next man in line. A tiny glow of pride warmed Utu. He'd lasted longer than the next man. He chuckled to himself. His pride would be paid with aching muscles the next day.

Did Inanna know he'd be leaving today? He hadn't seen any glimpse of her outside since the day by the stream. Was she no longer assigned to the laundry, or had he simply missed seeing her? Was she safe? That bothered him most. She was so impulsive. What if she said or did things that led to her being beaten? Or worse? Utu clenched his fist. She was so slender and fragile. He'd seen beatings where the skin was stripped off people's backs. Some didn't survive. *Keep her safe*, he breathed.

Ever since they were children, he'd sensed when she was in trouble. Lately he'd felt nothing. Did that mean there was no trouble, or had the connection between them somehow broken?

The fourth tent lay ready to be picked up by the carters. Utu opened the waterskin and gulped down the now warm water before passing it to the next man.

"Well done," Eliezer said, striding over. "I've been watching your work and think you're the best team to do the main tent."

A glow settled in his belly, and Utu grinned at the others.

"Once you've finished, you'll have time for a quick dip in the river before we head north." Eliezer moved off to the next group to give more instructions.

Utu looked around. Already the vast majority of the tents were neat piles on the ground. Soon all that would be left to mark their camp would be areas of flattened grass and the blackened stones of their fires. Once the rain came, those marks would disappear under new growth.

The team picked up their tools and moved to the center of the camp. Avram's tent was not only the biggest but had a colored door flap with tufted wool embroidery. Avram often sat at the doorway so people could find him and ask for his counsel.

Practiced now, the team moved into place. The senior member of the team went to the entrance of the tent and called out. A woman answered, and a small group of women moved out of the shade of the tent. Utu and the team went into the now-gloomy interior. Utu's skin goose bumped with the cooler temperature. Two women were just finishing rolling the final carpet.

The women straightened up and headed for the entrance. Someone removed the embroidered entrance panel, and light flooded into the space.

"Utu!" exclaimed one of the women.

"Inanna?"

Inanna threw back her veil, revealing the cheeky grin he knew so well.

He swallowed tears. He'd been so worried they'd never see each other again. Yet here she was, laughing at him. "Are you coming with us?"

"Yes!" She nodded vigorously. "I've come as a maid to Sarai."

Who was Sarai? Maybe she was the wife he still hadn't seen. Whenever he'd asked questions about Avram's wife, no one would talk about her. "But how?"

Inanna pointed at the tent team with her chin. "No time now to tell you, but I'll come and find you later. I've got to go. We're in the next group to set off." She and the other woman moved rapidly out of the tent.

Inanna! Thank the gods for this mercy. His heart sang and he grinned broadly at the men.

"And who was that?" one of them asked with a wink.

"My sister."

"Yeah, yeah, we've heard that before." The man sniggered.

"My twin sister," Utu said firmly. "Strictly off limits."

Four of them leaned down and hoisted the main carpet on their shoulders. They took it out into the bright sunshine to the waiting cart and loaded it with much grunting. Then it was back to work on the main tent, which they took down in record time. In the months of travel ahead they'd be getting plenty of practice. Utu's stomach fluttered with excitement. After nearly four summers in Egypt, he was headed in the direction of home.

And the gods be praised, he wasn't going alone.

CHAPTER FIVE

*I*nanna shivered in the cool before dawn. They had settled into a pattern on their travels. The women and shepherds left just before dawn to do their day of walking. The men would strike camp, then move ahead with the carts and camels to set up the next camp.

She still couldn't believe she was headed towards home. The distance and the desert had always been huge barriers, and now she had company. There was security in such a large group. If only they could hurry, but being a group this size had its disadvantages as well. The flocks could not be hurried. They went at their own pace, eating as they went. It would be many months before they reached Canaan, and there were plenty of dangers along the way.

Someone spat loudly outside the tent, startling Inanna. She got up, plaited her hair, and folded up her bedding. Utu would be along soon to pack up their tent. Before then, she and Hagar and the other women would prepare the bread dough to take with them. They'd be at the new campsite by early afternoon and would swing into action, baking the bread on hot coals and preparing food. Most of the food they prepared themselves: goat's milk, curds, and dried fruit. Fresh onions, leeks, and fruit could be bought along the way from local farmers.

Inanna spent the majority of her time with Hagar. Sarai had been moody since her time in Pharaoh's palace and didn't talk much with anyone. Inanna had assumed the connection they'd had in the palace would continue, but she'd been wrong. Poor Hagar was the one who bore the brunt of Sarai's outbursts of anger. Inanna would have to ask Hagar why Sarai was so moody. After all, Avram's god had rescued her, hadn't he? Sarai was safe. Sarai now commanded slaves rather than suffer enslavement, so what did she have to complain about?

They were soon on their way. Since they'd left the temples and palaces of the capital, they'd only seen villages and endless small farms. They avoided Egyptians as much as possible. She'd heard that was what had got Avram and Sarai in trouble last time. Too many people had seen Sarai, and they'd been too close to the capital. Avram wouldn't make the same mistake again, so Sarai had to wear a veil at all times. Perhaps that was what was wrong with her. All the rest of them had enjoyed going about without veils since early in the journey.

The first days of their travels, Inanna had walked too quickly, as though her speed would ensure they'd reach Canaan sooner. Now she'd learned it made no difference. Inanna glanced sideways at the soldiers Pharaoh had sent along. They kept to themselves. Some said they were the gift of Pharaoh for their protection, but the more cynical said they were there to ensure Avram and his followers left the borders of Egypt as quickly as possible.

* * *

*I*nanna and Hagar were cutting onions. For once, Inanna was veiled. It helped a little, but the onions still made her eyes sting. They would stir fry them with a little olive oil and precious salt to have with the fresh-baked bread and curds. While they chopped the onions, Inanna taught Hagar the languages she'd need in their future home.

They chatted together in Amorite until Hagar said, "Spare me. I need a rest."

"I remember," Inanna said. When she came to Egypt, she'd been lonely until she'd learned enough of the language to communicate beyond polite greetings and murmurs of assent to commands. The first words she'd come to understand were all related to commands— pick this up or put that there.

Inanna glanced over at Hagar. She often seemed quite down lately. It made sense, as every step took her further away from all that was familiar. Hagar hadn't chosen to be given to Avram and Sarai or to leave Egypt. All slaves were passed from one household to another at the whim of their owners. Slaves had no choices. They couldn't choose what tasks they did or when, but were expected to do all tasks well. They couldn't choose when to stop and rest. They couldn't choose to take the day off and go fishing or climb trees.

Hagar preferred cooking to being a maidservant, although cooking here must be restrictive with the same few ingredients day after day.

Hagar was older and more experienced than Inanna. Would she be able to explain Sarai's recent moods? Inanna paused to think about how to best raise the topic. "I'm sorry that the mistress has been making your life difficult lately."

"It hasn't been easy, but I understand."

Inanna leaned in so she couldn't be overheard. "I don't."

Hagar stopped her chopping and pursed her lips. "How would you feel if your husband allowed you to be taken into another man's household?"

Inanna blinked. She had been focusing on the fact that Sarai had been rescued from the situation.

"And now she has to wear a veil all the time to prevent others noticing her."

Inanna had only worn a veil for a few days. She'd found it stifling. The veil made it difficult to speak to anyone, because she'd had to project her voice that much more, and because no one could see her facial expressions. In the end, she'd gone silent rather than make the extra effort.

"The mistress has too much time to think. It would be natural if she's reliving her whole experience in the palace. Perhaps she distrusts Avram. After all, he put his own safety above hers."

Hagar's explanations made a certain kind of sense. "If her problem is with Avram, why is she taking it out on us?"

Hagar clicked her tongue. "Didn't you ever take your annoyances with other family members out on your brother when you were a child?"

Yes, she'd often been snappy with Utu after she'd been reprimanded by her mother.

"If Sarai was cross with Avram, everyone would know and be gossiping about it. We're a much easier target."

Inanna sighed. "I wish we weren't."

"Try not to take it to heart. She isn't angry at us." Hagar tipped the onions into a serving dish. "Perhaps the mistress isn't sure herself what she's feeling. Feelings are tricky things."

Inanna might not know much, but she knew that. She still didn't understand why she so often felt stifled by her life while Utu seemed content in his situation. He actually seemed to like being Eliezer's assistant and didn't seem to be bothered by the fact that he was merely a slave.

"And you've heard her at night," Hagar said.

They couldn't help hearing Sarai cry and the murmur of Avram's voice as he tried to comfort her.

There'd been other things about Sarai that had puzzled Inanna. She'd seen Sarai turn away from any woman nursing a child. The women she kept around her were single or childless. Was that deliberate? Inanna tried to frame a question.

"Not having a child weighs on her," Hagar said before Inanna could come up with a question.

Inanna blinked.

"It would weigh on any woman," Hagar continued. "A woman without a child is like a ... a day without the sun ... or a year without a harvest."

A year without a harvest. Inanna knew what that was like. She'd seen famine when she was a small child. Remembered the stomach pains and craving. The words lodged in her heart. She'd never thought about children as she'd been too busy trying to fly free, but would she one day long for children as Sarai did? Would she long so much that tears came?

Inanna looked over at Hagar. Most women of Hagar's age were married with several children. Did she too feel the lack that caused Sarai's tears?

CHAPTER SIX

A few months later

"*L*ook!" The camp lookout pointed to the horizon. Great dark gray and yellow billows spread across the sky.

"Sandstorm," Eliezer yelled. "Everyone to their positions."

Utu dashed for one of the medium-sized tents. They'd been practicing what to do in a sandstorm for weeks. His job was to check all the main ropes on the tent and to place heavy objects along the tent's bottom edge on the side closest to the approaching storm.

His new and already closest friend, Job, was responsible for using stakes and tough cloth to build a temporary wall for the sheep. The sheep and their shepherds would crouch within the three-sided structure and wait out any storm.

Utu finished checking the ropes and found a heap of rocks to lay along the tent edges. He partially secured the entrance flap so that there was just enough space for people to enter. A messenger arrived as he finished.

"Utu," the messenger said. "Eliezer wants to see you the moment your tent is secure."

"It's done," Utu said, and ran towards the central tent. Eliezer had been giving him a few extra jobs lately. Whatever task Utu did, he'd look up to find Eliezer's eyes on him. He didn't know if this was a good or a bad thing.

Eliezer was supervising four other slaves to saddle a group of camels. He stepped aside as Utu approached. "Hagar and Inanna and eight other women, including my daughter, went to the second spring to bathe."

Utu's heart pounded. They'd be out in the open without any protection. He'd experienced two sandstorms on their trip to Egypt but they hadn't been too bad. He'd heard the worst could flay the skin off an adult or smother those caught unprepared.

"I want each of you to ride hard and take an extra camel tied to your saddle." Eliezer indicated the five young men around himself. "You must not get separated. If you get separated, you could die." He gave Utu a stern look.

Utu licked suddenly dry lips.

"When you find the women, put two on each camel and try to get back here. If the sandstorm hits, shelter behind the camels. I've put in extra coverings for you to shelter underneath, along with water and supplies." He fixed his gaze on Utu. "Now repeat my instructions."

Utu repeated them.

"Good. Don't let me down."

Utu nodded and vaulted onto the camel. He'd been practicing riding and loading and unloading the camels. One of the grooms slapped his camel, and the camel went up to its knees. Utu held on, ready to be pitched forward as the camel straightened its back legs. Once upright, he checked the other four riders were ready and glanced over at the storm front. It was already noticeably closer. Bolts of lightning shot through the darker parts.

Utu slapped his camel. It bawled in protest but took off at a gallop. Had the women even seen the approaching storm, or were they bliss-fully enjoying their bath? *Keep them safe.* The camels sensed his urgency and sped forward, but it was going to be a close race. Already the roar of the storm was making itself heard. He glanced around to check that the camels were bunched close together.

Ahead he could see the date palms of the oasis but no sign of Inanna and the others. He raised his voice and hollered in the way of his own people if they had to call from peak to peak. If Inanna was still there, she'd know it was him.

A head appeared at the rim of the shallow saucer that led down to the spring. Then another. He pointed towards the looming clouds and was close enough to see Inanna's look of horror. She turned and disappeared. He hoped the others were clothed and ready to leave.

The camels no longer needed urging. It was as if they sensed the oasis provided the greatest shelter. They reached the edge of the oasis just as the front edge of the storm hit with a roar and a blast of sand. It was suddenly pitch black.

Utu crouched low and hauled on the camel's halter to bring it to a stop. He yelled to the others, but his words were whipped away. He slid down beside the camel, keeping its body between him and the storm. The protection made a difference, but it was minimal, and the camels weren't going to cope long with walking forward. They had to find the women and shelter here.

Had the other camels even made it to the edge of the oasis? One pair loomed out of the gloom. Utu linked the newcomers to his camels, praying the others were nearby. Utu wove his long head scarf around his nose and mouth and breathed through a few layers of cloth. The darkness meant that they'd never find the others if they weren't close by. His camel pulled to his far side and another linked pair of camels loomed out of the gloom. Six. Maybe the camels were their best chance of finding each other. Their ears and senses were more attuned to what was happening, and they'd lived through sandstorms before.

Where were the other two riders? The wind howled and the bare skin of his feet and legs was peppered with thousands of grains of sand. Another camel and rider appeared, but the trailing camel was missing.

They waited for the final rider.

Sweat trickled down the side of Utu's face. It was hot, like the inside of a furnace, much hotter than it had been before the storm arrived. Lightning flashed and lit up their tight group. The gods had been kind. They'd been close enough to the edge of the dip in the land to be protected a little.

They waited but the final camel did not come. Its rider would have to trust fate. Right now, they needed to find Inanna and the other women. The safest place would be in the pool itself. Utu gestured forward. If they went down into the oasis, they should find the pool. Hopefully the women would be there.

They shuffled forward. The camel grunted beside him as its bulk absorbed the worst of the blast. Utu couldn't see or hear the others but trusted they were still following.

The camel stopped without warning and pulled against its halter. Something slithered in front of them. Probably a snake. Utu stroked the trembling camel's neck until it settled. Then he cupped his hands around his mouth, still keeping a firm grip on the halter, and bellowed. Behind him, he heard one or two of the others join in. They might achieve something if they could coordinate their shouts. He took a deep breath and bellowed again, holding it as long as possible. This time they were louder. Once more might do it. He filled his lungs and let out another long yell, then listened.

He heard a faint answer. His camel turned its head to the left. It was as good a direction as any. Utu allowed the camel to lead, following cautiously in the darkness. The camel led him around some rocks and into the water where it paused for a short drink, then walked along the edge.

There! He glimpsed something pale and then another. They'd found the women—or rather, his camel had. The women were crouched on the ground behind a rock, much too small to shelter them. They had their backs to the wind and their heads hidden between their knees.

"Inanna," Utu called.

One of the women looked up, but all he saw was the blur of her face. He couldn't tell if it was his sister. She stood up and came and threw her arms around him. She was trembling, and he hugged her back. He kept Inanna beside him as they got the camels to sit down behind them. Eliezer had provided spare goat's hair coverings and they got them out and then settled down with their backs to the camels and the coverings over their heads. Immediately the roaring lessened.

He clasped Inanna's hand. "Are you all here?"

She nodded.

"Everyone alright?"

"I think so. How long will we be here?"

"Long enough to get bored."

Sweat trickled down his cheeks. Apart from the constant roar, the biggest struggle was going to be the heat. He inched forward and put his feet in the water. Much better. Inanna followed his example.

Initially, he'd planned to get the women back to the main camp, but that was clearly impossible. Eliezer would be worried, but he would just have to wait. They were much safer here than getting lost in the desert.

He reached out to the other side from Inanna and touched another rider. He pointed to the water, and he too moved into its cool embrace. Utu reached down and scooped some water, then washed his face and poured it over his head.

Overhead the sandstorm continued to roar but down here, they'd survive. Had the fifth rider made it into the sheltered bowl of the oasis, or had he been caught out in the open? If the rider was injured, would Eliezer blame him?

After what seemed like an eternity, Utu crawled back to his camel and found the dried fruit. He handed some to Inanna and took some himself before passing it down the line. Then they waited. And waited. Utu tried not to worry, but it was hard. As long as the missing rider stayed with the camels and used them as a barrier, he should survive, but would he do that, or would he panic in the dark and heat?

It would be easy enough to become confused or trust himself rather than the camels.

* * *

"*U*tu, I think the storm has gone," Inanna said.

He must have fallen into a doze, because she was right. He couldn't hear the roar any longer. He cautiously pushed the goatskin aside, then coughed as sand cascaded over him. Outside the storm was gone.

"You can come out," he called.

He had to assist Inanna, and then helped Jemimah. She thanked him profusely, and he stammered a polite reply and turned away before she saw his flushed face. He counted the women. Yes, no one was missing.

"Can anyone see the other rider or the missing camels?"

The riders peered around the oasis area.

"There's one of the camels," Job called. "Shall I go and get it?"

Utu nodded. Job had some sort of magical connection with camels, and a frightened camel was more likely to follow Job than anyone else.

"Come on, everyone else help me to fold the coverings. We'll start with this one."

The camels didn't wait for a command but staggered to their feet, showering them with more sand.

It took a bit of work to clear the sand, but they had everything loaded and were giving the camels a drink by the time Job returned with the missing camel.

"I'm going to go up to the lip of the oasis and see if I can spot the other two camels." He didn't mention the missing rider. "You may as well rinse the sand off before we go."

He'd like a quick dip himself, as his hair was full of sand and his skin itched.

"I'll come with you," Inanna said.

He nodded and set off for the nearest edge. They were puffing by the time they'd reached the top as new, soft sand covered everything, and it was hard to walk through it.

Turning in a slow circle they scanned the desert. Nothing to the north. He turned and looked to the east. Still nothing. Putting his hand up to shade his eyes, he looked south and west. Nothing, nothing, nothing. The desert looked flat, but it undulated. A man or camel could easily be hidden, even fairly close by.

"Let's wash and get back to camp," Utu said.

Back at the oasis, Utu asked Job to get the group ready to go. He'd be better at choosing who went on which camel. Utu just had time to plunge into the water and scrub his hair and body. There weren't enough camels unless they found the two missing ones, so he'd be walking home.

As they headed back to the main camp, they scoured each dip in the desert for the missing rider and animals. Nothing. Wherever the other camels had gone, they weren't in this direction.

Ahead of them, Utu could see someone waiting for them. Eliezer. As they drew closer, Eliezer ran towards them, searching the riders on each camel. His face creased into a broad smile when he recognized Jemimah. He ran over to her camel, and Jemimah slid off and dropped into his arms. After he'd hugged her, he approached Utu who was walking alongside the others.

"What happened?"

Utu waited until the camels had moved forward and then went over to Eliezer.

"The storm hit us right on the edge of the oasis, and we lost one rider and two camels."

Eliezer frowned. "Two camels returned, but there was no rider."

Utu clenched his jaw. "I was afraid of that."

Would Eliezer be angry at him because he hadn't protected everyone? His sister and Jemimah and the others were safe, but someone might even now be grieving that a youth they loved had not returned.

"I'll send out a search party, just in case," Eliezer said.

They searched for the missing rider until nightfall but found nothing. Not a body, not a water bag, not a mound. It was as if he'd never existed.

Utu returned to the camp tired and dirty. Eliezer did not reprimand him, but Utu blamed himself for assuming all the camels and their riders were together. Would the man have lived if Utu had stopped and gathered everyone together instead of trying to outrun the storm?

CHAPTER SEVEN

"Those shepherds drive me crazy." Job slumped down on the ground near Utu.

"Lot's shepherds?" Utu asked. Job had been complaining about Lot's shepherds ever since the sandstorm.

"They seem to think they deserve to go first because they're older and have been with the family ever since Harran."

Or it might simply be because they followed their master's example. Lot and his wife were not well liked around the camp. They ordered their servants around and didn't hesitate to order Avram's servants around as well. In contrast, Avram never held himself aloof. If something needed to be done, he did it without calling a servant. He talked to all those around him as equals. Lot looked down his nose at them like the haughtiest of the camels, and his wife was even worse. Utu had seen servant girls slapped harshly for small misdemeanors.

"Does Avram know?' Utu asked.

"I don't think anyone dares tell him. He seems to think Lot can do no wrong."

Utu shrugged. "He's the only other family Avram has here. Maybe Avram thinks of him more as a son than a nephew."

Job spat on the ground. "Well, it looks like he'll be the kind of son who breaks his father's heart."

"Do Avram and Sarai have children?" Utu asked.

Job checked over his shoulder and spoke quietly. "Sarai is barren."

"Then why hasn't Avram taken another wife?"

"I don't think it's the custom with these people."

Odd. Utu's mother was his father's tenth wife. Amorite chiefs paraded their status with numerous wives and children. His father had never been more than a distant larger-than-life figure during his childhood, although he'd seemed to take a shine to Inanna. It used to make him jealous, but he'd soon realized his father only bothered because Inanna amused him.

It was Utu's mother who'd raised them amidst a bickering crowd of women and children.

"I thought Avram's god told him that he'd become a great nation," Utu said. "That's impossible without a son. Maybe he thinks the line will be through Lot."

"But Lot only has daughters."

Utu frowned. "Avram has been blessed with flocks and herds, but he'd probably exchange half of them for a son."

"Possibly." Job looked at Utu and changed the subject. "How's your new job going? No more smelling like sheep for you."

"I'm liking it so far." Truth be told, he was a little embarrassed to have been chosen as Eliezer's assistant. A few had shown their resentment, but he'd remained friends with Job. Job preferred working with the camels, and the camels liked Job. Even the ornery ones nuzzled his hair.

Job sighed. "Things are going to get tougher from tomorrow. We'll be in the Negev."

The craggy hills of the Negev had been looming closer all day. Now the setting sun turned them to dusky pink. In the Negev, they'd be forced to travel in the valley bottoms where there'd be even more competition for water.

* * *

47

"*Utu*, I want you to go and help Job water his camels," Eliezer said.

Utu raised an eyebrow.

"To report on any issues at the watering hole. There was a fight yesterday."

Eliezer seemed to know what was going on before anyone else.

"We cannot have disunity in the camp, because a group of our size is always in danger."

"Danger?"

"Our herds are a temptation to local chieftains, and we also make locals feel threatened. They worry that we might attack them."

"Avram wouldn't do that."

"But no one knows that. Any disunity makes us vulnerable to outside attack, and it is often the innocent who get hurt."

Women and children. Utu's stomach turned over at the thought of Inanna or Jemimah injured, or captured, or worse.

"You're intelligent enough to know what to look for, although I suspect you know all about it anyway." Eliezer's eyes twinkled. "I need to have my facts correct before I speak to Avram."

Utu had heard all about the fight from Job, who had avoided being swept up in the scuffle because the camels were always watered last.

Utu jogged off to find Job. The back of a camel would give him a high seat to study the crowd.

As they approached, he saw Lot's herdsman pushing to the front. Behind them, Avram's herdsmen muttered and looked sullen.

Lot's group didn't hurry, almost as if they were taunting the others. They didn't bother cleaning up the droppings their animals left behind either. Avram's herdsmen, already cranky at the long wait, had to wade through the droppings to reach the troughs.

Utu stayed to help Job water the camels. Each camel slurped up several days' worth of water, so it was almost dark before they made it back to their tents. Utu went immediately to Eliezer and reported what he'd seen.

Eliezer stroked his beard. "I'll talk to Avram in the morning."

Utu turned to go.

"Would you like to eat with us?" Eliezer asked.

Utu accepted, working to school his voice so it didn't show his eagerness to be around Eliezer and Jemimah. The way the two of them related always made his heart yearn to be part of a family. Not that his own had been close but he'd like to see his mother again.

* * *

*U*tu, Inanna, and Job were watching Avram who stood near a stone altar. He'd repaired the altar, sacrificed a lamb, and now stood with his arms raised.

"What's he doing?" Inanna whispered to Utu.

They'd been traveling north ever since they'd crossed the Negev and were now camped somewhere between Bethel and Ai, according to those who knew such things.

"Eliezer said that Avram built that altar to his god the last time he was here," Utu said.

"And?"

"And I think he's asking his god for wisdom. Something has to be done about the situation with Lot."

"I thought Eliezer already talked to him about that," Job said from beyond Utu.

"Several times, but Avram hasn't dealt with it yet."

"What do you think he'll do?" Inanna asked.

"I imagine they'll have to separate."

Inanna looked at him, expression fierce. "As long as they don't separate us."

He smiled at her, affection filling his chest. "Or you'll do what?"

"I don't know. Something."

She was still as fierce as the ibex he and Job had seen fighting in the desert. The clash of their long, curved horns had echoed across the canyons.

"I don't think we'll be separated." Lot's wife might take some extra slaves from Avram, but she wouldn't want someone with Inanna's strength of will.

"I guess we'll be leaving the hills then," Inanna said. "I know it isn't easy to find enough pasture here, but they make me feel safer somehow."

And the hills reminded them both of home.

* * *

*T*he next day, Utu saw Avram walk towards Lot with his head bowed. His heart sped up. Was this it then? Were the men going to talk about their futures? Futures that would impact his life and Inanna's too. He drifted towards the main tent and alerted Inanna. Together, they watched as the two men headed for the ridge and out of sight of the camp.

They didn't return for a long time, and Utu couldn't help noticing that Avram looked sad when they did return. Did that mean the men would separate or not? Had they had a fight? Were they still in disagreement?

He had to contain his fidgets until the next day. Now he, Inanna, and Job sat on a rock looking down to the plain below. Dust still lingered in the air. Lot had set off just after dawn, taking all his flocks and herds.

"I never expected to still be sitting up here in the hills," Utu said.

"No, me neither," Inanna said. "I was sure that Avram would choose the most fertile land and go down to the plain."

"Apparently he gave the first choice to Lot."

"But Avram is older. He should have had first choice," Inanna said.

Utu laughed. "It might not be what should have happened but it's what Avram chose to do."

"Even if Avram did that, Lot should have known that the best land must go to the more senior family member," Inanna said.

"Apparently not," Job said.

"He knew." Utu drew his knees up to his chest. "Lot was never one to hesitate about something he wanted."

"I think it stinks," Inanna said. "Avram has far more animals, and now he'll have to work much harder to find the feed they need in the hills."

"Eliezer says that Avram trusts that his god has a plan and will bless him anywhere." Eliezer had said more than that, but Utu realized that if he was going to be Eliezer's assistant, he couldn't pass on everything Eliezer said to him. Utu had heard Eliezer remonstrating with Avram when he was told what Lot had chosen. Eliezer had insisted that Avram rebuke Lot for his greed, but Avram said his god had promised him everything his eyes could see, from the north to south and to the east and west. Everything would belong to him and his offspring for ever and ever, and his offspring would one day be as numerous as the dust of the earth.

Avram seemed a sensible man, but Utu was beginning to doubt that his god really was speaking to him. For there was still no son, not one. The man was in his eighties, and Sarai was only ten years younger.

Inanna had confirmed that Sarai was past childbearing years. A woman's flux wasn't something that could be hidden from those who lived with her.

"Look." Job pointed to the east. "Lot is headed for that big town. What did Eliezer say it was called?"

"Sodom," Utu said. "Eliezer said it was a wicked place."

"Then it sounds like the right kind of place for Lot," Inanna said, turning her back on the plain, and pointing to the sky. "Look. Eagle."

They watched the bird doing its final hunting before dark. Soaring up and up, barely moving its wings. Inanna sighed. She always identified with the birds, longing for the same freedom they had. Was she ever going to be content with the confines of a woman's life?

Utu sighed. He loved working with Eliezer and doing something worthwhile with his life, but Inanna wanted freedom and never thought of the costs involved. Here, their every need was generously provided for—food, clothing, shelter. If they were free, they'd be struggling to eke out an existence in rocky places.

The eagle plummeted to the ground, talons extended, and disappeared from view.

"Wait for it," Job said.

"There!" Inanna said as the eagle rose from the ground bearing the limp body of a plump hyrax in its talons.

Utu could see the desire on Inanna's face as she watched the eagle soar and dreamt of freedom for herself. She never saw that the eagle was bound by its needs and the needs of those dependent on it. Even the eagle had responsibilities. Utu was only a few breaths older than Inanna but sometimes he felt years older. Why was it that some people only seemed to learn the hard way?

CHAPTER EIGHT

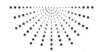

*E*ver since they'd arrived in Canaan, Inanna had been thinking about how to escape. Dreaming of going home and being free from slavery had kept her going in Egypt, but she hadn't been foolish enough to try. Not with half the length of Egypt and a series of deserts between her and the oak trees at Kiriath Arba. Leaving Egypt with Avram was almost enough to make her believe that the gods answered prayers. Almost, but not quite. They'd let her down too often in the past to be altogether trusted ... if they even existed at all.

Now they were somewhat north of her home. Today, it had been announced they were moving south. She'd talk with Utu. They could wait until they got as close as possible before making the run for it. She still had to convince Utu to come with her. He'd agree, eventually. She was sure of it. Even as a child, he'd always been content with the situation he was in but always followed her if she gave a good prod. She'd never understood his placid acceptance of everything. She could never accept being a slave.

Inanna headed for her tent to help the other women pack up the carpets and their few personal items, not that there were many. Just a pretty stone or two she'd picked up and a wooden comb Utu had made her. Each slave wore the same clothes until they wore out. She'd recently received a new tunic and grudgingly had to admit Avram was good to his slaves. Once the clothes wore thin, they were replaced and the cloth reused for cleaning or made into other items.

They wouldn't move far, just to new pastures. They'd camp there until the grass had been eaten by their ever-hungry flocks. Then they'd move on. She sighed. It was hard to curb her impatience.

* * *

Through all their wanderings Inanna had debated when to escape, but as they kept moving closer and closer to her old home, she kept putting off the attempt, waiting for the perfect timing.

Last month she'd finally seen something she recognized, a mountain her father, Mamre, had once pointed out to her, which looked like a crouching animal.

She waited until Utu was alone. "Utu, is that the mountain Father pointed out to us when we went to grandfather's funeral?" It was the only trip they'd ever made with their father, so it had been significant. It probably hadn't been far, but it had felt a long way to her little legs at the time. She remembered how tired she'd been, and that her father had pointed out the mountain to distract her. It was one of the few times he'd ever talked with just the two of them, and she treasured it. Sometimes, when she struggled to get to sleep, she imagined how thrilled her father would be to see her again, imagining him ruffling her hair as he used to, and calling her his little bright spark. She'd loved the name and the fact he'd singled her out.

Utu squinted at the mountain and pursed his lips. "Probably. Home should be that way, I think." He pointed, then looked sharply at her. "You're not thinking of leaving, are you?"

"What if I was?"

He sighed. "Then you're not as intelligent as I thought."

Her stomach tensed. "Are you calling me a fool?"

He was quiet for a long moment. She hated the way he did that.

Taking the time to make sure his words were the most persuasive he could make them, to convince her out of her chosen path.

"Fool is a little strong, but I do think your dreams aren't always based on reality."

He was calling her a foolish dreamer then. Dreams were better than his placid plodding. Dreams kept her from giving up. Dreams kept her alive.

She muttered something noncommittal.

"Don't do anything stupid, will you?" he said, concern tinging his voice.

She shook her head. No, she wouldn't do anything stupid. She'd wait as patiently as she could until they either arrived in the actual area or looked to be moving further away again.

* * *

They'd been moving in what she thought was the correct direction all day. Just on midday, she spotted the place that was most dear to her in all the world, the great oaks of Mamre at Kiriath Arba. A tossing glade of dappled green. The scene of so many of her childhood adventures and imaginings. Her brother had been right. They were heading right for home. She tamped down her excitement. She mustn't let her face reveal what was in her heart. Much as she wanted to, she must not climb her favorite tree, the tree that had gotten them in trouble so long ago.

They stopped a good distance from the town, and Avram had them set up camp. True to his policy, he was keeping a good distance away from any town, and he had Sarai veil herself again. Poor woman. He was definitely paranoid about her beauty. Their father had always had an eye for a pretty woman, but even he wouldn't look at a woman in her seventies.

In the morning, the lookout called out, "Men approaching!"

Inanna looked up and joy flooded her whole being. Her father! He hadn't changed a bit. He was still head and shoulders above anyone else, and his well-muscled body exuded power. He wasn't waiting around for Avram to make his intentions clear. He was coming to find out whether there was any danger. Pride warmed her heart. He'd never been scared of anyone.

Avram waited at the entrance of his main tent with Eliezer at his shoulder. He turned and said something to the veiled Sarai at his side, and she retreated into the tent. Inanna headed for the back entrance. She'd listen if she possibly could. Tent walls made that easy.

Inanna grabbed some raw wool. It wouldn't be as obvious that she was listening if her hands were occupied with combing wool ready for spinning. Not that she needed to hide her purpose, as Sarai and Hagar were already seated as close to the tent entrance as they could be.

"Welcome, esteemed stranger," Mamre boomed from the back of his unusually pale-colored horse. "Where have you come from, and where are you going?"

"I have come from the north, and I am seeking pastures for my livestock and a place to settle. Please stay and eat with me."

Mamre and his men had probably just eaten.

"We would be delighted to."

Avram clapped his hands and two of the girls in the room went to get the carpets and cushions to lay outside in the shade of the best tree. Sarai looked around. "Eliezer will have the lamb killed and cooked outside. Hagar, would you and Inanna take out some dried fruit, and the milk that has been keeping cool in the stream. I'll get some of the others to get the bread started."

Inanna grabbed her veil. She doubted her father would recognize her, but she wasn't taking the risk. She needed to think carefully about when and how she'd contact her father. Utu might think she was a fool, but she'd prove she could plan carefully. No rushing into anything. She wasn't a child anymore.

Inanna prepared the selection of dried figs, dates, and raisins, and they took them out to lay in dishes on the carpet. The men were already seated in a circle on the carpet and parted to let her through. One of them she recognized. He'd been on that same trip to their grandfather's funeral. She kept quiet and escaped back towards the tent. It was going to be more difficult to hear from the tent now the men were a little further away. Thankfully her father had been blessed with a voice that carried.

"Why do you speak our language so well?" Mamre asked.

"We originally came from Ur of the Chaldeans," Avram said.

"Our ancestors came from the same area. But why would a man like yourself leave such a city? I have heard that it is a wondrous place."

"It's a long story," Avram said, settling back on his cushion.

"All the better," Mamre said. "I love long tales."

Inanna could hear Avram's voice but not what he was saying. Was he telling the story of what his god had said to him? Did Avram ever doubt it? After all, he still had no son, and surely he wasn't blind to Lot's faults. He had no man worthy of being his heir, and the thought of Avram dying and Lot taking over was depressing.

Sarai called Inanna over. They made the bread and left it to rise. Inanna could see the smoke of the fire. The sun would have moved well across the sky before the lamb was cooked.

"Inanna and Hagar, can you please go and forage for some herbs? We'll need some for the meat and some to add to the yogurt."

Inanna's mouth watered. They only ate meat on feast days or when they had guests. She looked around for Utu. She hadn't seen anything of him since their father arrived.

During the serving of the meal, Inanna heard her father say, "You would be most welcome to come and base yourselves at our grove of oak trees. I can see mutual benefits to having you there."

Clever man. So large a group camping outside his town walls would spare Mamre the depredations of the desert raiders. It also vastly improved his security and provided buyers for many of the town's goods.

"I'll send some men ahead of me to plan the best place for us to settle without inconveniencing you," Avram said, bowing his head towards Mamre.

It was all Inanna could do not to cheer. She'd wanted to reach her home, and now she knew exactly how to do it. The only question left was choosing the best timing. Utu would be watching her carefully. He'd made himself clear, quite clear. He wasn't coming with her. So be it. She'd go alone. Once she was back home, she'd get their father to ask for Utu's release. If Avram wanted to be in Mamre's favor, he'd have to agree.

CHAPTER NINE

Some months later

"*U*tu, what is that over there? Your eyes are sharper than mine," Eliezer said.

Utu shaded his eyes from the noonday shimmer and stared across the river. For a moment he didn't see anything. Then he saw a blur of movement. "It's a man, close to exhaustion."

"Call Job and his three workmates and tell them to bring their heavy staffs. I'll alert Avram." Eliezer spun on his heel, and Utu ran for where the camels were picketed.

It was hard for Utu to keep his mind on this new threat when he couldn't help being consumed by being back outside the walls of his hometown. It was great to be back in this area that was so familiar to him, but it also made him nervous. Inanna fantasized about being welcomed by their parents, but Utu had no illusions. He was the youngest son of a man who had too many sons. As he remembered it, his older brothers had spent all their time fighting for their father's approval. Even as a child, he'd realized he had no chance of winning. There was something satisfying about being Eliezer's assistant and ensuring the camp ran harmoniously.

Utu forced his mind back on the task in front of him.

Soon they were gathered around Eliezer. "Keep your eyes open in case it is some sort of trick."

Utu's chest tightened. Avram's men had recently beaten off the desert raiders. Maybe this was another attempt.

They waded through the knee-deep river. The man was lying on the ground on the other side. As they reached him, Eliezer gestured for three of the men to fan out and keep facing outwards to watch for any possible attack. He and Utu approached the man.

"Who are you and what do you want?" Eliezer asked.

The man rolled over. "Avram ..." His voice was raspy.

"What do you want with Avram?" Eliezer said.

"Water. Give me water."

Eliezer unslung the water bag he was carrying across his back and handed it to the man. The man's hand shook as he held it to his mouth, and most of the first mouthful was wasted as it splashed down his chin. He gulped in one mouthful and another and another.

"I need to see Avram," he said when he finished drinking. "I've come about Lot. He's been captured."

Eliezer sucked in a breath. "You'd better come with us."

Utu and Job helped the man to his feet and supported him across the river. Then Eliezer sent Job ahead to alert Avram.

Avram came out to meet them. The man sank down on a rock and had another drink.

"Take your time." Avram handed him some raisins.

Once they'd all gathered around, the man spoke. "How much do you know about what has been happening down in Sodom and Gomorrah?"

"We know it's been subject to King Kedorlaomer of Elam for some years," Avram said.

"Yes, for thirteen harvests. Recently Kedorlaomer has conquered the Amalekites, and as far as the hill country of Seir."

Avram and Eliezer exchanged worried looks.

"The kings of our area knew they hadn't a chance on their own, so they united."

"Which kings?" Avram asked.

"Sodom, Gomorrah, Admah, Zeboiim, and Zoar. Our five kings against their four."

"And?" Avram leaned forward.

"They met in the Valley of Siddim and fought among the tar pits."

"And I'm guessing they were defeated?"

The man shuddered. "It was terrible. Some of them fell in the tar pits. When it was obvious that we were losing, many ran away into the hills." He took a shaky breath. "Kedorlaomer seized all the people who were left unprotected, plundered the towns, and headed north."

Avram looked sick. "And Lot and his family are among those captured?"

Utu clenched his fist. He might not like Lot, but he'd follow Avram.

The man nodded. "I escaped out the back gate but had to travel the long way round to find you."

That explained the man's exhaustion. Sodom wasn't that far as the ravens flew.

"When were they captured?" Eliezer asked.

The man pursed his lips. "Two nights and days."

Eliezer turned to Avram. "They'll be well ahead and traveling fast."

"Yes, but the children will slow them down, and they might be overconfident after so many victories."

"Eliezer, you know how many men we have. Bring anyone capable of fighting. They'll need supplies for a week."

Eliezer's careful records had always seemed a little excessive to Utu, but now they made sense. In an uncertain world, it was good to be prepared for emergencies.

"Three hundred and sixteen at last count, excluding us," Eliezer said.

"No, I'm going," Avram said, standing up. "And I think Mamre will go with us and bring some of his men."

Eliezer turned to Utu and the three others who'd crossed the river with them. "You heard Avram. Run and gather the men. We leave the minute we've eaten. And Job, bring the best of the camels."

* * *

"*I* would never have believed that they could get so far," Utu panted to Job.

"And I never could have believed I was so unfit," Job said between puffs.

"Just unfit for running." They'd been running for four days. The older men, including Avram, Mamre and two other Amorite chiefs, were on camels, but the younger men ran. They rested and slept in the midday heat, then ran again from late afternoon into the cool of the evenings.

Job mopped his brow with his arm. "I'm thankful it's not yet summer."

Utu nodded, too tired to summon the breath for any more conversation, although he pointed at yet another abandoned sandal. The army and its captives had obviously slowed their pace, because the campfires they'd passed were now closer together and the last fires had still been warm.

One of the scouts Eliezer had sent ahead came towards them, pulling his camel to a stop as he came up to Avram and Eliezer.

"They're just over the hill," the scout said. "Nearly ran over the top of them but heard their voices in time."

"And how many could you see?"

"At least double our numbers, although there may have been soldiers I couldn't see."

"Then we'll wait until dark," Avram said. "Eliezer, let's gather the more experienced men to make a plan."

"Blast," Utu muttered to Job. "We'll have to wait to hear what's happening,"

Avram turned to them. "You can rest and eat but be silent. If we've sent scouts ahead of us, they might have sent scouts behind. Spread out among the bushes and prepare yourselves for battle."

Utu went over to the nearest camel, where dried fruit was being distributed. He'd give up sleep for fresh bread. The bread they'd brought had been finished on the second day and now they had only fruit or an occasional wild vegetable they snatched along the way. He went with Job to lead the camels back to a stream they'd just crossed to allow the beasts to drink their fill. Then they tethered the camels among the trees and lay down in the shade to rest.

Utu woke with a start at twilight. A line of ants was crawling over his foot. He brushed them off.

"Welcome back, sleepyhead," Job said. "You were snoring loud enough to warn the enemy."

Utu punched Job on the shoulder. "Have you heard what's happening?"

Job nodded. "We're going to split into four groups and get into position before sunset. When it's fully dark, Avram will beat his shield and we are all to scream and yell." Job rubbed his ear. "The idea is to frighten the soldiers so they abandon the captives."

"Let's hope it works," Utu muttered.

"It had better, or you might not get to see the pretty Jemimah again."

Utu felt his face warm. "I didn't think you'd noticed."

"Not notice! You flush and stammer any time she comes near. I'm your best friend, and I'm not blind."

"Well, nothing will come of it." Eliezer might have chosen Utu as his assistant but welcoming him into the family would be something else entirely.

* * *

*I*t had taken them a long time to get into position but below them they could see the glimmer of fires and smell the roasting meat. It was a good sign. If Kedorlaomer and his soldiers dared to light fires and were feasting, they were not expecting any attack.

A mosquito buzzed in Utu's ear, and he shook his head rather than risk slapping it. It buzzed again and he stuffed some moss in his ears. It was better to be bitten by a swarm of mosquitoes than to endanger their plan.

Job was standing silently at his shoulder. If the worst should happen, then he was glad he would die with Job at his side. He'd been a good friend.

But he didn't want to die or be captured. He might not have a chance with Jemimah, but being around her was better than nothing. And who would protect Inanna from her own impulsiveness?

It was fully dark now, and the fires below were dying down to mere coals. Surely they would attack soon.

A little breeze lifted the hair at his neck. He strained his ears, and after long moments, he heard the thud of a stick against a shield. Finally! Utu opened his mouth to yell and swung his sturdy staff with a crash against the nearest tree. All around him and on all sides of the enemy below, there were more loud crashes and bangs and shouts.

"Come on," Job said from beside him.

Utu's stomach churned but he followed Job, who didn't seem scared at all. They ran, crashing through trees and yelling. Below them came a series of screams. Utu could see the campsite clearly and the silhouettes of people in panic. Several people ran right through the fires, scattered the coals before them, and howled in pain. People were already running north, away from Avram's men.

Utu arrived at the campsite along with most of the younger members of their group. They raced towards the last people fleeing and struck them with wooden staves. The weapons shepherds used against wolves and lions worked equally well on men.

"Lot, are you here?" Avram called behind them. "Lot?"

Utu turned and went back into the camp, skirting the still glowing coals and abandoned possessions.

A man emerged cautiously into the firelight. "Uncle, is that really you?"

Avram hugged Lot and greeted Lot's wife and their daughters.

One good ending then.

"No time for celebration yet," Eliezer called above the chatter. He turned and talked to one of the fitter men with fighting experience. The man started calling out names and Eliezer turned to Job and Utu.

"You'll be part of the group pursuing the soldiers. Just keep making noise and don't get separated."

They went to join the others, ready for instructions.

Eliezer stood next to the man he'd chosen to lead them. "Your job is to give Avram and the rest of us time to get away," Eliezer said. "Eat a little food now from the provisions abandoned by the raiders. Only pursue them until dawn, then turn back."

After Eliezer finished his instructions, Utu and Job headed for one of the campfires further away. The still-warm chickpeas in an abandoned pot were more than welcome.

"All those on camels and all the captives, leave now and head for home," Eliezer said to those heading towards home. "Anyone elderly or injured can ride. The rest of you will have to walk." He turned to indicate another group. "Make sure you pick up all the belongings and spoils. Don't leave anything behind."

Utu finished his meal with a long drink, then he and Job attached themselves to the group heading north. The leader set off at a steady pace, one suitable for the pursuit of an unknown length. If the gods smiled on them, there would be no need to fight. They just had to keep the enemy more intent on fleeing and saving their lives than turning and fighting.

* * *

"There they are," Job called as they topped a hill the following afternoon.

As instructed, they'd pursued the raiders well to the north, then turned south again at dawn to follow Avram and the others. Avram could clearly be seen below them, on top of his heavily laden camel. Around him were the freed captives and the rest of the band. The walls of a city were not far ahead.

"Someone's coming out of the city to meet them," their leader said. He turned to yell to the group around him, "Come on. Let's get down there."

Despite the soreness of Utu's feet and all his cuts and bruises from their night of running without anything more than the faint light of the crescent moon to guide them, he picked up speed.

Before long, they reached the outskirts of Avram's group where everyone was feasting from baskets of bread. Where had the bread come from?

Utu looked for Avram and saw him talking to a man dressed in much finer clothes than anyone surrounding him. The man offered Avram wine.

Utu and the others stopped on the outskirts of the group, chests heaving and smelling like a herd of animals themselves. He'd definitely be taking a long bath in the river when they made it home. Maybe tomorrow or the next day.

Utu and Job inched towards the front where Eliezer stood next to Avram and the stranger. "Who is he?" Utu whispered to the man next to him.

"Melchizedek, king of Salem," the man murmured.

Utu had never heard of him, but Avram was treating him with great respect.

"And that's the King of Sodom over there," his informant continued.

Now, Sodom he'd heard far too much about. The King of Sodom was huge and flabby with the red face of a heavy drinker. Utu crept closer to hear what the mysterious Melchizedek was saying.

Melchizedek raised his hands towards heaven. "As priest of the most high God, I bless you."

The most high God. Was this another name for Avram's god? It seemed so, for Avram had bowed his head and raised open hands to receive the blessing.

"Blessed be Avram by God Most High, Creator of heaven and earth. And blessed be God Most High who delivered your enemies into your hand."

Surely it was their plan and strength that had won the fight? Avram stood silent receiving the blessing, then he lowered his hands, smiled, and turned to Eliezer.

"A tenth of all the spoils are to go to Melchizedek," Avram said.

A tenth for a man who hadn't done anything except offer a blessing? It didn't seem right. This Melchizedek hadn't done any of the hard work.

Eliezer looked around, and beckoned Utu off to the side. There'd be no eating for Utu until after the sorting. He swallowed his disappointment. He was hot and tired and hungry, and sorting wasn't what he wanted to be doing but he also couldn't leave the work to Eliezer.

"Save me something," he mouthed to Job.

It took ages to divide the spoils, but once Melchizedek returned to Salem with his portion, the King of Sodom came over to Avram.

"Give me the people who were captured, but keep the goods for yourself," the King of Sodom said.

"Thank you for your kind offer," Avram said. "But I have raised my hand to the Lord Most High, Creator of heaven and earth, and I have taken an oath that I won't accept anything belonging to you. Not a single thread of cloth, or the thong of a sandal, so you will never be able to say, 'I made Avram rich.'"

Utu blinked. His father would see such an act as foolish and even weak. A man's power was increased by his wealth, and no man ever turned down opportunities to increase it.

Avram turned to indicate the three men nearby. "But I will accept the food my men have eaten and let Mamre and the Amorite chiefs have their share, for they have fought alongside me."

The King of Sodom remonstrated for politeness' sake, but Avram was firm, and Avram won.

CHAPTER TEN

*H*er chance had come. Inanna had known her stars would align and now they had. Ever since they'd arrived at Kiriath Arba, she'd been watching for her chance, but there'd always been too many people around. Too many people with not enough to do except watch what everyone else was doing.

But now 318 pairs of eyes had gone elsewhere, including Utu's. Ever since they'd arrived home, he'd been watching her. He knew her well enough to know she didn't give up easily. A sliver of disappointment lanced her heart. He hadn't been willing to come with her. He'd always valued stability, and now he was choosing that over her. Or maybe Jemimah and her father had been the deciding factor.

Perhaps she was being unfair. If he'd been here, he might have followed her at the last moment, as he had the day they were captured. She hardened her heart. She wasn't going to wait for him, but she still had to be patient. She had been hurrying to prepare food for the men before they left and had overhead Lot's servant saying the captives had a two-day head start. By her reckoning, it would be at least the third or fourth day before they caught up with Lot and his family, and as many days again until they returned. She'd go on the night of the third day, when it was darkest. She'd managed to check her route while collecting herbs, and it was still as familiar to her as the smell of her mother's hair.

"You seem anxious," Hagar said as they cooked lentil and onion stew together. "I'm sure Utu will be fine. Avram and Eliezer are careful men. They won't do anything foolish."

"Thank you for your reassurances," Inanna murmured, although her mind had been far away from Utu.

"You were talking in your sleep last night," Hagar said, stirring the pot.

Inanna's heart started to race. "Did I say anything?"

"You were calling for your mother."

Inanna released the breath she'd been holding. She'd always been a sleep talker, so murmuring for her mother wouldn't be viewed as anything unusual. A few more days and she'd feel Mama's arms around her.

Her shoulders tensed. She longed for her mother, but what if her mother still thought of her as a little girl? Even as a little girl, she'd only submitted to a hug for brief moments before struggling to be free. Struggling to assert her independence.

Inanna shook her head. It was now or never, and she must not give any hint of her plans. Patience. That was all she needed.

* * *

*I*nanna waited for the shadows to lengthen towards evening on the third day. She'd volunteered to collect herbs and had been busy down near the river. She timed her return to the tent for when people would be elsewhere and put the herbs in the cool area. Then, as casually as possible, she drifted in the direction of the oak trees.

All she wanted to do was to dash forward into the branches where she felt so at home, but she meandered this way and that, that way and this, until at last she was under the dark coolness of the outer trees.

She turned to look behind her, willing herself to look like she had not a care in the world. No one was looking in her direction. Casually, oh so casually, she flitted from tree trunk to tree trunk. There was no sound but the wind in the grass, the distant burbling of the river, and one solitary bird pouring out its heart in song. Finally, she was standing behind the tree that had started her long journey away from all that was familiar. She checked all around and then reached up her hands and scrambled into the protective embrace of the old oak. The higher she climbed, the more it felt like home. In the very place where she'd hidden from the desert raiders, she straddled the branch and wrapped her arms around the trunk of the tree. It had grown faster than she had. She placed her ear against the trunk and imagined the tree talking to her. Telling her that she was safe. That she'd soon be home where she belonged.

The darkness amongst the trees deepened and the bird stopped singing. Only the breeze continued to rustle the leaves, and somewhere, two branches creaked and rubbed together.

* * *

The muffled sound of voices in Avram's camp had died down long ago. Inanna cautiously descended from her tree. She must not be caught. She'd seen the horrible things that happened to recaptured slaves in Egypt.

She wound her way carefully to the edge of the grove and tested the wind's direction on a wet finger. It was blowing from behind the camp and towards her. Perfect. Taking her time, she headed for the edge of the town wall and used its shadow to move silently around to the far side.

As a child she'd found a secret entrance into the town after the gates were locked, and she was counting on it still being possible. If not, she might have to sneak back into camp and pretend she hadn't been missing for hours. Tonight, if all went well, she'd be back where she belonged. She swallowed the lump in her throat. She'd miss Utu and Hagar, but Utu had made his decision. Tears prickled her eyelashes.

Don't think about Utu.

Inanna tripped over a stone, and it clattered against the wall. She froze, holding her breath for a long moment, before letting it out again. Praise be. The guards on the wall must be on a different section of their rounds.

It seemed an age before she found the tumble of rocks marking the spot where she used to stand. She cupped her hands around her mouth and made the sound of an owl but with a rhythm all her own. Hoo-hoo-hooo-hooooo. She called twice and waited. Then twice more.

Could her mother's brother have moved? Or had it been too long, and he'd forgotten? She hooted again. Hoo-hoo-hooo-hooooo.

There! A tiny flicker of light. She called again before she saw a man's head silhouetted against the lowest window, peering out towards the rocks. She hooted again and waved the sleeve of her tunic. The paleness of the cloth should be visible to her uncle on the wall.

"Is it you, little owl?" he whispered.

She hooted again and came to the base of the wall. She heard a scrape from the top of the wall and then silence. Did he still own the rope?

Above her there was a slither, and she jumped when the rope touched her shoulder. She gave a firm tug and it held. Now to see if her limbs still remembered how to climb. She reached up and held on tight, then placed her feet on the wall. Moving one limb at a time she walked up the wall with her legs straight out in front of her. The man above her grunted. He'd better still be fit enough to hold her, or she'd fall and break all the bones in her body.

Her arms trembled with the strain, but the window was now just one body length away. She moved her hands up. Near the top she lunged and grasped the window ledge with one hand, then the other, and wrapped her legs around the rope for the last shimmy. He grabbed her under her arms and hauled her into the room.

"Well," her uncle said, laughter in his voice. "I never expected to see you again."

Inanna scrambled to her feet and smoothed down her tunic. "Or me you, uncle."

"Where have you been all these years?" he asked as he coiled the rope.

"Egypt." She squeezed the word out between breaths.

"I hope you're not going to make a habit of climbing my wall. I'm not as young as I used to be." He wheezed. "And you're not a child anymore." He raised the tiny oil lamp and peered at her. "You look like your mother."

"I've come to see her," Inanna said.

"Ah," he said, avoiding her gaze.

A trembling began in her legs. Had something happened to her mother? Inanna had spent so much energy planning how to reach home that she'd never considered her mother wouldn't be waiting.

"We don't know where she is," he said, sinking to the floor. "After you were taken by the raiders, she was crazy with grief. One day she left to look for you." He sighed. "And we've never heard of her again."

"So you don't even know if she's still alive?" Inanna asked, a catch in her voice.

He shook his head. "I try not to think about what may have happened to her." He placed his hand on Inanna's shoulder. "Like I tried not to imagine what happened to you both. Where's your brother?"

"Off chasing Kedorlaomer's soldiers."

"So you're part of Avram's household?"

She nodded and quickly told him how that had come to be.

"And are you going to get beaten for being here tonight?"

"I'm not going back. I want to be free."

He whistled softly between his teeth. "Girl, no one is ever free."

"My father can do whatever he wants."

"Can he really?" He laughed ruefully. "The responsibility of this whole town rests on his shoulders. If there is famine, he has to find food. When the desert raiders come, he is blamed. When it doesn't rain, he must find a solution. Me, I have no desire to be the chief. I'm content to have enough to eat." He patted his expansive stomach. "And somewhere warm and dry to sleep. I have no great ambitions. Great ambitions will enslave you as much as anything else."

She shook her head. No. She didn't want to believe it.

"The smartest thing you could do would be to go back the way you came before you're missed."

And not do what she'd come to do. No way. If her mother wasn't here, she was going to see her father. Or her brothers.

"Now what are you plotting?" Her uncle raised one quizzical eyebrow. "There's no point in going to see your family. They won't even remember your name."

Her uncle might be a nice man, but he didn't know everything. Her father and some of her brothers would certainly remember her. Her father had loved her even if he'd never said the words. In her years in Pharaoh's household, she'd nursed the memories of his hearty laugh when she said something witty and the trip they'd all made together to her grandfather's funeral. He'd pat her curly hair and remark how much she was like him.

After spending so long planning how to escape, she wasn't going to leave without at least trying to see him.

"I'll stay until morning," she said, curling into a ball.

"Girl, you're going to be the death of me," her uncle muttered as he stomped off. He returned a few minutes later with a cloak and laid it over her.

"You might be as stubborn as any donkey," he said, patting her cheek, "but it is good to see you. Life hasn't been the same without you three."

* * *

She'd always woken early. At the first birdsong of dawn, she got to her feet, folded the cloak, and found some bread under a cloth. Then she put on the veil she'd hidden beneath her tunic and crept out the door, into the street. The streets were relatively quiet, but the first vendors were already laying out their wares in the marketplace: woven cloth, excess fruit, and honey from a secret find.

She ignored those trying to sell her things, for she had nothing to barter. Instead, she headed towards the place her father had always had breakfast, up on the town wall where he could keep an eye on everything in the town.

When she reached the bottom of the wall, she paused near the kitchen and took a dish of curds when the cook's back was turned. It might be better not to turn up empty-handed. She climbed the stairs, heart racing in anticipation. Soon she'd see her father. Would he be as pleased to see her as she would be to see him? Uncle said not, but he'd never had any children of his own. What did he know of the bond between fathers and daughters?

She heard the men's laughter before she saw them, lounging in their usual spot. She scanned the backs of their heads but couldn't see her father. Perhaps he would be joining them later.

"Hey, you," one of the men called. "Bring that over here. You're late."

Heart in throat, she clutched the dish and moved forward.

"Put it there," said the man she now recognized as her fifth brother. She'd never liked him.

She hesitated, unsure what to do next. Did she dare to question them?

"Don't stand there all day. Bring the rest," the same brother said.

It was now or never.

"Where's your father?" she asked, a tremble in her voice.

"What does it matter to the likes of you?" her sixth brother said. It was the scorn in his voice, as though she was cow manure underfoot, that got to her.

"He might be interested to know that I'm not dead," she said.

"You're very bold for a stranger," the fifth brother said, menace in his voice.

She backed away but stumbled over someone's outstretched leg.

"Careful girl," a voice said and grabbed her arm.

"Unveil her," said another voice. "Let's see what we've caught."

She wasn't going to wait for them to do the job. She whipped off her veil and stood before them, knees trembling but head held high.

"I can certainly see the family resemblance," said another of the men, one of her many cousins.

"Where's father?"

"Are you claiming to be related to him?"

"Of course. I'm Inanna, daughter of Mamre and Attar."

Her fifth brother spun her around and peered at her. "Inanna, it's about time you turned up."

She thought he was happy to see her for the length of a single heartbeat, but his expression changed as fast as the sky in a summer storm. Her gut twisted.

"You and your mother caused me a great deal of trouble," he said. "Got me a beating when your mother ran off, then I had to waste my time searching for her. Father was not happy she'd left without asking permission."

"Father," she stammered. "Where is he?"

"Nowhere he can help you." The mockery in his voice sent shivers up her spine. "Gone off with Avram and our big brothers to chase the captives."

She'd assumed her father wouldn't have gone to a fight that didn't concern him.

She whipped around to her seventh brother, staying quiet as he usually did. He'd always been kind to her and Utu. "Can I wait with you for Father to return?"

"There's no point," he said gently. "At last count, Father had forty children, and your mother was one of the lesser wives."

His words struck her like blows. She'd dismissed her uncle's warnings, but perhaps he'd been right after all.

"I'll go then," she said, moving towards the kinder brother.

"Not so fast, little sister," her fifth brother said, surging to his feet and grabbing her roughly. "I still owe you a beating."

She looked towards her other brothers, but they turned away and didn't say a word as she was propelled down the stairs. It was no use struggling or screaming for help. If her own family wouldn't help, no one else would.

* * *

*T*he whip whistled through the air and struck her back, setting her skin on fire. She clamped her jaw. She'd never give him the satisfaction of hearing her scream.

"You're a tough one, eh?" he grunted.

The whip came down again. And again. Three thin stripes of fire traversed her back and her buttocks. She waited for the fourth stroke.

"Now you know how I felt. Father said it was my fault when your mother left, because I was supposed to have been watching her."

The whip landed again. She bit her lip, tasting blood. It roused her from a stupor of pain, and she heard approaching footsteps.

"Enough," her uncle's voice said behind her. "This girl is not to blame for your situation."

There was a brief scuffle and she staggered to the wall, letting it hold her upright.

"It's finished, girlie," her uncle said. "Let's get you home."

He threw a cloak over her back and supported her on his arm to take the slow and painful steps back to his home. There was an older woman waiting, and she bathed Inanna's back and gave her something to drink that made her sleep.

* * *

"*G*ood to see you awake, Inanna," her uncle said, coming into the room. "How are you feeling?"

"Sore, but much better." She'd spent the last two days sleeping on her stomach, but now she pushed herself up to her hands and knees. Her back groaned in protest.

A great lump filled her throat and tears prickled her lashes. She clamped her lips together. She must not cry. Must not show how much it meant to her that her dreams weren't going to be fulfilled. While she'd been recovering she'd thought a lot about her childhood. Memories of herself with her father were actually very few. But they were so treasured that they had taken over a large part of her heart.

Inanna grimaced and combed her fingers through her tangled hair. "Better enough to go back to your mistress?"

"I suppose there's no other option."

Utu had tried to warn her that her dreams might be fantasies, but she hadn't listened.

"Not really," her uncle said, his voice gentle as though he sensed her devastation. "Your fifth brother now has another reason to hold a grudge against you. You won't be safe here."

The tears threatened again. "Why does he hate me?"

Her uncle handed her a drink. "It's not you. He's frustrated to be a lesser son in a big family."

"But the other younger brothers seem content." She swiftly plaited her long hair.

"They're smart enough to realize they can't change things."

Smart like Utu, who didn't long for things that would never be his. She'd looked down on what she called his lack of ambition, but maybe he was wiser than her. He was focusing on things that were achievable instead of trying to fly with the eagles.

Her uncle took the cup from her and turned to go. "Come and eat when you're ready."

She waited for him to leave and then dealt with her urgent physical needs before heading out to the main room.

Her uncle had fresh bread, curds, and olive oil waiting for her. "Eat. Then I'll accompany you back to Avram's camp."

"Utu and the others aren't back yet?"

"No, but a messenger arrived to tell us they succeeded in rescuing the captives without any loss of life."

Some of the tension in her neck relaxed. She'd blocked Utu out of her mind while she pursued her own plans. Refusing to think about him and the danger he'd been in had been the only way she could cope with leaving him behind.

Her uncle sat with her while she ate hungrily. "You were right," she said when she'd finished.

"About what?"

"That I am unimportant to this family." The words stung her heart.

It wasn't fair. Why were only the first few sons important in a family like hers? Every wise man must have a few backups in case the first met with an accident or succumbed to a disease. Daughters only had importance because they could be strategically married off to further alliances and keep the town prosperous and secure.

Tears welled in her eyes. Birth order and being a son shouldn't determine importance.

"Don't take things so much to heart." He leaned forward and patted her shoulder. "Although, as I remember, you always did."

He had been her favorite uncle, and she'd often poured out her childish sorrows to him. The time her mother had first spanked her. The time she'd been stung by multiple bees. The many times she'd been frustrated by Utu's overprotectiveness.

"Your brother was always easygoing, and that's a good thing in this life. You can't change the fact that you have no status. You can fight against it all you like, but you and I aren't in a position to change anything."

She clenched her fists and her jaw. Why did he have to state things so starkly? She wanted to belong to a world where she mattered more than an ant that gets crushed underfoot. She wanted to belong to a world where her father cared about her and wanted her around. Confusion swirled in her gut. Why had she wanted her parents so much when being around them clashed with her desire to be free? How could one be free and still be important to others? She didn't know, but it looked like none of her wishes were going to come true, no matter how much she longed for them.

Her uncle handed her some more fruit. "I'm mighty glad you're still alive and fighting. You always were my favorite niece."

"I'm your only niece," she muttered.

"There is that as well, but I suspect you'd have been my favorite even if I'd had as many as the stones in our river."

"Thank you." She leaned over and tentatively gave him a hug. "I guess I'd better be going."

"You'd be safer if I accompanied you back to your camp once the gate opens. That way you might avoid another beating."

"I don't think I'll get a beating." Avram wasn't that sort of man. He'd be disappointed in her, but he wasn't vindictive or cruel.

"You have a good master then."

And gladness flooded her heart. "Yes. Yes, I do."

She'd had a much better life with this household than she ever would have in her father's. She might not be important, but she had been happier than most with plenty of food and no beatings to show for it. The desert raiders and Pharaoh's household had not been nearly so lenient. If she'd broken a dish or tripped and drawn attention to herself, she'd been beaten and left without food for a day. She still had a few scars to show from when she'd been labelled cheeky.

She'd go back and make any explanations she needed to and take any punishment Avram or Sarai decreed. Utu was going to growl at her, but she'd handle him. She might be knocked down now, but things would change one day.

She'd keep her eyes open for opportunities. And if she saw one, she'd grab it with both hands.

CHAPTER ELEVEN

*U*tu looked at his sister. "You've been avoiding me."

Inanna was the type to rush forward and throw her arms around him, not hang back as she'd done yesterday when they'd all returned from rescuing the captives. No matter how many times he tried to find her, all he'd heard was, "She was just here." When he saw her heading for the oak grove to collect firewood, he'd pursued her.

Inanna gave a grunt. Also not like her. Normally the words were tumbling out of her. His mouth went dry.

"What's wrong?" he asked.

"Nothing," she mumbled as she stooped awkwardly to pick up a fallen branch.

Awkward? She was never awkward. He reached out and touched her shoulder, but she pulled away with a gasp. His heart raced.

"Inanna, you're hurt."

"I'll be better soon."

"That's not the point," he said. "Who hurt you?"

She sighed and sat down on a fallen tree trunk. "Are you going to go all big brother on me?"

"It sounds like I need to."

She brushed the corner of her eye. "I did something stupid."

He'd already worked that out. "Does it have anything to do with there?" He gestured at the town over their shoulder.

She hung her head. "You warned me not to go."

Pity twisted his gut. Why was it that she always had to learn everything the hard way? "What did you do?"

"You probably didn't know I had a secret way into the town."

He hadn't.

"I went outside Uncle's place and whistled for him to let down a rope."

He swallowed. The thought of the dangers involved in that were enough to give him palpitations.

"Don't look at me like that. I'd done it often before, and it was easy enough."

"You should have told me what you planned."

"And have you talk me out of it?"

He already tried that, a conversation that had made as much of an impression as holding up his hand to stop the rain. "And did you see her?"

"Mama?"

He nodded. Who else would he mean?

"She wasn't there," Inanna's voice cracked. "She went looking for us."

His eyes widened.

"Father refused to search for us, so she went on her own."

His mouth twisted. Mother was just like Inanna. "And she hasn't returned?"

Inanna shook her head.

He saw the fear in her eyes, and he reached out to lay a hand on her forearm. Someone else for him to worry about. Mama could be anywhere. She might not even be alive, but he wasn't going to raise that possibility.

"Tell me what happened and who hurt you."

"Only if you don't interrupt."

He promised, but her story made it hard for him to keep the promise. She joked about it, but he couldn't miss the disappointment and

81

deep hurt in her voice. If only she had spoken to him. He could have told her their father had gone to chase after the captives. He could have warned her about some of their brothers. He'd learned early to keep well away from the brother who'd whipped her. He was a bully who said and did nasty things that had twisted his gut as a small child. Their fifth brother always managed to seem a model of perfection while getting others in trouble.

"… none of our brothers seemed happy to see me." She gave a huge sob.

"I'm sorry. Sorry you had to go through all this without me." He shifted closer to her on the log and took her hand. "I've thought a lot about our family over the years."

She looked at him. "I never knew that."

"You know me. I don't speak much—"

"But inside, you're thinking," she said.

"I think it would have made things better in the family if our oldest brother was the heir, but father has always hinted he'd choose his heir when the time came." He sighed. "So each brother keeps competing for father's favor."

He'd been reminded of how ambition could curdle a man's heart as he'd watched their four oldest brothers trying to prove themselves during the last week. It had made them take unnecessary risks, but it had also protected him, because his father hadn't noticed there was an extra son hidden in Avram's household.

"But you and our seventh brother aren't like the others," Inanna said with a sniff.

He chuckled. "There are some good things about your boring brother."

"I don't think you're boring."

He was sure she'd thought it often enough and got frustrated with his lack of ambition. It was just that he longed for satisfying work and a family. He had satisfying work now, and he continued to hope for the other. One day, when he was able to consider someone besides Jemimah.

CHAPTER TWELVE

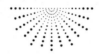

$\mathcal{U}$tu tossed and turned. It was stifling hot in the tent. A twig cracked outside, followed by the cautious tread of someone's feet. Utu crept to the entrance of the tent and peered out. Avram! Utu left the tent and ghosted after him. It felt uncomfortable spying on Avram but only that morning, Eliezer had taken him aside and made an unusual request.

"'Keep an eye on Avram. If you see him wander off, follow him. He tried to get Lot to send his daughters up here, as he's worried about them in Sodom. It certainly isn't a place I'd like my daughter to live," Eliezer had muttered.

Was Avram going to meet someone? He walked with purpose. Once Avram reached the shelter of the oak trees, Utu abandoned caution and sped up.

Utu knew every stone and root in the wooded area. He made sure to keep at least one tree trunk between himself and Avram at all times.

Avram stopped without warning. Utu ducked behind a tree, leaves crackling beneath his unplanned sidestep. He held his breath. Had Avram heard him? He peeked around the tree, and his eyes widened. In front of Avram there was a shimmering, shifting something. Was it light? Maybe. Certainly there were parts of rainbows in it.

Avram bowed low and then a voice spoke. Utu bit his lip to stop himself crying out.

"Do not be afraid, Avram. I am your shield. Your reward will be great."

Utu looked around. There was no one else here, and surely no human had a voice like this. The voice was somehow deeper and wilder and older than any he'd ever heard. If the shimmer hadn't been there, Utu might have thought it was the biggest oak tree talking.

Why was the voice telling Avram not to be afraid?

"Sovereign Lord," Avram said. "What can you give me, since I remain childless and the one who will inherit my estate is Eliezer of Damascus?"

Eliezer? What about Lot? Surely a blood relative was the more likely heir? Long life and wealth obviously wasn't enough. Maybe when someone was old, lack of descendants was what they feared the most. To die and leave no son behind him. Did Avram envy Eliezer because he had a child?

Eliezer had never mentioned he was the heir. Maybe he didn't know. Did Lot? Eliezer was more worthy to be heir. After their rescue, Lot had once again lost everyone's respect by not offering a word of thanks. In fact, Lot seemed to resent that Avram got all the praise.

"Oh, Lord, you have given me no children." Avram rocked back and forth.

Utu looked away. He couldn't bear to watch Avram's grief. The grief of an old man approaching eighty-five and without a son. Avram loved Sarai—that was obvious to all of them—but love hadn't been enough.

"Instead a servant in my household will be my heir."

Utu knew Avram loved Eliezer like a son, but even Utu could see it wasn't the same. Inanna longed for freedom, but Utu, though still young, had begun to dream of a son of his own. His face warmed, thinking of the dark eyes of Eliezer's daughter.

The light shimmered and pulsed, and the voice spoke again. "This man will not be your heir ..."

Avram raised his head.

"But a son who will be your own flesh and blood will be your heir."

Avram gasped and choked back a sob.

"Look up above you and count the stars, if you can."

Avram tilted his head back, and Utu did the same. The dark canopy of the sky was pricked with a multitude of points of light.

"Your offspring will be as many as the stars."

Avram fell prostrate on the ground.

"I am the Lord, who brought you out of Ur of the Chaldeans to give you this land to take possession of it."

Avram scrambled to his knees and looked up at the light. "But Sovereign Lord, how can I know that I will gain possession of it?"

"Tomorrow, bring me a heifer, a goat, and a ram, each three years old, along with a dove, and a young pigeon."

Avram was still nodding his head when the shimmer faded and disappeared. He stared up at the sky for a long time, gently rocking back and forth, before finally getting stiffly to his feet.

Utu waited until Avram had passed before he returned to the tent as silently as he'd come. Utu lay down. Tomorrow he'd be on the lookout for Avram taking the animals to wherever this god intended him to go.

A god who revealed himself, communicated, and made promises was well outside anything Utu had ever heard. Sure, the Amorite priests claimed the gods spoke to them, but he'd never seen any evidence of it. There'd been little more than smoke and incantations to deceive the gullible and put them into debt. Avram's god gave gifts, generous gifts. Even if he asked for sacrifices, they were perfectly reasonable for a man of Avram's wealth.

Utu shut his eyes. He needed sleep if he was to be awake to watch Avram tomorrow.

* * *

*U*tu was leaning against the oak tree he and Inanna still called their own. The cicadas pulsed in his ears, and he had almost dozed off in the midday heat when Avram walked by, leading a heifer, a goat, and a ram, and carrying a cage with two birds in it.

Utu stood up and looked around. No one was following, so he cautiously set off in pursuit.

Avram seemed to know where he was going. He reached a canyon with a stream coming out of its mouth, and he turned down into it. He tied the animals to a nearby tree, and placed the cage with the birds on the ground.

Utu dropped to his belly and crawled behind a pile of rocks that were shaded by twisted trees. He found a cool spot and watched for what Avram would do next.

Avram did nothing except stand motionless. Was he waiting, or was he communing with his god?

Utu had expected Avram to gather stones for an altar. Instead, Avram reached below his robes and untied the knife attached to his thigh. He went and put his arm around the heifer to calm it and, quick as lightning, cut the animal's neck. Blood poured out on the ground and was soaked up by the thirsty earth. The heifer struggled and gave a strangled gurgle before collapsing. Avram lowered the corpse to the ground, then did the same with the goat and the ram.

He divided the two smaller animals in half before returning to the heifer.

Utu had seen this once before. A cutting ceremony. Long ago, Utu's father cut a covenant with another tribal chief. They'd divided the animals as Avram was doing and both parties walked through the divided corpses signifying what would happen if they failed to live up to their promises. Mamre had sealed the deal by marrying one of the other chieftain's daughters and promising him a daughter for his son.

The smell of blood filled Utu's nostrils as Avram dragged the corpses to the flat area, laying them out in matching pairs with a clear space in between. Then he reached into the cage, drew out the dove, and quickly killed it. Once the blood had drained, he lay the intact corpse on the ground. The pigeon soon joined it.

Then Avram went to the stream and washed the knife and his blood-spattered arms and clothes. As he was finishing, there was a strident squawk that bounced off the canyon walls. Utu looked up. Already, two vultures were circling. With more cries, several others joined them. They flew in ever lower and tightening circles.

Avram came out of the water. As the birds came nearer, Avram rushed towards the animal corpses, flapping his arms to protect them. The vultures screeched and rose but soon descended again. Again, Avram ran to flap his arms. Again, the birds flew out of range.

Utu looked around. It seemed strange that Avram had killed the animals before the arrival of the other party. Now he was forced to protect them from the eager interest of the birds.

Again and again, Avram had to protect the corpses. Utu's eyelids grew heavy, and his head dropped to his chest. He woke to see the sun dropping down behind the rocks. Right in front of him, Avram fell to the ground as though dead.

Utu leapt to his feet. Now what should he do?

Avram rolled over and grunted. Some sort of darkness hovered over him. Utu hesitated, unsure what to do. The vultures had given up, with the divided animals still untouched by them, yet still the other party for the covenant had not arrived.

The sun disappeared and the sky was dark and starless. A bright light appeared from nowhere, almost blinding Utu. He covered his eyes and looked through the gaps between his fingers. Avram was struggling to his feet. Overhead, a pot full of flames moved slowly between the animals Avram had cut in half. The voice Utu had heard last night spoke again.

"To your descendants I give this land, from the Wadi of Egypt to the great river, the Euphrates, the land of the Kenites, Kenizzites, Kamonites ..."

As the names were announced slowly and sonorously, Utu pictured the different tribes. Some he'd encountered as a child as they formed alliances with his father. Some he'd met as the desert raiders passed through their territories.

"... Hittites, Perizzites, Rephaites, Amorites, Canaanites, Girgashites, and Jebusites."

Amorites! His people were in the list. Would they too disappear like water into the desert sands? How was that possible? Avram and Sarai were old. Too old for children. Where were Avram's descendants going to come from? And how?

So many questions. Questions that seemed to conflict with the absolute certainty in the voice of Avram's god.

* * *

*U*tu woke to a silent tent the next morning. Somehow everyone had left the tent without him hearing a thing. He jumped to his feet, folded his covering, and put it in the box in the corner, then hurried out of the tent.

Eliezer was nearby and beckoned him over.

"Sorry. I was dead to the world." Utu flushed. He'd never slept so late before.

"You and Avram both. Whatever happened out there seems to have overwhelmed you. Avram wouldn't speak much of it last night, but we've had a talk this morning."

"How did you know I was there?"

Eliezer smiled. "I saw you following him."

The man seemed to have eyes on all sides of his head. "Did Avram tell you about the two …" How could he describe what had happened? He swallowed noisily. "… encounters?"

Eliezer nodded.

Good, because Utu doubted he could find the words to describe something so … so otherworldly. He wasn't scared by the experiences. Not in a negative sense, at least, but he was overwhelmed by awe. It was as if he was only an ant and this being was so far above him that the contrast was laughable. The question that lingered in his mind was simple. Why had he been permitted to see and hear what he'd seen and heard? And what must it be like for Avram to be chosen by such a god? To be part of such great and weighty plans?

CHAPTER THIRTEEN

Two years later
Kiriath Arba

*U*tu loved the return to the rhythms of his childhood. Rather than moving on, Avram had settled in Kiriath Arba, near the oaks of Mamre.

The barley planting was done, and his body ached from the constant stooping. Eliezer had noticed that the birds ate most of the seed when they sowed using the traditional seed scattering method. This year they'd planted each seed individually and covered it. It was much harder work, but less wasteful. Now there would be a few slower days before the next task on the yearly calendar, and he and Job had been invited to eat with Eliezer and Jemimah.

Utu clutched a handful of white and purple wildflowers. Job had teased him, but Utu didn't care. Jemimah had seemed appreciative the last time he'd taken the time to pick flowers.

He'd come early, so he could complete any tasks Jemimah needed help with.

Jemimah was outside, using a large rock as a platform to crush the grain. She looked up as Utu approached and colored prettily. He held out his hand with the flowers. "As a thank you."

"You didn't have to. Your company ... I mean yours and Job's, is always a pleasure." She took the flowers and busied herself finding a bowl to put them in.

Did Job really rate equally with him in her eyes? Utu had begun to hope that Jemimah saw him differently from the others. If her father had been anyone other than Eliezer, he would have spoken before this, but if Eliezer wouldn't consider Utu for a son-in-law, then Utu might lose his job too.

"Do you need any help?' Utu asked Jemimah.

She pointed to the waterskins. "Abba was going to get some more water. I didn't put the stopper in tight enough and lost half a bag."

He stooped and picked up the two bags. "It won't take long."

Getting water from the well was usually considered women's work, but why should women have to do the heavy hauling? Although Inanna would always fight for the right to collect water, because she preferred that task to making bread.

By the time Utu had been to the well and back, Job had arrived.

Jemimah served them lentil stew and herbs with fresh bread, and they eagerly went back for seconds. After the meal, they munched on raisins and dried figs and chatted about the planting.

Job leaned back against the nearest tree trunk with a contented sigh. "Eliezer, I never did hear how you came to work for Avram."

Utu sat up straight. He'd long wanted to ask this question but hadn't, hoping Eliezer would tell the story on his own. And 'work for Avram' was the key phrase. Unlike himself and Job, Eliezer wasn't a slave. This fact alone made Utu doubt he had a chance with Jemimah. What father would let his precious only child marry a slave?

"It's a bit of a long story," Eliezer said.

Job leaned forward. "I'm not ready for sleep yet."

Eliezer drank some water. "You know I'm from Damascus. I was raised as the only son of the man in charge of feeding the army." A tiny smile quirked the corner of his mouth. "From my earliest childhood, I ran after my father to buy supplies."

Eliezer still ran from place to place.

"He taught me to calculate the amount of meat on an animal and how to check it was healthy. He also taught me how to save money by buying things in quantity from the local growers." Eliezer's voice had warmed. "My father knew all the local farmers and shopkeepers. He knew when someone was trying to cheat him, and sellers soon learned that he'd never buy from a cheat."

"It sounds like a useful education," Utu said.

"It was, and Abba made sure I could read and figure."

Utu had seen how fast Eliezer could calculate the size of a flock or herd. Eliezer had told him, "Don't compare yourself with me. You have your own strengths. Learn to read people, and get reliable help in your weaker areas."

Eliezer stroked his beard. "My father was soon so trusted that he began to deal in other things—ropes and halters for the animals, leather goods, and footwear. All the time he was training me to take over one day."

Something must have gone wrong, because Eliezer had previously said he'd been working for Avram since his mid-twenties. Surely he wouldn't have done that if his father was still around.

"By the time I reached adulthood, my father's business was so huge that it occupied another partner and myself. Along the way, my parents arranged my marriage."

Jemimah had told Utu how much Eliezer had loved her mother. Eliezer's parents had chosen wisely.

Eliezer picked up a log and placed it in the fire. "For a few years, things were blissful. I had a wonderful wife and belonged to a wealthy family. Everywhere we went, my father was treated with respect and that respect was extended to me."

Jemimah brought out some milk and they drank. Eliezer gestured towards the stars. "But we knew nothing about the Creator."

"What gods did you worship?" Job asked.

"We weren't a religious family," Eliezer said. "Too busy making money, I guess. My father considered the local gods mere superstitions." He shrugged. "He attributed his success to hard work and honesty."

"But sometimes hard work can't protect you," Jemimah said, sitting down near her father.

Utu loved the warm affection and respect between Jemimah and her father. This was the partnership, the relationship, he dreamed of for his own home.

Eliezer moved over to give her more room. "No, it can't." He took a deep breath. "First, my wife was with child but lost the baby. Then it happened twice more." He sighed. "Then my father's partner ran away with most of the silver. My father was so distraught, he became ill. He died not long afterwards, even though he was still a relatively young man."

Eliezer's voice had dropped, and he stared at the fire. "I was young, and people didn't trust me like they'd trusted my father. Overnight most of what we'd been doing went to another."

It must have been a devastating series of losses.

"Life can be so unfair," Job said.

"It certainly seemed unfair to me at the time," Eliezer looked up with a smile. "But Jemimah was still to come. I didn't know what a gift she would be."

Jemimah blushed and Utu's mouth went dry. Did he have a chance? One precious jewel in the family. Who was he to think that Eliezer would even consider him?

"On the anniversary of my father's death, we found out a baby was coming. This time, there were no major problems. Jemimah was born. For a short while, there was joy in our household." He paused as though to summon the strength for the rest of the story. "But in the hottest days of summer, fevers swept Damascus. Both my wife and mother succumbed within a week of each other." He swallowed loudly. "Only Jemimah was left."

"And I was only a baby and couldn't bring much of a comfort," Jemimah said.

Eliezer gripped her hand. "You became my comfort later, but I was too blind to see it at first."

Anyone would have been mired in grief after such a series of losses.

Eliezer put the last log on the fire. "I buried myself in work and handed Jemimah over to a relative. But work didn't help. I was empty, and I could see no real way forward."

"And Jemimah?" Utu asked.

"She only reminded me of my wife, so I avoided seeing her."

Jemimah might have given him a reason to live.

"Things got so dark I convinced myself that Jemimah would be better off without me."

"Papa you've never told me that!" Jemimah pulled her knees up to her chest and hugged them.

"You didn't need to know."

"But something happened to give you hope, didn't it, Abba?"

Eliezer nodded. "Something happened, but I didn't understand it at the time."

"Sir," Job said. "You don't need to tell us anything that's too private."

No! Utu wanted to hear what Eliezer had to say. He'd had unanswered questions ever since he'd first met Eliezer. Like why was someone from Damascus in Avram's household? And why was Avram's heir a non-relative?

"Neither of you are blabbermouths, and it's no secret anyway."

Utu almost cheered.

"It's not a secret, but it's also hard for me to talk about, because it was like nothing I'd ever experienced before."

Utu leaned forward.

"One night, I had a dream. At least, I think I was asleep. It's a bit difficult to know for sure. I saw someone in a long, shining robe. Dazzling white, like when the sun gleams off the snow on Mount Hermon."

Utu had only seen snow once, but he understood the allusion.

"I think it was a man, but the brightness made everything unclear. He told me to wrap up my affairs, take Jemimah, and walk to a certain crossroad some way from Damascus." Eliezer closed his eyes. "He didn't say when, but he said I would meet an older man and I was to go with him. In my dream I asked how I'd know he was the correct person. He didn't answer, but somehow I knew that when the time came, I would know."

"And that was all?" Utu asked.

"Not quite. The heavenly being told me I would find life and light. When I woke, I knew I must obey, or I'd regret it for the rest of my life."

"What happened next, Abba?"

It sounded like even Jemimah hadn't heard this part of the story.

"There was a sense of urgency, so I cut all my ties with Damascus and chose a few things to take with us. On that final day, I felt like I was pushed out of Damascus."

Eliezer touched Jemimah's arm. "It wasn't long before I had to hoist you on my shoulders. By the time we reached the crossroads, you were screaming for something to eat."

"And how long was it before Avram came along?" Job asked.

"With a caravan the size of Avram's, it wasn't a single arrival. They were passing for a long, long time."

"When did you know that the moment had come?" Utu asked.

Eliezer laughed. "Some of the sheep ran away, and I saw this older man yell at the shepherds. I told Jemimah to sit and wait for me, and went to help round up the sheep."

"And?"

"And it took a while for all those sheep to be gathered up. At the end, Avram apologized for yelling at the young shepherd. He said he hadn't known the two older shepherds were too sick to move and had had to be left to recover at the previous night's campsite." Eliezer laughed. "I'd never heard a man apologize. Apologies were considered a sign of weakness in Damascus."

"Was I still sitting by the roadside?" Jemimah asked.

"Yes, but you weren't alone. You were standing behind a woman, and she was letting you play with her hair. You'd tucked a few sprigs of flowers in the braids."

Jemimah giggled. "I wouldn't have done it if I'd known it was Sarai."

Sarai! Utu would never have imagined Sarai playing with a child, but maybe she'd been different before she'd been taken into Pharaoh's palace. Jemimah spent plenty of time with Sarai and always glowed when she returned.

"We were invited for a meal, and Avram found out more than I'd wanted to tell," Eliezer said. "When he heard about my father's business, he asked lots of probing questions. Before I knew what had happened, I was agreeing to work for him."

"And Aunt Sarai agreed to help look after me," Jemimah said. "I was too young to remember our arrival, but Abba has told me this part of the story many times." She looked sternly at Eliezer. "Although there were bits of the story you skipped over."

He held up his hands in mock surrender. "Sorry. I won't do it again. You're old enough to know life isn't always sunshine."

Utu suspected she'd known that for a long time, but Jemimah reminded him of the stream they lived beside. Most of the time she was an ordinary girl, but every now and then she'd sparkle like sunlight glistening off the water's surface.

CHAPTER FOURTEEN

"What's wrong, Hagar?" Inanna asked.

"Nothing," Hagar murmured, turning her wet, blotchy face away.

It definitely wasn't nothing. Inanna hesitated, debating whether to push the matter. "I've never seen you crying before."

Hagar sniffed. "I haven't had much to c-cry about before."

Hagar was an orphan, without any extended family, so she wasn't crying for family. Maybe she was crying for that lack. Maybe someone had laughed at her accent. No, not likely. She'd always laughed that off in the past.

"I thought I was plain enough to escape notice." Hagar sniffed again.

Inanna couldn't help smiling. "Someone wants to marry you? Surely that's not so terrible." On the rare occasions when just the two of them were together, Hagar had shared her dreams of a family of her own. Why was she so upset about it?

Hagar put her head in her hands and cried harder.

Oops.

"He's o-old."

Oh. Poor Hagar. If a woman dreamed of getting married, she dreamed of someone young and handsome.

"Can't you say no?"

Hagar shook her head. "Not this situation. I'm a slave. Slaves do what they're told."

"Avram has always seemed reasonable. Why don't you ask him to intervene?"

"Ohhh," Hagar moaned. "I wish it was that easy."

Should Inanna push for more details or leave it? She was probably Hagar's closest friend. Inanna had often protected her from anyone who treated her as lesser, simply because she looked, and sounded, foreign.

Hagar sniffed. "You've heard Sarai crying, because she longs for a child more than anything and feels her god has let her down."

"They specialize in that," Inanna said, sarcasm dripping from her tongue.

"Well, you and I are just slaves. Sarai has higher expectations of her god."

And maybe she had reason to. Utu had told Inanna about his experiences. They'd sounded like some made-up tale, but Utu had obviously seen something unusual. Whatever he'd seen, he no longer questioned that Avram had been led by this god to Canaan and that he would have a son. He'd be an impressive god if he could conjure a baby from a seventy-five-year-old woman's womb.

"... has chosen me."

Inanna had been off with her own thoughts and missed the key point. "I'm sorry, Hagar. I wasn't paying attention."

Hagar looked sorrowfully at her.

Inanna flushed. "I was trying to imagine myself in Sarai's position."

"I see her flinch when we have visitors, and they ask about children. She has always blamed herself. Now she blames her god. She wants to build a family through me." Hagar's voice was harsh and broken.

"Through you? Do you mean ..." Inanna's voice trailed off.

"Yes. Sarai has told me that I must marry Avram. And have a son."

Hagar hung her head, and the tears ran down her cheeks again. She swiped them off her face with her hand. "There's no point in crying. I'm a means to an end. My womb will belong to Sarai." Her voice cracked. "And my son will be hers."

Inanna clenched her fists, the tension radiating across her head. It was unfair. Unfair that Sarai could use Hagar to achieve her own desires. Unfair that Hagar had no say in the matter. Unfair that Hagar's dreams were lying smashed on the ground.

And any day the same kind of thing could happen to Inanna. If she'd stayed in Mamre's household, she would probably already have been married off to seal some deal. That's what daughters were for. No father wanted to keep providing for a daughter. Fathers thought it better to send them off to another household to feed and clothe. Inanna ground her teeth. So unfair.

Outside, eagles called. Once again, Inanna yearned to soar with them. Away from all the messiness around her.

"When will all this happen?" Inanna asked gently.

"Tomorrow."

Unfair again! Hagar would have no time to adjust to her new situation. She was being moved around like a carpet for the convenience of others. And like a carpet, others put their feet on her and trampled her feelings and desires underfoot.

Tension gripped Inanna's stomach. If Hagar was treated like this, would this be her lot too? To be treated as possessions that could be passed from one person to another, rather than as a woman to be consulted? The familiar desire to be free coursed through her body. Oh, to be able to make her own decisions.

* * *

*I*nanna had washed in the women's section of the river, downstream from where water was drawn.

"Inanna," Sarai said. "I forgot my comb. Could you please go and get it."

Inanna was more than ready to leave the group of women. Hagar's sadness made it hard to participate in the chatter. She scrambled up the bank and approached their tent from behind.

"I don't think this decision is wise," said a voice Inanna recognized as Eliezer's.

Inanna halted, unsure what to do. She couldn't go in and get the comb during what was obviously a private conversation.

"I don't see any other alternative," Avram said.

"Are you sure God would approve of this path?"

Avram was quiet for a long moment. "He has promised me descendants, and it's clearly impossible for Sarai to have a baby now. I must build a path."

"But didn't the promises imply the child would be Sarai's?"

"The promises never specified her name, only mine." Avram sighed. "Sarai is low, very low. All these years without a child. People are always making comments about how she must be cursed. It wears a person down."

Sarai and Avram had been married for sixty years. For sixty years, Sarai had been hoping and praying. Her god didn't seem to hear her prayers any more than Inanna's had, yet Utu insisted the god who'd appeared to Avram was nothing like the Amorite gods. He was a god who spoke and who spoke in ways that brought hope and life. Inanna wouldn't believe in such a god until she had heard him herself.

"Men who take a second wife make things more complicated," Eliezer said. "More quarrels and more fights."

Avram sighed again. "Then I'm caught between two impossible choices. I don't need another wife, but I do need a son. If I agree, then the outcome might be as you say. If I don't, I don't know what to say to Sarai."

Inanna stifled a sneeze. Yes, tears could wear a person down.

"You face a difficult choice," Eliezer said.

"Thank you for your advice, but I'm not sure that I have a choice."

"Sometimes we fear making the choice, but it might still be the right choice," Eliezer said as their footsteps walked away from Inanna.

* * *

Four months later

*I*nanna held Hagar as she vomited. Hagar retched again, the bitter smell of her vomit turning Inanna's stomach. She poured some water on Hagar's hand, and Hagar rinsed out her mouth and washed her face.

"Sorry," Hagar said, weakly. "That's the worst yet."

"How long have you been sick?"

"I doubt it's an ordinary sickness," Hagar said. "I think I'm with child."

Inanna didn't know whether to congratulate Hagar or not.

"I'll tell Avram, so he'll know to leave me alone." Hagar flushed. "I won't be able to hide it from Sarai much longer. She watches me all the time." She turned to Inanna. "It's a comfort having you around."

"Hagar," Sarai called from inside the tent.

Hagar got to her feet and gave Inanna a twisted smile before heading back to answer Sarai's summons.

Inanna could give little in the way of practical help to Hagar. She was Sarai's slave, not Hagar's. Hagar hadn't been assigned a maid, and Avram didn't seem to notice. As a man, he left all the household management to Sarai. Sarai might have given Hagar to Avram, but that was the end of the matter in her eyes. Hagar was still to do her share of the many tasks that needed doing, although Sarai was clever enough to only make her work when Avram wasn't around.

Poor Hagar. There'd been no party for Hagar's wedding. No celebration, no pride, no joy. Nothing to honor Hagar at all. Just a tiny handing over ceremony with a few people as witnesses. Hagar couldn't even understand why she'd been chosen. Inanna had been afraid to voice her suspicion that Hagar's plain looks had sealed the deal. Sarai need not be scared of Hagar ever being a real rival for Avram's affections.

As Inanna had said to Utu afterwards, the whole thing was colder than a business deal. Utu hadn't said much, but she sensed he was disappointed in Avram. Utu practically hero-worshiped the man. Inanna was far less likely to make any man a hero. Either they didn't work at all and let women serve them, or they chose all the more enjoyable jobs for themselves and left the monotonous jobs for the women. Given the choice, she would have done more of the work Utu enjoyed. As often as possible, she fled from the stifling tents and performed her tasks outside, under the nearest tree. Outside, where she could feel the breeze on her face, hear the birds, and watch others.

There was a gagging sound in the tent and Hagar scurried out through the entrance, covering her mouth with her hand. She didn't make it to the cover of the trees before she fell to her knees and vomited.

Inanna looked up at Sarai standing in the entrance of the tent. For a woman whose whole idea this was, she didn't look happy about the results.

CHAPTER FIFTEEN

"*W*hat did you say?" Sarai's voice rose. "Who do you think you are? You're a nobody. An Egyptian nobody."

"I only asked for a drink." Hagar's voice shook.

"It's not your place to ask me for anything."

Inanna's instinct was to run away, but Hagar was now six months with child and Inanna had somehow elected herself to protect Hagar. She didn't really know why. Maybe it was because Utu needed her less and less and Hagar had no one else. Inanna walked towards the tent and went into the dim interior just as Sarai spoke.

"Ever since you've been with child, you think you're superior to me."

"And whose fault is it that I am with child?" Hagar said, her voice stretched thin. "I didn't ask to be in this position. You have only yourself to blame if my being with child bothers you." Hagar clambered up from the carpet to her feet and headed towards Inanna.

Once out of the tent, a sob erupted out of Hagar's throat.

Inanna drew near and said in an undertone. "Please be careful. A jealous woman is dangerous."

"I try, but I have so much hatred for that woman I just can't help saying something."

"Please don't show her your hatred. You have your baby to think of."

Hagar cradled her belly. "But she'll take it away when it's born."

"Unless it's a girl."

"Maybe, but I think she'll take a girl too." Hagar's voice wobbled. "Now that the baby is coming, I find myself wanting it with all my heart. Someone who is mine."

Having lived in Egypt, so far away from her own homeland, Inanna could understand Hagar's yearning. Hagar would miss familiar foods, and seasons, and even the way the sun kissed her skin. But the most difficult thing was the loss of familiar people. Hagar had no family. No one like Utu. Without Utu, Inanna would be missing part of herself.

* * *

hree evenings later, Inanna and Utu took their daily walk before dark.

"You need to stick close to Hagar until her baby is born," Utu said. "I heard Sarai exploding at Avram. She claimed that Hagar despised her and that everything she was suffering was his fault."

"Pfft," Inanna said. "Sarai's mental anguish is caused by Sarai's own choices. What was she thinking, giving Hagar to Avram?"

"Eliezer warned Avram it would only cause trouble."

Inanna kicked a stone. "Sarai wore him down until he couldn't think straight."

"Maybe." Utu gnawed his lip. "But Avram should have held firm, for everyone's sake. Jealousy combined with a sense of failure is dangerous."

They reached the river and looked over the biggest pool. Utu picked up a flat stone and sent it skimming over the surface. Three, four, five, six skips before it sank out of sight. "I don't understand why his god made the promises about descendants, yet hasn't fulfilled them. It's been ten years since Avram and Sarai were in Harran and their god promised them a son. Avram's god seems to be toying with him."

"And that makes you angry?" Inanna asked.

"Yes, and disappointed. I thought this god was different."

Utu was a faithful person. He wanted a trustworthy god and was disappointed to discover Avram's god was a fickle tease, like all the others. She wasn't disappointed, because she had no such expectations.

She picked up another stone and made it skip seven times. "Beat that."

He stooped for another stone and the competition was on. Even though he won, she could see his heart wasn't in it.

As they scrambled up the riverbank, he laid an arm on her shoulder. "I mean it. Look after Hagar."

* * *

*T*he slap resounded through the air. "How dare you, you Egyptian upstart."

After days of sticking close to Hagar, Inanna had needed to leave the tent to relieve herself. She rushed back inside. Hagar sat hunched over with her arms curved around her belly and the mark of Sarai's hand clear on her cheek.

"Pick up your own shoes," Sarai hissed and stomped out of the doorway, eyes averted from Inanna.

"My back is sore. Why can't she help me for once?" Hagar asked.

Inanna had warned Hagar not to give Sarai any excuses to claim that Hagar was looking down on her. Hagar couldn't possibly win in this situation.

"I'm sorry I had to go out. Next time I'll take you with me." Inanna knelt down to put the shoes on Hagar's feet. "Don't take it to heart. She's insecure and jealous."

Hagar touched her red cheek. "I don't know how much more I can take. She's getting worse."

104

Utu had told Inanna he'd overheard Avram saying Sarai could do whatever she liked with Hagar. Avram might have abdicated responsibility, but he was a kind man. He wouldn't have intended for Sarai to mistreat Hagar. He probably didn't think his precious wife would do such a thing.

"That's the first time she's hit me, but there have been lots of whispered insults." Hagar sniffed. "The insults I can handle, but I'm not sure about the other."

And it looked like the other would only increase. What if Sarai's jealousy threatened the baby? What would Hagar do then?

* * *

*I*nanna opened bleary eyes. It was early, much earlier than she normally woke up. The first of the birds was chirping outside. She shivered and drew her covering up over her ears and then lowered it again. Something was missing.

She rolled over to her other side. Hagar was not making her little whiffling sounds as she dreamed. Inanna patted the mat beside her. Empty. Where was Hagar? Ever since her condition had become obvious, Hagar had been back in her accustomed spot next to Inanna, not in the special tent where Avram had visited Hagar regularly. The first of many insults.

Inanna rose to her hands and knees and patted the mat again. There was no lingering warmth. She searched in ever widening circles. Nothing. Her chest tightened. Would Hagar run? It was a risk, a huge risk, but what if she judged running to be less risky than staying?

The insults had come more often in the last two weeks. Sarai had slapped Hagar twice more, but that wasn't what had really scared Hagar. She'd told Inanna that Sarai had tripped her, and Hagar had barely avoided falling face first. In that moment of anger, Sarai had forgotten her plans for the baby and wanted to harm it instead.

What should Inanna do? Approaching Sarai would likely be met with scorn, and she couldn't approach Avram—not at this time in the morning, and not in his private quarters. It would have to be Utu. Utu could find Eliezer, and Eliezer would know what to do.

Inanna stood up and moved cautiously. She successfully avoided all the sleepers' feet. Outside, a half-moon peeked between clouds, and an owl hooted in the oak grove. She shivered. Was Hagar out there somewhere, alone and afraid, but desperate enough to run?

Inanna wrapped her cloak more tightly around her and walked through the dew-laden grass towards Utu's sleeping area. He'd shown her exactly where he lay each night in case she ever needed him. She flicked the outer skin of the tent with her finger. There was no break in the gentle snores inside. She flicked again and heard a snort. She flicked a third time and after a short pause she heard him flick back.

She drew away from the edge of the tent and stood on one leg. Her bare feet were tingling with the cold.

Utu joined her, and they moved away from the tents.

"What's wrong?" he said in her ear.

"Hagar's gone." The words sent waves of panic down her spine. Out there it was dangerous for women, and a heavily pregnant woman was especially vulnerable.

"Run away?"

She nodded. "Her mat is cold, and her few possessions are missing."

"I'll wake Eliezer."

He hurried away, and she was left with her fears. Fears that gripped her by the throat and made her stomach churn. "Oh Hagar, keep safe," she murmured.

The sky was beginning to lighten towards the east, but the signs of a new day didn't brighten her own heart. Deep inside was the hollow Hagar's friendship had started to fill, but now a cold wind of fear whistled in its emptiness.

Hurry, Utu.

But the search had to wait until dawn, when they could thoroughly search the camp. Utu volunteered to search down near the river. Since Sarai didn't need Inanna yet, Utu sent her and Job to search the oak grove. Inanna set off with a shudder.

Please, don't let anything happen to her.

She didn't know if it was a prayer. If it was a prayer, she didn't know to which god the prayer was directed, but it made her feel better all the same.

"You're checking those trees most thoroughly," Job said, laughter in his voice. "I'm not sure a lady in her situation would have climbed one."

"Depends how determined she is," Inanna said, and told him about the two times she'd hidden among the branches.

"You are certainly different from other girls." Job laughed, his voice warm with admiration.

Inanna flushed and pretended to be looking behind the nearest tree.

They finished the task and hurried back to report to Eliezer.

"No sign of her near the river," Utu said.

That was what Inanna had been most afraid of. She liked to think Hagar would never hurt the baby, but what if she'd rather kill herself than lose the baby to Sarai?

"Job, Utu, take five pairs of men mounted on camels and move out to search in different directions. We'll do our best to find her, but one of the camels is missing, so she might have gone quite a distance."

The young men rushed off to get ready. In no time, they had saddled the camels, grabbed a few supplies and were off.

CHAPTER SIXTEEN

*T*he searchers had returned without Hagar and now the harvest had started. Inanna's stomach still churned with fear when she thought of Hagar out there alone. Was she safe?

In front of her, Job and Utu and the other younger men swung their scythes. Sweat glistened on their bare backs and she averted her eyes from Job. Ever since they'd searched the oak grove for Hagar together, it had been more and more obvious that he was interested in her. He would have been a good match if she'd been interested in finding a husband, but she wasn't, and that was that. Utu obviously thought quite differently to her on the matter of marriage. Whenever they rested, he would contrive to be as close as possible to Jemimah.

Inanna moved to gather the stalks of barley and tie them together with a longer stem to form a sheaf. The women's job was to keep up with the men. Later, once the grain had dried, they'd be part of the threshing team.

Soon after Avram and his household had arrived in the area, they'd begun to help Mamre's men with all of the farming. This was a win for both clan leaders and their dependents. Mamre had enough workers to plant a far greater area with crops while Avram's household did any of the necessary watering. Their presence also meant that raiders and thieves kept away. In exchange, Avram had all the fruit and grain he needed.

Avram also did things differently from her father's men. Avram insisted that a tree be planted for every tree they cut down. "No pillaging and spoiling God's good earth. You've got to think of the next generation and leave the world a better place for them." It gladdened her heart to see new oak trees and fruit trees planted.

It was a perfect harvest day with not a cloud in the sky. Inanna stooped down, gathered the next pile of stalks, and tightened them into a bundle. Then another and another. Sheaf after back-breaking sheaf. She'd wake up tomorrow stiff and sore, but by the third day her body would adjust and she'd enjoy the change of work and maybe it would help her sleep better. Harvest also gave her the chance to be away from Sarai, who'd been even more difficult than before Hagar disappeared. Avram obviously hadn't believed Sarai's protestations that she had no idea why Hagar had left. He must have been more aware of the situation than Inanna had realized. A band of tension gripped Inanna's neck. Where, oh where, was Hagar? She almost wished she believed in Avram's god so she could ease her worry by praying.

Utu had found Hagar's camel wandering back towards home. Seeing the camel had given Inanna a grim sense of satisfaction. She'd never believed Hagar would steal a camel. She borrowed it to get well on her way, then switched to traveling by foot.

Let her be safe. The birth must be close now.

Utu and Job reached the end of the row and turned back to help the women. "We'll eat when we've finished this."

This was always Inanna's favorite time of harvest, sitting in the shade eating and drinking after all the hard work. Once the harvest was fully gathered in, Avram would kill and roast some of the flock and everyone would celebrate.

* * *

U nanna, come quickly," Utu said, as he found her by the well.

She scurried after him. "What's happened?"

"Hagar's back and it looks like the baby will arrive at any moment."

Joy flooded Inanna's heart. "Where is she?"

"Waiting in the oak grove. I didn't want her to face Sarai without you."

Inanna flashed him a grateful smile and headed for the trees. Hagar was seated on a log, looking tired but surprisingly relaxed.

"Weren't you afraid to come back?" Inanna asked.

"No." Hagar smiled a smile of peaceful contentment. "I have seen the messenger of Avram's God."

Inanna gasped. "How did you know who he served?"

Hagar shrugged. "I didn't at first. I was scared because I was alone at the spring. It was one of the springs we passed on our way from Egypt, the one on the road to Shur."

"Eliezer guessed you'd head towards Egypt." What foreigner would dare to head north and further away from home? It had given Inanna nightmares, thinking of Hagar crossing that desert on her own.

"I guess it was instinct, but I hadn't really thought it out. I had no one to take me in even if I reached Egypt. I was sitting next to that spring with no plans at all."

That was the problem for women. There were no real options. There was marriage or there was slavery, and the line between them was narrow. Hagar would probably have lost her baby in either situation.

"The man himself wasn't scary. He was kind of reassuring really, until he called me by name. To have someone in the middle of nowhere say, 'Hagar, slave of Sarai, where have you come from and where are you going?' Those words really caught my attention."

"I'd have been terrified."

"I was and I wasn't. I knew he wasn't anyone from Kiriath Arba, but somehow I also knew I didn't have anything to fear. He wasn't there to harm me. And the way he said my name!" Tears pooled in Hagar's eyes. "I can't describe it. How could the way someone said my name make me feel safe? He said it the way my mother used to. Full of love. Better than a warm hug." She shook her head. "I know it sounds crazy, but he was the first person to say my name like that in a long time." Hagar touched Inanna's arm. "You call me by name, but Sarai never says my name at all, it's just a 'Get yourself over here,' or worse."

Inanna had noticed this. Sarai labeled Hagar by her status or country of origin—slave, or Egypt. Both implied she was foreign and more an object than a real person with feelings.

"And did you answer him?" Inanna asked.

"I wouldn't have dared not to."

"So he was scary?"

"No, not scary." Hagar pursed her lips. "It was more that he spoke with authority. I told him I was running away from here, and he commanded me to return and submit to Sarai."

Submit. There was the word that made Inanna grind her teeth. Her mother loved to use the word. "Obey. Submit. You're like a wild horse. Be more like your brother. He is much more biddable." And boring, she'd thought at the time. Not that Utu seemed to mind. She was the only one who found submission difficult. She still did, even if it was just revulsion on Hagar's behalf. Hagar, who'd had to submit too much. To things she would not have chosen if she'd had the freedom to say no.

"I didn't want to listen, but the messenger gave me a promise. 'I will increase your descendants so much they will be too numerous to count.'"

"That sounds like the promise Avram said his god gave him." The promise it seemed would never be fulfilled. Not that she'd mention that to Hagar. Hagar needed all the encouragement she could get if she was going to have to submit to Sarai again. Although she should be safer this time, because Avram would be more alert to what Sarai might do.

"And the messenger had more words for me." Hagar cleared her throat and closed her eyes. "You are now with child, and you will give birth to a son. You shall name him Yishmael, for the Lord heard of your misery. He will be a wild donkey of a man; his hand will be against everyone and everyone's hand against him, and he will live in hostility toward all his brothers."

Inanna knew plenty about hostile brothers. The man's words sounded like both a curse and a blessing. A promise of a son was always a good promise, but the prediction that his life would be full of conflicts didn't sound pleasant.

"Yishmael." Hagar said the name like a caress. "'God will hear' and that is what he has done. Every time Avram says our boy's name, he will remember that God will hear."

But why the future tense in the meaning? Surely the child's name should have been god heard or god hears, not god will hear? Maybe Inanna was being too sensitive to the deeper meanings. She hoped so, or there would be more family trouble coming.

"Beer Lahai Roi," Hagar murmured. "That's what I called the spring on the road to Shur. I have now seen the One who sees me."

The thought obviously gave Hagar comfort, for she almost looked beautiful as she murmured the words. No one else had seen her as a real person. Not Pharaoh, who gave her away as part of a group of slaves. Not Avram or Sarai, who thought of her as a means to an end. And not many of the others in the camp. Hagar, slave of Sarai, had been noticed and called by name. Inanna almost envied her. Almost but not quite. She was better off without any god telling her what to do.

* * *

"*A*rgh," Hagar moaned through clenched teeth. "That was a bad one."

The first contractions had come during the early morning, and Inanna had helped Hagar move to the birthing tent and sent Utu to call the midwife. Within a camp this size, there was more than enough work to keep a midwife busy.

"You're doing well," the midwife said as she readied a clean cloth to swaddle the baby. "It won't be long now."

Hagar moaned and her moan grew in volume. She clenched her

fists and rocked side to side. She was determined not to shriek, saying she didn't want to give Sarai the satisfaction.

The midwife examined Hagar and then gestured to her assistant.

"Time for you to kneel. The baby's head is showing."

Inanna grasped one of Hagar's hands and the assistant the other. Together they steadied Hagar so she could kneel. Another contraction came, then another.

"On the next contraction, I want you to push," the midwife said.

As the next contraction built, Hagar pushed with a loud groan. Inanna winced in pain as Hagar crushed her hand. Ouch.

"Just a few more. The baby's head is visible."

"Is my son—" Hagar panted. "Healthy?"

"We don't know if you have a son."

Inanna grinned. There wouldn't have been many women who'd had a divine messenger tell them who was arriving.

Inanna's hand was crushed again as Hagar pushed. The sweat poured off her as she labored.

"That's it, almost here," the midwife said. "One more big push."

"I can't," Hagar moaned.

"One more," Inanna urged. "Then you'll be meeting Yishmael."

"Oh." Hagar groaned, and pushed.

With a slither of fluid and blood, the baby slid into the midwife's hands. The woman grabbed a soft cloth and rubbed the infant's skin. "A boy. A fine, healthy boy."

The baby gave a wail, as though he knew they were talking about him. The wail grew in volume.

"Let me see him." Sarai pushed open the flap of the tent.

"Inanna, hand him to me, quick," Hagar whispered.

Inanna took the baby off the midwife before she grasped the situation and handed him to Hagar. Hagar cradled him close and put her head down to kiss his forehead. "My love, my little love."

Yishmael struggled to free himself.

"Let me see," Sarai said.

Still cradling him close, Hagar lifted her head but kept her eyes lowered. Perhaps she feared what would show in them if she looked at

Sarai. Sarai, who had upended Hagar's life, then walked in here as though she'd done all the hard work.

"He's handsome enough, I suppose." Sarai turned to the midwife. "Get him cleaned up. I'll go and tell Avram he has a son." Her voice wobbled, but she lifted her head high and exited the tent.

"Inanna, can you wash him?"

Joy burst through, but Inanna gnawed her lip. "You'd be better off choosing someone else. I haven't had much experience with babies."

"I want you to do it."

A warm glow filled Inanna's belly at this statement of trust. She walked to the tent entrance and brought in the waterskin which she'd left lying in the sun to warm up. It was a bit early to introduce the little man to cold water.

Taking a cloth, she wet it before laying the baby on the mat and wiping his legs. Yishmael kicked and she giggled. Already on the move. She wiped the tiny toes. Amazing. Each one so cute, so tiny, so perfect.

By the time she'd finished cleaning him, her heart was hopelessly entangled. She who'd longed for freedom was bound as tightly as a fowler's snare by this tiny scrap of humankind.

CHAPTER SEVENTEEN

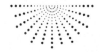

Seven years later
Still Kiriath Arba

"What are your intentions towards my daughter?"

Utu choked on the drink Eliezer had given him as they sat outside the tent in the late afternoon sun. Sweat broke out on his upper lip. He'd tried so hard to hide his love for Jemimah. He'd even tried to convince himself to love someone else, but he couldn't. Was he about to lose everything? He'd miss working with Eliezer, but no father would keep him around if it made his daughter feel uncomfortable.

"You have a wonderful daughter," Utu stammered, heat warming his cheeks.

"I know I have a wonderful daughter, but I don't want her feeling she has to take care of me. She should have a husband of her own," Eliezer said.

Utu swallowed. Had Eliezer arranged a marriage for Jemimah? He wanted to cry out in protest but held himself back. "She'll make a terrific wife and mother."

"I thought you were interested in her, but obviously I was mistaken."

Utu's heart pounded in his ears. Not interested! He was more than interested, but surely Eliezer wouldn't give his beloved daughter to him? Inanna would declare her love if she was in this situation, but he was too cautious. Speaking might lose him his job, yet caution might lose Jemimah.

"I do love Jemimah," he said.

"Then why have you not spoken?"

Utu frowned. "Surely you must know." He touched his chest. "She is free, but I'm only a slave. Why would you accept me?"

"Jemimah thought that must be the problem."

Utu's cheeks burned. Jemimah had talked to her father. A warmth filled his chest. He was not mistaken. Jemimah cared for him. He wanted to jump up and dance wildly but instead he said, "It's a big problem to me. Your daughter deserves the best."

Eliezer stroked his beard.

Utu's stomach ached. Were these moments about to change his future? *Avram's god. If you listen to slaves, help! You know I love Jemimah, and I think she loves me. Please do a miracle.*

"I took a long time to choose you as my assistant, because I would only choose an assistant who was also suitable to become my son."

What! Utu's eyes nearly popped out of his head.

"It was inevitable that my apprentice would spend much time here. I would not introduce a bad influence to Jemimah. I chose you, because you were steady and humble and eager to learn. You were the kind of boy who might become the right man for my daughter."

"Thank you," Utu said. The words seemed vastly inadequate. In his heart, hope was beginning to bloom.

"You have my permission to speak to Jemimah, if that is what you want."

Utu shook his head in wonder. Then he grabbed Eliezer's hand and pumped it up and down. "Thank you, thank you, thank you."

Eliezer smiled. "It sounds like we're in agreement." He turned and called over his shoulder. "Jemimah, why don't you and Utu go for a walk."

Utu's face heated again as he scrambled to his feet. Had she heard everything they'd said?

Jemimah came out of the tent. Her face glowed. Could that look of serene joy be because of him? He swallowed. Maybe Avram's god did listen to slaves.

"We won't be long, Papa," Jemimah said as she came and kissed her father on his forehead.

In a daze, Utu took his place next to her and they headed for the relative privacy of the oak grove. Once in its quiet confines, he turned to her. "Oh, Jemimah, I can't believe it."

She smiled gently. "You still need to ask me, you know."

"Can't believe I forgot," he stammered. "I'm overwhelmed."

"With joy, I hope," she said.

He took her two hands in his. "Jemimah, you are more special to me than I can ever express. More than anything I would count it the greatest of privileges to be your husband. Would you do me the honor of becoming my wife?"

She squeezed his hands, sending tingles up his arms. "I will. Most gladly I will."

* * *

A tambourine jangled and joined in with the pounding of handheld drums and a wedding song. Inanna craned her neck and looked back towards Eliezer's tent. Job and a group of other attendants held up the tent flap, and Eliezer emerged with a heavily veiled Jemimah. She was wearing a long tunic dyed with swirls of red, and wore gold ornaments around her neck and wrists.

Utu was getting married. It was an amazing thought. The little boy who'd trailed after her everywhere and tried his best to protect her, was a man. A man who was now seeing the fulfillment of a dream.

Not only had Eliezer done the asking but he'd handed Utu a clay tablet with a mark that proclaimed he was now free. Inanna clenched her teeth. Utu, who had never desired freedom, was free, and she, who had always longed for freedom, was still a slave. Yet another injustice in a long list. For freedom, even she might be induced to marry.

Eliezer and the crowd of young men now led Jemimah forward to where Utu stood beneath a tree. It was a stiflingly hot day. Poor Jemimah must be finding it difficult to breathe underneath the veil, her beauty only to be revealed to her new husband after the feast. An archaic custom. Shouldn't the woman be allowed to enjoy the food and see her guests?

Eliezer came forward and took Jemimah's hand and placed it in Utu's. He spoke up so they could all hear. "May you be a blessing to each other. A protection from the cold winds of life. May you always trust and bring joy to one other, and may you be fruitful."

In the front row, Sarai flinched. There'd probably been prayers for fruitfulness at her wedding too. It was brave of Sarai to be here. A trickle of pity entered Inanna's chest. Jemimah considered Sarai the only mother she could remember. As soon as Sarai had heard Jemimah was getting married she'd started work on a woven blanket. Sarai had also given Jemimah a complete set of storage jars and cooking utensils for her new household. Not that they'd be moving far. Jemimah and Utu had worked on making the goat's hide for their own tent. They'd invited Eliezer to go with them, but he'd said children should leave their parents' household. If he needed assistance sometime in the future, then he would be happy to rethink.

Avram walked behind the couple as they stood facing each other and holding hands. Then he stood and faced all the guests. "Welcome, to all of you and to Eliezer, who has been the Creator's gift to me. God knew organization wasn't my strength, and he sent me the best possible gift. You have been a faithful friend and have saved me from more mistakes than I can possibly repay." He bowed towards Eliezer. "We are here to celebrate the marriage of your precious daughter to Utu. The man you carefully chose as your assistant today becomes your son as well. You made a wise choice. Utu has shown over and over that he can be trusted. He is steady and faithful. Jemimah, you will be blessed."

Inanna's heart swelled with pride. It was true, and it was wonderful to hear her humble brother praised in public.

Avram turned towards Utu. "And Utu, you have won a prize of great worth. Jemimah has a quiet faithfulness that will bless you. Eliezer calls her his jewel beyond price. May you both have much joy."

If only she could have had a father who loved her in the way Eliezer loved Jemimah. Inanna brushed a tear from the corner of her eye. When would she learn not to yearn for impossible dreams?

Avram raised his hands. "May the Lord, the Creator, shine his face upon you. May he bless when you leave and when you come home. May he make you a blessing to all you meet, and may the generations to come rise up and honor you." He placed his hands on their heads, then Utu and Jemimah turned to face all those standing witnessing the event.

Utu's smile was so proud and excited, it looked like it would jump off his face. A dagger of jealousy stabbed Inanna in the gut. For the first time, Utu was going ahead of her to a place she couldn't follow. Jemimah would now be the first to hear his thoughts, not her. And as children came, Utu would be further and further from her, distracted by a myriad of responsibilities. Inanna swallowed the sting of loneliness and forced her lips to curve upwards. She and Jemimah were friends. She could do this.

The new couple walked through the onlookers and towards the pavilion that had been set up. The rest of the day would be spent feasting on the many sheep and bull calves that had been killed two days before and had been roasting since dawn. They'd prepared all the bread and accompaniments beforehand. As a member of the family, she had no responsibilities for once, and she'd be seated under the wedding pavilion with Eliezer, Avram, and Sarai. The full weight of responsibility for the serving fell on Hagar.

Inanna scanned the area for young Yishmael. He was running around with other children his age, hair flying, free as a young deer. He'd find her if there was a problem.

* * *

*U*nanna heard a wail and spotted Yishmael looking round wildly. She got up as quickly as she could from her place on the carpet and hurried towards Yishmael to head him off before he reached the wedding pavilion. If he was upset, he wouldn't think of any consequences, and Sarai would be angry if Yishmael burst into where they were finishing up the last of the meat and bread.

Yishmael rushed at her and threw his arms around her waist. "It's not fair, Aunty."

"Shh. Come further away and tell me what's the problem." Inanna untangled his arms and led him away from the wedding celebration.

Once far enough away from the guests she sat on a stone so she could see Yishmael's face. "Now, what's the problem?" she asked gently, although she'd already guessed the answer as it was an almost daily issue.

"Japheth pinched me and called me a nasty name." His voice cracked and tears brimmed.

Japheth, son of one of the shepherds, was the bane of Yishmael's life. He was older and bigger and faster. He liked to throw his weight around, and he treated the younger children like his personal slaves.

"I hate him! If Father would give me a bow and arrow, I'd shoot him."

Which was exactly why Avram hadn't yet given him a bow and arrow.

"Have you tried walking away from him?" Inanna asked. This was only one of many suggestions she'd made to him, but nothing had worked. Young Japheth simply delighted in tormenting Yishmael. Maybe he sensed that Avram wouldn't come after him. She'd have to speak to Job and Utu and see what ideas they had.

"I never remember what you say. He just makes me—" Yishmael screwed up his face while he thought of something suitable to say. "He makes me want to spit on him."

Inanna choked back a laugh. At Yishmael's age, it was hard to think of something terrible enough to do to an enemy. She'd had an enemy once and had taken great satisfaction in pushing him face-first into a mud puddle. He hadn't bothered her again but that didn't seem like good advice to pass along to Yishmael.

She gave Yishmael a hug. "Next time, come and find me."

"You're the best, Aunty Inanna. You'd scare him."

The glow of his trust in her filled her heart. "Now, why don't you come and sit with me? They'll be bringing out fruit and nuts soon."

He shook his head. "I don't want to sit with you." He shifted his feet. "You know, because she's there."

He didn't need to say Sarai's name. Yishmael had only been four when he worked out that Sarai didn't like him and wanted to know why. Inanna had tried to put him off, but he'd known she was avoiding some truth that was hidden from him. It was only going to get harder as he matured.

CHAPTER EIGHTEEN

Six years later
Kiriath Arba

"Son, it's going to be a painful day," Eliezer said to Utu. "I need your help choosing the best men for the job."

Utu frowned. "Painful day?" A strange thing to say.

Eliezer nodded. "Avram." His tongue tripped over the word. "No, Avraham. Avraham has heard from God again."

"Avraham?"

"That was part of the message. God has changed both Avram's and Sarai's names."

This was all rather confusing.

"You remember how you and Jemimah considered all sorts of names for your baby? You wanted the name to express something about your and Jemimah's hopes for your child. Well, God seems to be doing the same. The new name is part of God's promises to Avram."

Avram meant "exalted father." It couldn't mean a literal father, since Avram's father, Terah, had given the name to a baby. It was more likely a reflection of the respect they hoped that Avram would experience as he grew. But the new name meant "father of multitudes."

"Abba, I know what the new name means but ..." Utu cleared his throat.

"Yes, it does seem a bit of a joke for a ninety-nine-year-old man with one teenage son, but that was part of the message. Next year, he and Sarai—now Sara—will have a son."

Utu swallowed the date seed he'd been ready to spit out. He coughed and Eliezer pounded him on the back.

"Avraham laughed too," Eliezer said as he offered Utu a drink of water. "He too thought a woman of ninety having a child was impossible, and he asked God if Yishmael might live under God's blessing."

Utu leaned forward. Ever since hearing this god speak to Avram—ah, Avraham—he'd been hungry to hear more of this god. "And what did god say?"

"He said Yishmael would be blessed. He would become the father of twelve rulers and a great nation as well, but the main blessing would go to Yitzchak."

"'Yitzchak?'" Are you saying god has already named the coming son?"

Eliezer beamed as he nodded. "Yes. He will be called Yitzchak. Sara too will be the mother of nations, and kings will be descended from her."

Princess indeed.

"But you said something about it being a painful day. This doesn't sound painful." Utu rubbed his eyebrow. "Although there will be a painful day for Sara." He'd been terrified when Jemimah's pains had gripped her for Peleg's birth. There had been several miscarriages first, and during Jemimah's labors, he'd had to remind himself often that joy would come after the pain.

"Does Avram—Avraham—know you tell me all about what god says to him?" Utu asked.

"He told me long ago that he trusted my discretion in whom I told."

Utu always told Inanna and now Jemimah, but neither of them were gossips.

"And this time God revealed another name of his own: El Shaddai."

123

El Shaddai, God Almighty. Utu rolled the name over in his mind. It had a ring to it that he liked. If parents took such care to prepare names for children, then god's revelation of his own names wasn't an accident. Every night, Utu looked up at the stars and remembered god had told Avraham that he was the creator of all and would be Avraham's shield and protector. Now there was another name to ponder.

"Once again, El Shaddai promised to make a covenant between himself and Avraham. It's an everlasting covenant for the many who will be descended from Avraham, generation after generation. One day they will own all this land."

Whoever this god was, he certainly had his own sense of timing. He made grand promises but he also kept people waiting. Avraham and Sara had already been waiting twenty-five years for the fulfillment of the promises they'd heard in Harran. Now god was saying Sara was going to have a baby next year. Inanna wouldn't believe it. She hadn't believed Sara could have a baby all those years ago when Utu had told her about what he'd seen and heard. She'd said the coming child couldn't possibly be birthed by Sara. That she was well past such things. Well, time would tell whether El Shaddai lived up to his name. A baby for a ninety-year-old would be something none of them had ever seen.

"And the painful bit?" Utu asked.

Eliezer grimaced. "Apparently the sign of the covenant is going to be circumcision."

Circumcision! That was an Egyptian custom. Utu raised an eyebrow. "I don't get it."

"El Shaddai says it is to be the sign of the covenant. Every male born from now on must be circumcised at eight days old. I guess circumcision is an outward symbol of an inward commitment to follow God."

"Phew." Utu mopped his brow. "We're older than eight days old."

"Mmm," Eliezer said. "Avraham has been told that all the males of the household, including himself and Yishmael, must be circumcised."

"Even us?"

"Perhaps we could wriggle out of it, because God said, 'Every male, including those born in your household or bought with money from a foreigner.'"

"I wasn't bought," Utu said. "I was given to Avraham by Pharaoh."

"I guess you could argue that, but you need to also work out if you want to be excluded or not. Do you want to be part of this household or not? For El Shaddai also warned that any who don't have the sign of the covenant, will be considered to have broken the covenant, and will be cut off from God's people." Eliezer grimaced. "I will be getting circumcised and Peleg and any other sons you have will also be included."

"And my sons might want to know why I am not circumcised."

Eliezer nodded.

Utu could get out of the whole thing, and he liked to think no one would say anything, but choosing not to be circumcised would actually be a strong statement—one he didn't want to make. He would be choosing to say he was different to everyone else.

Avraham and Eliezer had been more than good to him, and now he was a member of Eliezer's own household. He belonged in his heart, even though he had not yet chosen to follow El Shaddai for himself. It was hard to follow a god he knew so little about. Yes, he knew El Shaddai existed, and that he was powerful and eternal. He'd seen evidence of this god's existence for himself, but he still had doubts and questions. Questions about whether Avraham's god really kept his word and whether he really wanted Utu's best. All the gods he'd ever known were capricious, demanding loyalty without giving anything in return. There was no point in abandoning one set of gods and getting the same treatment from the next.

"I need three or four men to do the actual circumcisions," Eliezer said. "I thought you might know the shepherds with the steadiest hands with a knife."

Utu shuddered at the picture in his mind, but he listed off three or four names.

Utu shifted uncomfortably on his sleeping mat. It had indeed been an unpleasant day, and he'd sting for a few more to come. Poor Peleg had been inconsolable by anyone but Jemimah. He may as well get up and fetch the day's water. Jemimah had been up several times during the night tending to Peleg's needs.

Utu got up carefully. Outside the stars were pale against the gold-washed sky.

What did Avraham's god want with them? He'd made glorious promises to Avraham, promises he'd only partially fulfilled. Avraham had one son, a son he could hardly embrace fully because of Sara's attitude, but one son was a long way from being a great nation. Being a great nation didn't just require a people group but the land itself, and Avraham didn't own a single clod of earth. He worked together with the people of Kiriath Arba for every harvest on land he didn't own. How did Avraham feel about it all? Did he ever doubt El Shaddai's promises? Did he wonder if his god was simply boasting with his grand names? After all there was still no real proof that the rest of the promises would come to pass.

Utu had asked Eliezer some of his questions.

"This God doesn't work like any other I've ever known about. Trust him," Eliezer had said.

But how did he trust a god he couldn't see, a god no one else seemed to worship? Surely it made sense to trust gods who were worshiped by many people? The more the better.

CHAPTER NINETEEN

*I*t was a breathlessly hot day. Inanna took yet another drink, then poured water into her hand and wiped it over her face. Ah, so much better. She and Hagar and some of the others had moved their bread making outside, under the shade of one of the oaks, where there was the possibility of an occasional gentle breeze.

"Yishmael, come and get a drink," Inanna said.

He came over, and she held the skin water bag for him while he gulped down a few mouthfuls then laughed when some trickled down his chin. Her heart clenched with love for him. It was hard work to keep him occupied, but oh how she loved him.

"How much longer are you going to be making bread? I'm bored," he said.

He was easily bored, even though he had plenty of chores to do. That was the problem. If he was acknowledged as Avraham's heir, he would be trained for the role and treated like the heir, but Yishmael was not in favour. Not with his father. Not with the others in the extended household. No one but her dared to show him favor in case the situation changed, but they also didn't dare to exclude him entirely. It made her angry and more than ever determined to champion him.

"Why don't you shoot some arrows?"

Avraham had given Yishmael his most prized possession, a bow and arrows, and Yishmael practiced every day.

Avraham had promised to take him hunting when he could shoot accurately, and he'd been able to do that for some time. Inanna sighed. When would Avraham treat Yishmael as his son?

"Thanks, Inanna," Hagar said as Yishmael bounded away. "That boy has far more energy than I have. What a pity we can't harness it to get him to do our work for us."

Inanna laughed. "He's too clever to fall for that trick." He was too clever for most things. The other children didn't like him much because he often led them into trouble, and then they were all punished.

They settled to their task of grinding barley for the next day's bread and kneading that day's dough.

Inanna looked towards the hills, in the opposite direction from the town. It was hot enough for there to be a haze. The buzz of cicadas pulsed in her ears. Was something moving out there? She brushed flour off her hand and shaded her eyes. Out of the shimmer, three men materialized and walked towards the camp. As they came closer, they moved towards the main tent where Avraham was sitting at the entrance with a cool drink at his side and someone fanning him.

Avraham got up, hurried towards the men, and bowed low in greeting. In the breezeless air she heard exactly what he said.

"If I have found favor in your eyes, my lord, do not pass your servant by. Let a little water be brought." He signaled to the boy assigned to such tasks. "And come and rest under this tree."

Even before he'd finished saying the words, Utu appeared with two younger boys carrying a carpet, which they unrolled under the tree.

The three men sat down, and the young boy washed their feet and handed each of the guests a damp cloth to wash their face and hands.

"Let me get you something to eat," Avraham said. "So you can be refreshed and go on your way."

"Very well," they answered. "Do as you say."

Inanna got to her feet and headed for the tent. The instructions would be given to Sara, but it was she and the others who would have to carry them out. Avraham bowed again and went into the tent in front of her.

"Sara, my love, quickly. Get three seahs of the finest flour and knead it and bake some bread."

As Inanna approached where Sara was standing, Avraham passed her and headed towards the herds. It was unusual for him to go and personally select an animal.

Three seahs of flour was a lot of flour. Inanna went to the storage area to get the wheat. No coarse barley for this bread. Avraham must know these men, and they must be important. She poured out the wheat to measure it. It cascaded out of the jar onto the cloths she'd prepared. She measured it with an experienced eye. Just enough. There'd be plenty of time to grind it into fine flour and make the bread. Killing the calf and roasting the meat would take the better part of the afternoon. Meanwhile, Sara would have made sure there was a selection of dried fruits and nuts laid before the guests.

It took three trips to carry the wheat out to the women under the tree. She'd do the grinding and let them keep going with the ordinary bread for the household. If they ate elsewhere, she'd be free to help with the serving when the time came.

* * *

The mouthwatering scent of roasted calf permeated the camp. Inanna had seen people licking their lips. Most would receive some before the day ended. Avraham was generous and would likely have roasted several animals at the same time, especially on such a hot day when Utu and the others would be over-heated from working so close to the fire.

Inanna maneuvered the paddle into the oven to dislodge the first of the loaves, then drew it out of the chamber. The braiding she'd done on top had turned out better than she'd hoped. She poured on a tiny amount of olive oil and rubbed it across the surface of the loaf to make it shine. Even though she'd had her meal, she longed to munch on the fragrant crust.

Yishmael appeared at her elbow. "Can I have some?"

"Soon. I have to make sure the guests are served first."

"But I'm the son. Surely I'm more important."

Only thirteen and already using his status to gain privileges.

She pointed to one of the loaves. "I'm keeping that one for you."

He stood on tiptoes and kissed her cheek. "You're the best."

She flapped her hand at him. "Don't try to wheedle your way into more privileges."

"But it works, doesn't it?" He winked and headed outside to his bow and arrows.

It did work. The boy had her even more tightly in thrall than when she'd first held him. Maybe it was because she had to watch him so closely to keep him away from Sara. Sara wasn't cruel to the boy, but seeing him reminded her of her failures and no one wants to be reminded of their failures.

Inanna placed the loaves of bread in a basket. Utu would bring platters of carved meat in, and Eliezer would eat with Avraham and the guests. Yishmael might possibly wheedle a place too. It was amazing how good he could be if food was the reward.

She carried the bread out to Avraham. He immediately held it up to thank his god, then broke it and handed pieces to each guest. They each dipped their bread in a bowl of olive oil. She hurried out with the accompanying dishes: curds, fragrant onions, and herbs.

Utu came and laid the platter of meat in the center, then stood near Avraham in case he was needed. He'd be alert to who these men might be and where they'd come from. She wanted to know what their business was, but as a woman, she was supposed to be out of sight in the stifling heat of the tent. She was too far away to hear, although she could glance over towards the guests every now and then.

Inanna tried not to fidget, but the meal dragged on and on as they always did when important guests were being entertained. The guests wouldn't leave until the cool of the evening.

Inanna stood to check how things were going outside. Avraham signaled for the servant to bring out a basin with a towel for the guests to wash the grease from their fingers.

One of the guests raised his voice. "Where is your wife, Sara?"

"There, in the tent," Avraham said.

"I will surely return to you about this time next year," the man said. "By then, your wife Sara will have a son."

In the darkness near the entrance of the tent, Inanna saw Sara's shoulders shake with silent laughter. And no wonder. Did this man have the power to restore a dried-out womb? Ninety-year-olds didn't have babies.

Sara had been praying for a child for most of her life, and no god had ever heard her prayer. Yes, Utu said Avraham's god had promised a child, but Sara had never quickened. Whoever Avraham's god was, he was just like the rest. Cruel to make such false promises.

The man was speaking again, and Inanna closed her eyes to hear better. "Why did Sara laugh and say, 'Will I really have a child, now that I am old?'"

Inanna gasped. How did the man know Sara had laughed? There'd been no sound and Sara was well hidden.

"Is anything too hard for the Lord? I will return to you at the appointed time next year, and Sara will have a son."

"I did not laugh," Sara said, coming out of the tent.

The man looked at her for a long moment before speaking gently but firmly. "Yes, you did laugh."

He didn't repeat "Is anything too hard for the Lord?" but the words hung in their minds as though he'd shouted them.

If Inanna had dared to say anything she would have said, "Yes, some things are too hard for any god," but it wouldn't be too long until the man's words were proved one way or another. If Sara wasn't with child within four months, she wouldn't have a baby by this time next year. Inanna wasn't going to hold her breath.

* * *

a s the men got to their feet, Avraham signaled Eliezer and Utu. When they reached him, Avraham said, "I'm going to accompany my guests as they leave. Come with me."

Eliezer and Avraham walked with the three men, but Utu hung back a little. There was something unusual about these men, but he couldn't say what. They'd appeared out of nowhere, yet the camp sentry swore he hadn't been asleep on the job.

Another strange thing was their age. They looked to be men in their prime, and yet seemed older, much older. Two of them always deferred to the third, who was undeniably the leader. He didn't speak often, but when he did, everyone listened. His voice reminded Utu of someone, but he couldn't work out who. It wasn't his father or anyone from Kiriath Arba or even Egypt, but he'd heard the voice before. If only he could remember where.

They reached the top of the ridge, and the three men talked together.

"The outcry against Sodom and Gomorrah is so great and their sin so grievous that we must go down and see if what they have done is as bad as the outcry that has reached me," the leader said to the others. "If not, I will know."

The two others turned and headed towards Sodom. They wouldn't fit in there. They seemed too ... Utu struggled for the word. Too holy? Pure? Something like that.

Utu had never been to Sodom and had no plan to visit. Eliezer had gone some years ago to take some gifts to Lot and—yet again—to offer Lot's daughters a home with Avraham and Sara. He'd come back shaken, refusing to say much beyond that it was a place no self-respecting person would ever want to venture to.

The remaining man turned to Avraham. "I will not hide what I am about to do. The outcry against Sodom and Gomorrah is too great."

He said something quietly to Avraham, which Utu couldn't hear.

"Will you sweep away the righteous with the wicked?" Avraham asked. "What if there are fifty righteous in the city? Will you really sweep it away and not spare the place for the sake of the fifty righteous people in it?"

Was that this man's plan? To destroy the cities? He'd need a mighty big army for that, as the towns weren't small.

"Far be it from you to do such a thing—kill the righteous with the wicked, treating the righteous and the wicked alike." Avraham lifted up his eyes towards the man. "Far be it from you! Will not the Judge of all the earth do right?"

Utu's skin broke out in goosebumps. Judge of all the earth? Who was this man? Utu was rooted to the spot. He knew this voice. It was the voice he'd heard when Avraham had seen the visions of his god. Would a god come to earth in human form? Surely a god would come in smoke and flames and with rumbles of thunder. Not as a mere man.

"If I find fifty righteous people in the city of Sodom, I will spare the whole place for their sake," the visitor said.

Avraham licked his lips. "Now I have been so bold as to speak to the Lord, though I am nothing but dust and ashes. What if the number of the righteous is five less than fifty? Will you destroy the whole city for the lack of five people?"

Utu looked across at Eliezer, whose face was shining as he stared in rapt awe at the man. Avraham called their visitor "Lord" as if he were god. Eliezer seemed convinced that their visitor was no ordinary man. He and Avraham were behaving as if this man was far superior to themselves.

"If I find forty-five there, I will not destroy it."

Avraham swallowed. "What if there are only forty?"

"If there are forty, I will not destroy it."

"May the Lord not be angry." Avraham's voice shook. "What if only thirty can be found?"

The visitor chuckled. "I will not do it if I find thirty."

Utu couldn't believe it when Avraham dared to open his mouth twice more to ask about twenty and ten. Then the visitor turned and walked away, and they were left standing on the ridge. Utu didn't ask any of the questions burning in his mind. Talking seemed somehow inappropriate.

Avraham continued staring down at the city, the smoke of its fires hanging in a pall over the buildings. Then he turned abruptly and headed for home without saying another word.

CHAPTER TWENTY

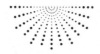

*B*oom, crash. The ground shuddered, and Jemimah clutched Utu's arm where they sat eating their first meal of the day. "What is it? What's happening?"

"I don't know."

Peleg wailed from his place in the corner. Utu rose from his seat on the ground and rushed over to his son.

Outside there was a cacophony of lowing and baa-ing and the terrified squealing of camels.

"Honey, run outside. It'll be safer," Utu said to Jemimah as he scooped up his son. "I'll go and see what's happening and what Eliezer needs done."

The ground shuddered again, and a child screamed outside. Utu put his arm around Jemimah and ushered her outside before handing Peleg to her. "Go and stand in that clearing with Inanna and the others. Keep away from the trees. I don't want anything falling on you."

The sky was a dark ominous green, streaked with fire, and the stink of something foul carried on the breeze from over the ridge.

"Utu, come with me," Eliezer called. "Hurry."

Somehow, despite the panic, Job had saddled four camels. Utu,

Eliezer, Avraham, and Job set off for the ridge they'd stood on yesterday.

Utu's heartbeat pounded in his ears. Was this judgment from Avraham's god? Or something entirely unrelated?

Once they reached the ridge, they dismounted and tied the camels to some trees.

"Careful now," Avraham said. The sun was hidden behind dense smoke. "Crawl to the edge and keep together."

Utu dropped to his belly and crawled, panting to the rocky edge. A strong smell of sulfur choked him, and he drew the edge of his head scarf over his nose and mouth. Fireballs rained down from the sky and lightning zig-zagged between heaven and earth. Deep rumbles shook the ground.

Next to him, Avraham moaned. In the flashes of light, Utu could see the glistening of tears running down Avraham's face. "Lot, oh Lot."

There was no way Lot could have survived unless he and his family had left Sodom hours ago. Nothing could survive such devastation. A tightness clutched Utu's chest. Yesterday he'd felt awe, but today he was terrified. He never wanted to fall into the hands of such a god, a god who could command the heavens to spit fire.

"Job and Utu, please ride back and tell the camp there's nothing to fear. Tell them it's the judgment of God on Sodom and Gomorrah, but it will not come to us." Avraham's voice cracked. "Then send someone to Mamre to reassure him, too."

* * *

The shaking continued for a long time, then disappeared as suddenly as it had started. A wind came up and blew away the smoke, and rain fell to clean the leaves and tents. Utu walked around in a daze. This god could hurl lightning like a spear then send rain to clean up all the devastation. Truly he was a god worthy of the name, 'creator' as Avraham called him.

The next day, as Utu approached the main tent, he heard Eliezer speak.

"Avraham, it's not safe."

Avraham was pacing up and down, wearing a furrow in the ground outside his tent. Utu sat down to listen and set about sharpening the knives he and Eliezer used every day.

"All that fire and brimstone. We couldn't send any of the men to look for Lot and his family," Eliezer said.

Avraham paced some more. "Not knowing is driving me mad. How long do you think we'll need to wait?"

Eliezer put his head to one side. "I'm guessing, about five days. We can't risk anyone getting burned, and whatever we find won't be a pleasant sight. I don't want to send any of the young ones. It will give them nightmares."

It would likely give Eliezer nightmares too.

"If Lot got away, won't he make his way here? He knows where you live."

"Maybe." Avraham stopped his pacing. "But he's a proud and stubborn man. He refused all my previous invitations."

He'd refused with a curt dismissal and an insistence that he'd continue to live in Sodom. Utu suspected Avraham had long had his doubts about Lot. Otherwise, why had Eliezer been his heir rather than a blood relative? Eliezer was an honorable man, and Utu was proud to be not only his assistant but his son by marriage. He wanted nothing more than his children to emulate their grandfather. He only wished that he'd known Eliezer's wife as well.

"We'll wait until the fifth day. Please choose a group of men to accompany us, and ready supplies and extra transport," Avraham said.

Avraham must be wound up. He would not usually have added the last commands because ever since he'd met Eliezer on the road near Damascus, Avraham hadn't bothered about details.

* * *

"*U*tu, where are you?" Eliezer's voice called from the entrance of Utu's tent.

"Coming." Utu scrambled up from where he'd been tickling his

137

son. He always grabbed the chance to spend time with Peleg while Jemimah was preparing the meal.

Utu picked up Peleg and carried him outside.

Eliezer checked over his shoulder. "A woman just arrived and said she's your mother," he said softly.

His mother! He'd assumed he'd never see her again.

"Where is she?"

"Job's giving her something to eat. She's eaten little since she escaped from Sodom."

Yet another surprise. They'd been waiting four days for news of Lot, but they'd heard nothing. Maybe this woman, who might be his mother, would know more. He handed Peleg over to Eliezer. He wasn't taking Peleg to meet the woman yet. Better he check her story first. He couldn't think of why the woman would lie, but in Canaan it was wise to check before accepting people's stories. Towns had been captured because they invited the enemy in by the front door.

Eliezer laid a hand on his shoulder. "I haven't said anything to Inanna."

Utu strode across the camp. Job shared a tent with several of the single cameleers. He didn't talk about it, but Job still seemed to be holding on to his fondness for Inanna. Utu shook his head. His foolish sister still wanted freedom more than she wanted a good man. Job was worth far more than any illusions.

The woman had her back to him and looked just like a thousand other Canaanites of her age. Slightly stooped and with her head covered in a scarf.

Job straightened up as Utu approached. The woman looked up with a glad cry. "Utu, my son."

The voice was right, despite the aging, but he'd only been nine when he'd last seen her. Back then, he'd remembered her as a beauty with smooth, capable hands. Now her hands were rough, with knobbly joints.

She put down the bread she had been dipping in the lentils and drew back her veil. "Do you not know me?"

He scanned her face. He didn't know the faded skin with its deep creases near the corners of her mouth or the fine lines around her eyes. But the eyes, the eyes were his mother's. Full of love for him.

He dropped to his knees in front of her, and she reached out and touched his face as though seeing it for the first time. Tears leaked out of her eyes, and he leaned forward and gathered her into his arms. She wept on his shoulder. His mother. He'd never hoped as Inanna had. Never believed he'd ever see her again.

He lifted his head and indicated the main tent. "Inanna," he mouthed to Job. Job set off to find his sister.

When his mother had finished weeping, she dried her eyes on her head scarf and sat upright again. "I'm so sorry."

"You don't need to be sorry. It is a miracle you are here. How did you know where to find me?"

"I'll tell you the whole story later, but I ended up in Lot's household."

Not the easiest of households to live with.

"One day Lot mentioned Utu, an assistant to Avram's steward."

And his name was unusual in the area.

"I asked some careful questions, and his story of how you joined Avram's household gave me hope that it really was you." She touched his arm as though assuring herself that he was real.

He put his hand over hers. "I can see Inanna coming."

"Inanna?" She whirled towards the direction he was looking. "I didn't expect her too."

"It's a bit of a story, which I'll tell when you've greeted her."

Inanna didn't hesitate. She left Job's side and ran towards them. Utu steadied his mother as she got to her feet. Then Inanna was there with a glad cry, nearly knocking Mama over in her enthusiasm. All over the camp, people were looking in their direction.

It was long moments before Utu could ask, "How did you end up in Sodom?"

"Like yours, it's a long story." She gestured for them and Job to sit down. "I set off a few days after the raiders when I realized no one was going to risk their lives to search for you." She dabbed the corner of her eye. "It would have been a different story if you'd been Mamre's oldest children."

Utu hadn't been surprised by this after Inanna had told them what their fifth brother had said and done, but Inanna had been deeply hurt. It had contributed to her distrust of men in general. She only allowed him, Job, and Eliezer into her heart. And Yishmael, of course, but she didn't consider him a man, although he insisted he most certainly was.

"I went south as far as the Negev then headed back north, but I strayed too close to Sodom and got caught by a slave trader."

Nausea surged in Utu's stomach.

"I had a dreadful few days before Lot bought me." She wrapped her arms around her middle as though cold. "I was lucky he wasn't a local because Sodomites are not anyone you'd like to know. I learned to never walk outside on my own."

It hurt to think that his mother had been in danger while he'd been safe here.

"What work did you do for the family?"

"Mostly running after those two daughters of theirs. They weren't bad girls, but their parents didn't discipline them."

Inanna touched their mother's knee. "And I didn't heed you enough."

A gentle smile glowed across Mama's face. "You were a bit wild and thoughtless, but you were never unkind."

"I certainly had a lot of growing up to do."

Mama reached out and cupped her hand under Inanna's chin. "And now you've done it."

"And have you been there all these years?" Utu asked.

"I have, until a few days ago."

"We thought everyone was killed," Inanna said.

"I might have been too, but two visitors arrived the night before the destruction. Lot brought them home and said they'd intended to stay in the city square." She shuddered. "Lot knew he couldn't let them spend the night outside, so he brought them home and gave them a meal. And …"

"And?" Utu asked.

"Really I'd prefer not to say in front of your sister."

"I'm not an over-protected young miss. I know of Sodom's reputation," Inanna said, voice full of indignation.

"I would prefer not to speak of it."

"Mama," Utu said. "Avraham and Eliezer also need to hear your story. Avraham is waiting to hear if Lot is alive."

"He was alive the last time I saw him."

Utu looked across at Job who'd been quiet during their mother's story. "Would you be able to go and alert Avraham and Eliezer? I'll bring my mother."

Job set off and they followed. When they reached the main tent, Avraham hurried out to meet them and welcomed their mother with a bow. Utu's heart swelled with pride at the way Avraham took the time to find out her name, Attar, and welcomed her, even though he must be desperate for any news she might have.

Once they were seated, Utu summarized the story so far, then touched his mother's arm. "Tell us as best you can what happened when the two guests entered your home."

"They mentioned they'd come from here, but before they could say anything more, the men of Sodom started pounding on the door." She stared at the floor. "They demanded that Lot send out the men so they could ..." She flushed. "C-could, you know, harm them."

Sourness filled Utu's mouth. It was obvious what his mother meant even if she couldn't actually say the words. Apart from the evil of the demand, it was an insult to all the rules of hospitality.

"And then?" Avraham asked, his tone full of revulsion.

"Lot went outside and tried to reason with the men. Even offered the two girls instead. I was terrified that the Sodomites would agree, but they didn't. They told Lot to get out of the way, complaining that he was a foreigner and had no right to act as a judge over them. Then they threatened him and started battering down the door."

Utu put a protective arm around his mother's shoulders.

"We were all shaking with fear. But not our guests ..." Awe flooded her voice, and she withdrew from Utu to sit up straight. "The men

141

opened the door, pulled Lot inside, and struck all the men with blindness."

"What do you mean, struck them with blindness?" Avraham asked.

"We didn't know at first what had happened. Everything suddenly went quiet, and we could hear them tapping the door. They started calling out, saying they couldn't see anything. They all sounded terrified."

Utu had suspected the men were messengers from Avraham's god, but now he was certain.

"The visitors turned around and asked Lot if he had any relatives in the city, then told him to leave the city because they were going to destroy it."

"Can you recall their exact words?" Avraham asked.

Mama closed her eyes for a long moment, then opened them again and spoke. "They said, 'Do you have anyone else here—sons-in-law, sons or daughters, or anyone else in the city who belongs to you? Get them out of here, because we are going to destroy this place. The outcry to the Lord against its people is so great that he has sent us to destroy it.' Lot went outside and talked to his two sons–in–law, but they thought Lot was joking."

"What did you think?" Avraham asked.

"I had no doubt. I packed a few possessions together and a little food and water. As I left, the two men were urging Lot to hurry so he wouldn't be swept away when the city was punished." She took a mouthful of water from the skin Inanna offered her. "No one was paying any attention to me. I just walked out the door and fled for the hills."

"But did you see Lot and the family leave?" Avraham leaned forward, his tone urgent.

"I think so. I made it to the edge of the hills. As the sun rose in the sky, I could make out four figures leaving the city. Three were definitely women."

"But you couldn't see who they were?"

"No, but the way they moved was familiar. They were headed towards Zoar when I last saw them."

"Mama, why did you take so long to reach us?" Utu asked.

"The closest hills weren't in the same direction as Kiriath Arba, and I didn't move while the cities were destroyed." Tears pooled in her eyes. "It was … you know … too terrible. I didn't know whether I was far enough away to be safe. I hid under a rock for two days."

The terror of that judgment would never leave Utu either.

"Utu?" Avraham asked.

"Yes, sir."

"Have you got space in your tent for your mother?"

"Of course." He'd already mentally prepared the minute he'd recognized her.

"Tomorrow morning, we will go to Zoar and look for Lot."

But even if they found Lot, would he be willing to return with them?

CHAPTER TWENTY-ONE

*U*p on the hills, the air had been washed clean and the sun shone, while down on the plain the air was thick and full of dust. There was no sound except the occasional gurgle of water. No twittering of birds, no sound of sheep, no voices. Nothing. It was eerie, and Utu wanted nothing more than to get out of here. He couldn't help checking over his shoulder, although he didn't know who he expected to see.

As they drew near to Sodom, the ground grew rougher. Great round boulders lay everywhere, and the camels had to wind their way in between them. In front of them was a giant hole filled with the boulders where Sodom used to be. Only an occasional bit of wall still stood, like broken teeth in an old person's mouth. Utu gagged at the stench of burned flesh. Ahead of him, two men vomited off to the side.

"There's no point in being here," Eliezer said.

Avraham turned his face towards them. His face was haggard, rough and pitted like the terrain. He pointed towards Zoar, the direction Utu's mother had said she'd seen Lot and his family take when leaving the city. They moved cautiously forward, skirting the worst of the boulders and putrid pits of tar. One stumble, and they'd disappear and never be seen again.

They plodded on. Utu's throat ached and his lips cracked. The sun slowly dropped in the sky. An angry orange ball through the murk.

"Let's stop and drink something," Eliezer said.

Eliezer had brought several spare camels and plenty of water. No one would dare to drink any water found on this plain for some months to come.

They gulped water from the waterskins without saying anything. What was there to say? Each was traumatized into silence. The area looked like something that might be encountered in a nightmare. Would plants ever grow here again?

"We'll keep going towards the hills," Avraham said, his voice harsh in the gloom.

They remounted the camels and stumbled forward. Utu's head drooped.

"What's that?" Job called, pointing.

Utu nearly fell off his camel at Job's words. He peered towards where Job pointed. Something glittered in the fading light. What was it? They moved nearer and dismounted to look more closely. The shape looked extraordinarily like a woman.

"That looks like an arm." Utu pointed.

"And those could be feet," Job said.

"Is that a face under a veil?" another man said. "And what is it made of?"

Eliezer licked his finger and rubbed it over the shiny surface. He licked his finger again and then spat. "Salt."

"But what's a statue of salt doing in the middle of a plain, far from the sea?" Avraham asked.

No one had an answer. They remounted and headed towards the hills, now looming closer.

"Stop, look over there," Eliezer called a short while later.

Utu looked where Eliezer was gesturing. They'd been riding through this scene of devastation for so long that he almost failed to recognize the regular shape of houses. Almost insignificant, but the first sign of life other than themselves that they'd seen since morning.

They changed direction and headed towards the closest building, which was covered in a layer of silt. There was nothing moving, nothing that indicated any life at all. Maybe it was deserted. But why was it not destroyed like everywhere else?

Eliezer held up his hand and silently pointed to divide them into pairs. One man was assigned to look after the camels and the rest moved towards the buildings.

Utu tapped Eliezer on the shoulder and mouthed, "I'll go ahead." If there was danger, he didn't want Eliezer encountering it first. Jemimah would never forgive him.

There were two front windows. He peeked in one. No people, but there was still food in dishes on the carpet. Had they interrupted a meal? He peeked in the other window. Still no one.

Moving quietly, Utu entered the main door. There they were. A huddle of cloaked figures, eyes wide, and the reek of fear in the room. Utu held up his hands so the group could see he didn't carry any weapon. "We come in peace. We are looking for Lot."

The group members looked at each other and pushed the oldest man forward. "What do you want with Lot?"

"His uncle has come to see if he's alright." Eliezer indicated over his shoulder.

"He's alive if that's what you mean," the man said.

"But we're not sure if he's alright," an older woman added.

That sounded ominous.

Eliezer stepped forward. "Can you show us where we might find him?"

"I'll go with you," the youngest boy said.

"Then come back straight away," the woman said. "We don't know if the skies will fall again."

"The judgment is finished," Eliezer said.

"Judgment? What judgment?" the woman asked.

"Judgment from the Creator God against the wickedness of Sodom and Gomorrah."

The adults frowned at each other. "Who is this god you talk of?"

Eliezer looked at the oldest man. "We'll go and find Lot. Then we'll come back and tell you more. Or you could come as our guests to Kiriath Arba, and we will tell you everything we know."

The woman clutched her cloak more tightly around herself. "We wouldn't dare. This is the only place we know."

"You might not be able to stay. It's total devastation in all directions. Nothing will be able to grow for some time."

The boy tugged on Eliezer's sleeve.

They followed him outside, into the rutted lane that functioned as a street. He led them towards the biggest building in the hamlet. Along the way, they gathered up the others and told them what they'd discovered. At the bigger building, Avraham turned to Job and the other men.

"Only Eliezer, myself, and Utu will go in."

They walked in silence up the slight slope to the building. Once again, Utu went first. He wasn't expecting any danger, but the locals were jumpy.

The only person in the room was sprawled in a corner. Even from the doorway, they could smell the alcohol.

"Lot?" Avraham said as he walked across the floor. "Is that you?"

Well he might ask. Utu wasn't sure either, for the man's beard was matted and unkempt, and his eyes were closed in his shriveled face.

"Lot," Avraham said again. He knelt near the man and gently slapped his face. "Utu, can you please go and get some water."

Utu took a deep breath as he went out the door to fetch one of the spare waterskins.

"We've found Lot," he told the other men but didn't say more. Avraham wouldn't want news of Lot's state to become a matter of gossip.

Back in the room, Utu's nose was assaulted by the sour smell of vomit from the new puddle on the floor next to Lot. The clean air of the hills seemed impossibly far away. Avraham found a cloth, poured water on it, and handed it to Lot to wash his face.

"Why are you here?" Lot mumbled.

"Looking for you and your family," Avraham answered.

Lot cursed. "There is no family. She's dead."

Avraham leaned in. "Who's dead?"

"M'wife. She looked back."

Utu crouched down and prepared for a long wait.

"We lingered too long in Sodom. Waiting for others to join us." Lot poured another handful of water and splashed it on his face. Beads of water trickled into his beard. "The messengers had to drag us out. Told us to flee to the mountains and n-not look back. But she didn't listen."

Did he mean his wife?

"I begged the messengers to let us come here instead of the mountains. Thought the mountains were too far."

El Shaddai would have delayed judgment until Lot and his family had reached the mountains. Utu didn't know how he knew that, but the god he'd seen interact with Avraham had never been unreasonable. God would have protected Lot even when he didn't deserve it, because of his promises to Avraham.

"And?" Avraham prompted.

"And the messengers said they'd protect Zoar for us."

"And?" Avraham repeated.

"But my wife couldn't help looking back. After all, we were leaving everything she'd ever known. The house, everything we owned ..." He wiped his nose with the back of his arm leaving a sticky smear on his skin. "All our flocks. We've got nothing."

"And what happened to your wife?"

"Your god turned her into a pillar of salt." Lot spat the words out, the smell of his breath foul in the close quarters of the room.

There was a sharp intake of air. The statue hadn't been merely like a woman—it had been a woman. Lot's wife. Bile rose in Utu's throat. He put a hand over his mouth and lurched to his feet. The image of the pillar of salt consumed his thoughts, and his heart pounded. He hurried out the back and vomited on the ground. Then he remained, leaning forward with his hands on his knees.

Revolting. Lot's wife was not the nicest of women, but he would never have wished that she become a pillar of salt. Warm flesh to brittle lifelessness. What kind of god was this that Avraham served? A god who had to be obeyed perfectly or he lashed out. Or was Utu being unreasonable? Avraham's god had given Lot and his family a clear warning. He had saved them. Had the woman hankered after what she'd had in an evil city rather than rejoicing that she was saved?

He found some brackish water in a covered pot and rinsed out his mouth before spitting the water on the ground.

Inside, Avraham was begging Lot to come with them, but Lot shook his head.

Avraham changed his methods. "This is no place for your daughters, and you know it." Avraham gestured around. "Do you want them seeing this? With us, they'll be able to live a normal life."

And it looked like Lot was in no fit state to look after anyone.

Lot glared up at Avraham. "You've already got everything. You're not taking my girls too."

Utu would have reminded Lot that he had chosen to live on the plain, but Avraham said nothing about Lot's choices. "I wouldn't be taking them. They'll always be your daughters and you can come anytime you want."

"Never," Lot mumbled. "'S-not fair."

Utu had had enough. He got to his feet and walked out. The air outside wasn't any better, but at least he didn't have to listen to a man who would never recognize or accept grace and mercy.

CHAPTER TWENTY-TWO

*I*nanna shook her head in disbelief. It had happened again. They'd recently packed up all the tents and left Kiriath Arba and headed south towards the Negev and now another man had sent for Sara, this time Abimelech of the Philistines. Yes, Sara was beautiful, but she was ninety years old. According to the word from god, she should be with child by now but there'd been no sign of it. Unless the new glow about her was a sign ... but no, that had been present ever since she'd been told she'd finally have a son.

Sara came out of the sleeping area, fully veiled except for her eyes. Her eyes were downcast, and why not? Avraham had let her down again. Eliezer and the others would have died protecting her if Avraham had given the word. What was wrong with the man? If a man wouldn't lay down his life for the woman he said he loved, then Inanna wanted nothing to do with marriage.

Job is different.

The thought floated into her mind, and she squelched it. She was not thinking about Job.

Sara stopped in front of the line of women and looked slowly at each one. Her eyes lingered on Inanna, maybe remembering how useful she'd been in Egypt. Then her gaze moved down the line. When they reached the end, Sara's gaze flicked back to Inanna.

"Inanna, would you go and find your mother please. I'll take her with me."

Mama. An interesting choice. Mama wouldn't be a threat to anyone in Abimelech's household. Life for a new woman among established wives and concubines was tricky.

* * *

Two moon cycles later

"*P*sst, Inanna."

Inanna jumped and turned her head. Mama was beckoning her from behind the tree next to hers.

She got up and crossed over to her mother.

"I wanted you to know we're okay." Her mother grinned. "Abimelech hasn't called for Sara."

Avraham would be pleased with the news although, she'd first have to relate it to Utu who would mention it to Eliezer, who would pass it on tactfully.

"Why not?" Inanna asked.

"It might be because Sara is with child."

Inanna's eyebrows rose towards her hairline. "Are you sure?"

Her mother nodded. "She's already showing."

But Abimelech wouldn't know that, not under the loose-fitting garments his women wore.

"I've got to go back before I'm missed," Mama said. "Give my love to Utu and the family."

And that was the last they heard until another few moons passed, and Utu came to see her.

"I have to accompany Eliezer and Avraham to see Abimelech, but Jemimah needs help with Peleg. Would you be able to stay with her?"

Inanna nodded. Jemimah was near her time and Utu had been sticking close to home.

* * *

*U*tu sat cross-legged on the carpets in an inner room of Abimelech's home. They'd been served drinks and snacks, but now Abimelech clapped his hands and dismissed all his servants. Once they'd left the room, he cleared his throat.

"Avraham, I want to speak with you, privately. Please send your men outside."

"I have no secrets from these two," Avraham said.

"As you wish." Abimelech looked at Avraham for a long moment. "I have had a dream. A dream in which your god appeared to me."

Avraham shifted in his seat. "What did he say?"

Abimelech paused as though deciding how to tell this story. "He said, 'You're as good as dead because of the woman you have taken; she is a married woman.'" Abimelech peered at Avraham from under bushy eyebrows. "I wonder why he would say something like that to me."

Avraham flushed and looked at the floor.

"I asked your god. 'Will you destroy an innocent nation? I have not touched her. Didn't Avraham say to me that she was his sister, and Sara say that Avraham was her brother? I have taken this woman as my wife with a clear conscience and clean hands.'"

Utu didn't enjoy watching Avraham squirm. The man had so many good qualities, but his fears kept getting in the way. It was a warning for Utu's own life.

"Then your god said, 'Yes, I know you did this with a clear conscience and so I have kept you from sinning against me. That is why I did not let you touch her.'"

Avraham swallowed.

Abimelech looked sternly at Avraham. "What have you done to us? How have I wronged you that you have brought such great guilt upon me and my kingdom? You have done things to me that should never be done. What was your reason for doing this?"

Avraham cleared his throat. "I said to myself, 'There is surely no fear of God in this place, and they will kill me because of my wife.'

152

Besides, she really is my sister—the daughter of my father, though not of my mother—and she became my wife. And when God had me wander from my father's household, I said to her, 'This is how you can show your love to me: Everywhere we go, say of me, 'He is my brother.' And so she has faithfully granted me this request.'"

"You have wronged us." Abimelech leaned forward, gaze intense. "I'm not some ruffian who kills a man because I want his wife. I have plenty of women. I don't need more."

Come on, Avraham. Now would be a good time to apologize. But Avraham just looked at the floor. Disappointment seeped into Utu's heart. Maybe Inanna was right not to make a hero of the man. Utu's face heated. Was he any better? Only last night, he'd been impatient with Jemimah. Her face had shown her hurt but he'd ignored it, hoping she'd get over it. He must make things right when he returned home.

"Your god told me to return Sara to you, and he warned me that if I didn't, all of us would die. He also said you were a prophet, and you are to pray for me so that we will live."

"I will pray."

Abimelech nodded. "Good. You will pray for me, and the women in my household will become fertile again."

Utu pursed his lips in a silent whistle. Once again, Avraham's god had protected Sara even though Avraham had failed.

They all stood, and Avraham raised his hands. "El Shaddai, maker of heaven and earth, thank you for your graciousness in speaking to Abimelech and his graciousness to me. Please restore health to the women of his household, and help us to live at peace."

"Thank you," Abimelech said. "I would have been happy to be your friend. Men such as us need all the friends we can get. Being the leader of men is a lonely job, is it not?"

"It is," Avraham said in a subdued voice.

Utu had never considered that Avraham might find his responsibilities isolating. He had Eliezer, but maybe that wasn't enough. He'd speak to Inanna and see what she thought. Perhaps this explained some of Sara's moods.

Abimelech struck his staff on the floor, and two officials opened the door and bowed. "Please summon Sara and her servant to join us."

When they arrived, Abimelech turned to Sara. "I am sincerely sorry for any offense or pain caused to you. I am giving Avraham a thousand shekels of silver. This is to cover the offense against all who are with you. You are completely vindicated." He turned to Avraham. "My land is before you; live wherever you like."

Admiration filled Utu. Truly Abimelech was a man worthy of respect, a man to emulate.

Avraham bowed his head and once Abimelech had left, he indicated for his people to leave. As Sara passed him, he touched her shoulder but she shook him off.

Sara had plenty of reason to have lost her trust in Avraham, but Utu must make sure that Jemimah did not do the same. Tonight he would apologize to her. She needed to hear the words, and he needed to learn the humility of admitting when he was wrong. A marriage needed this mutual humility and it was his responsibility to lead the way.

CHAPTER TWENTY-THREE

"Oh," moaned Sara. "Why did I wish for this?"

"Keep focusing on the thought of Yitzchak in your arms," Inanna's mother said.

Sara's pains had started in the early morning, and they'd called the midwife immediately. They couldn't risk anything going wrong. Sara had insisted she wanted Inanna's mother, Attar, there and Inanna had been relegated to the lesser tasks. This had included escorting Avraham outside and assuring him they'd call him when Yitzchak arrived.

Sara moaned again, her voice rising as she rode the wave of pain.

"Remind yourself that every pain is one step closer to meeting your little son," Attar said in her best reassuring tone. Sara and Mama had been inseparable since they had been in Abimelech's household. Sara had softened, and Inanna had even heard her laugh a few times. The laughter of joy, not scorn or skepticism, a sound she'd never associated with Sara in the past.

Inanna had now attended several births, but it wasn't normal to know if the baby would be a boy or a girl or even twins. And they didn't usually know if the baby, or the mother, would live. Knowing ahead of time that the baby would not only be a boy but would survive to go on and have children of his own, took the fear out of the process.

"Aar-gh." Sara's moans were building in intensity and coming more often. It would not be long now. This god even took care of the details, for he'd spared Sara a long, drawn-out process. Hagar would have said it was because this god saw, truly saw, and cared for women. Maybe. If so, it was a first. The gods of Canaan and Egypt certainly weren't known for their compassion or understanding.

"You're doing so well," Inanna's mother said and she wiped Sara's forehead.

"Attar, promise me you'll care for Yitzchak if something goes wrong," Sara said, gripping Attar's hand.

"You're going to be fine," the midwife said. "You'll be holding your son before you know it. I can see the top of his head already."

They worked together to help Sara into the birthing position.

"On the next pain, it's time to push." The midwife signaled to Inanna to bring in the warmed bath water and to hand her the knife, ready to cut the connecting cord between Yitzchak and his mother.

"Ohhh." Sara moaned as Inanna hurried to get the water.

"Push," the midwife and Attar chorused together from within the tent.

"I can't," Sara panted.

"You just did," the midwife said. "A few more of those, and your child will be here."

Inanna came back into the tent with the water. Sara gritted her teeth and took a deep breath, pushing into the next pain.

"Good," Inanna's mother said. "His shoulders are out. Here he comes."

With a final push and scream, the baby was in the midwife's hands. She turned him right way up and gently smacked his bottom. Yitzchak screwed his face up and let out a wail.

"Perfect, just perfect," the midwife said, tying, then cutting the cord.

"Let me see," Sara demanded.

The midwife placed the naked child in Sara's arms, and she cradled him close, staring at him in rapt silence.

"Can I come in?" Avraham's voice called from outside.

"We'll just clean up," the midwife said, but Avraham took no notice. He didn't look at the mess or pay any attention to the three other women. He just crossed the tent in great strides with his gaze fixed on Sara. At her side, he dropped to his knees and reached out his finger to stroke Yitzchak's cheek. "Welcome son," he said, voice wobbling with emotion. "We've been waiting for you a long time."

Avraham enfolded Sara and Yitzchak in a loose embrace. His shoulders shook and he stayed like that for a long moment. Inanna mopped her own eyes.

Finally, Yitzchak let out a wail and Avraham stood up straight again. "It's all right little man. It's just your arrival has overwhelmed me, and I'm so proud of your mother." He reached down and touched Sara's cheek. "So proud," he murmured.

"God has indeed brought me laughter, and everyone who hears about this will laugh with me," Sara said. "Who would have thought that Sara would nurse children? Yet I have borne Avraham a son in his old age."

* * *

On the eighth day after Yitzchak's birth, Avraham invited Eliezer, Abimelech, the Philistine ruler, and some of the key men in his household, to Yitzchak's circumcision ceremony.

Sara had decided not to come because she said she couldn't bear to see her child hurt, and the rest of the women had followed her lead. Utu wasn't looking forward to it himself, although Yitzchak would quickly forget the ceremony. Ever since god had commanded them to follow this ceremony, every new male child had been circumcised.

Yitzchak was wearing a new tunic and lying quietly in his father's arms.

Avraham looked down at his son, beaming with the same pride that often made Utu choke up. His oldest son, Peleg, loved to follow him and Eliezer, and Eliezer was already teaching him to write letters in the dirt. Peleg was picking up words and numbers much faster than Utu had.

"Let's pray first, before young Yitzchak shouts his indignation," Avraham said.

Eliezer and Utu raised their hands as Avraham did, and Abimelech and some of the others followed their lead. Utu had heard Abimelech questioning Avraham about his beliefs whenever they had opportunities to talk together.

"El Shaddai, Creator of heaven and earth and all that are in them." Avraham raised his voice so everyone could hear. "Thank you for the gift of life. Thank you that you keep your promises. May the miracle of Yitzchak's birth be told far and wide so that many, many people might know your name."

The priests of Kiriath Arba had prayed about protection from poor harvests, and plague, and victory over enemies. Avraham's prayers were full of praise of his god. The more his god revealed about himself, the richer Avraham's prayers became. Listening to them made Utu long for something beyond himself. To be a better husband and father, and to do something good and noble.

"May Yitzchak follow you all the days of his life, and may he be a man of strength tempered by mercy, vision tempered by kindness," Avraham continued. "May he be a man of integrity, generosity, and forgiveness. In all things may he honor you."

Utu's father would regard some of these virtues as weaknesses, but Utu had seen how hard it was to be consistently kind and patient in his own family. If he was distracted with the many tasks he had to do and brushed aside Peleg's request, the way his face fell was an immediate rebuke. His children needed his time and his attention. It took strength to be merciful and kind, and Abimelech had shown them that it took courage to forgive.

After the prayer, Avraham said, "We do this ceremony, because the God who spoke to me beyond the River Euphrates commanded it. Every male who is born into my household, or is bought and becomes a member of my household, must be circumcised on their eighth day.

Circumcision is an outward sign of the covenant between us and El Shaddai. He has promised to bless me and my descendants, and through our family all those who dwell on this earth will be blessed." He looked around at the group of men. "I don't understand why I have been chosen for I was not important beyond the river or here, in Canaan." He paused. "Maybe it has nothing to do with me. I don't know how El Shaddai will bless all peoples, but he has certainly blessed me." Avraham indicated the flocks and herds both near and far. "And the biggest blessing is this son of ours. Yitzchak is the guarantee that all God's other promises will be fulfilled, because if El Shaddai has the power to give a child to old people like us, then he can do anything."

He kissed Yitzchak on the forehead. "So we will circumcise Yitzchak as a sign that we trust God will fulfill his other promises."

Yitzchak kicked his chubby legs as Avraham unwrapped the cloths that swaddled him. Avraham held Yitzchak close while the designated man skillfully did the circumcision. Yitzchak gave a wail of protest, and Utu chuckled in rueful remembrance. He'd felt like squalling too, back on their circumcision day, but all he'd done was suck in a breath.

If Avraham's god had already done this miracle, what plans did he have for this child? And if Utu and Inanna and the rest of the family were within this covenant, what plans did god have for them?

CHAPTER TWENTY-FOUR

*I*t was good to be on camelback and traveling north once again. Utu looked over his shoulder. Avraham and Eliezer were in the middle, with Job riding at the tail end. Eliezer had spoken to him about the trip yesterday, saying Avraham was worried about Lot, and asked him not to mention the trip to anyone else.

Utu was going because Eliezer had asked him, but it seemed a waste of time. Lot had consistently rejected Avraham's kindness in the past, so why would he change now?

They'd left at dawn and should only be away two nights. If, that is, they found Lot quickly. He could be dead, for all they knew. The man hadn't even bothered to stay in contact with his uncle. Good riddance, Utu thought to himself. He didn't want to be away from home for long. Jemimah was big with child, but as she and his mother had become firm friends, he didn't need to worry. He'd asked Inanna to stay as well.

A hot desert wind blew from behind them, and Utu's camel gave a low grumbling roar. Utu patted its neck. "Don't sound so disgruntled. You love being on the road again."

They went to Zoar first. The place looked no better than when they'd last been here. Still the same scattered collection of messy houses. Still the same putrid drain running down the center of the muddy street. Utu wrinkled his nose and pulled his scarf up around his nose and mouth. At the inn where they'd last seen Lot, Job held their camels while Utu and Avraham pushed the oily curtain hanging over the entrance aside and went into the gloomy interior. No one was visible. After thumping on the counter, a man in a grime-encrusted tunic that had needed replacing a few seasons past answered their summons.

"We're here looking for Lot," Avraham said.

"Lot." The man spat on the ground. "I was glad to see the back of him. He was bad for business."

Avraham raised an eyebrow.

"Not that I object to selling wine to someone who has the money to pay, but he drank far too much and scared all my customers."

"Scared them? How?"

"Kept muttering about the judgment of god and how it was going to come here, too." The man scratched his belly. "As you can see, we're safe."

The town looked like it could destroy itself without any help from god, but the man was a fool. Little did he know they were only safe because of god's mercy.

"And where is Lot now?"

The man narrowed his eyes. "Maybe I know and maybe I don't. My memory is sometimes something shocking."

Eliezer leaned forward and touched Avraham's shoulder. "I'll look after this gentleman." His voice dripped with sarcasm on the last word.

Avraham headed back out to Job. Utu chuckled.

"Let me ask you again." Eliezer's voice was slow and deliberate. "Where did Lot and his family go?"

The man held up his hands, palms towards them. "No offense, no offense meant."

"Lot?"

"Um, ah, towards the mountains."

"You'll have to do better than that."

"He comes in about every month to get supplies."

"From which direction?" Eliezer snapped.

"I'll sh-show you," the man stammered, coming out from behind the counter. He stumbled as he pushed his way through the doorway.

Utu clenched his jaw on the laugh that threatened to spill out. The owner was much taller than Eliezer, but he was flabby and had picked the wrong person to try and swindle.

Once outside, the man eagerly showed them the direction Lot had come from, then scurried back inside.

They were soon headed for the mountains with the extra camels trailing behind. Avraham held out hope that Lot's family would come and live with them. Utu didn't think that that was likely, but he kept his mouth shut. It was not his place to disagree with Avraham's false optimism.

There was no clear path, and they rode two abreast, silent at the enormity of what had happened on this plain. The whole area was still desolate, although here and there, tender shoots were pushing through the dry soil. There must have been recent rain. Maybe someday no one would remember that this area had experienced the judgment of Avraham's god.

"We'll need a miracle to find them," Eliezer said. "The inn owner mentioned something about a cave."

"It's a good thing El Shaddai specializes in miracles," Avraham said. Let's ask him to lead us to the correct spot." With almost no pause, Avraham launched into prayer. "El Shaddai, maker of heaven and earth, we do not know where Lot and his family are, but you do, for nothing is hidden from you. Help us to find Lot. Help him be willing to come back with us."

Eliezer's head was bent. Was he praying too?

The camels plodded on and on. Slowly the path began to rise. Perhaps the heat wouldn't be as oppressive higher up. Ahead was the first grove of trees. A cave might be simple, but maybe it was better than living back in Zoar. The question was why had Lot lingered in the area at all? Why hadn't he left and gone somewhere more pleasant? Perhaps it was simply because this area was familiar.

"Eliezer, where would you look?" Avraham asked.

"He'd have to be near water."

"There's a stream over there." Avraham pointed.

"And there's another on this side," Utu said.

"Job and I will follow this stream," Avraham said. "Eliezer, you and Utu go the other way."

"Whistle if you see anything," Job said.

Utu and Eliezer soon found a vague path that wound along beside their stream, twisting and turning up the hill. Sometimes they had to dismount from their camels. They reached a series of pools and stopped to scan the area.

"There," Eliezer said, pointing. "What's that?"

Utu looked to where Eliezer indicated. There was a pile of something that looked like rags lying near the water. Could it be a man?

"Let's go and see first, but carefully. It might be a trick," Utu said.

They dismounted from their camels, and both took out knives and held them ready.

"I'll go first," Utu whispered. They crept towards the water's edge. Up to their left was a big cave, well above the water. The rags didn't move. If it was man, he might already be dead. If so, there was no evidence of what had killed him.

As they drew close, the rags jerked and the man cried out. The reek of alcohol and vomit lingered like a fog. Eliezer prodded the man with his foot, but he only grunted.

"Help me turn him over," Eliezer said.

"I'll do it. You keep watch, just in case," Utu said. He handed his knife to Eliezer and turned the man over with much effort and accompanied by the man's groans. The man's beard was matted and unruly, but he opened one bleary eye. Lot.

"Lot, where are your daughters?" Eliezer said.

"Left me," he mumbled.

"Utu, please call the others. I'll try and get Lot presentable."

It was going to take more than a little water to make Lot presentable, but Utu headed back to the high point of the track and whistled. He listened for Job to answer, and waited until he could signal where they were. Then he untied the camels he and Eliezer had ridden and brought them down to the stream. There'd been little fresh water on the plain, so the animals walked straight into the water, lowered their heads, and slurped noisily.

Avraham and Job arrived, and Job led the remaining camels to the water.

"Nephew, I'm sorry to see you in this state." Avraham seated himself on a rock.

"N-not-my-fault," Lot mumbled.

Avraham pursed his lips but said nothing.

"Where are the girls?"

Lot grimaced. "D-disgusting. Not-welcome-here."

Whatever they'd done, they'd hardly had an inspiring model for anything better.

"Where are they?" Avraham said again but more softly.

"D-don't know. D-don't care."

Eliezer gestured towards Utu with his hand and slowly moved back out of Lot's line of sight. Utu did the same. Eliezer leaned close. "He's more likely to talk to Avraham if he forgets we're here."

Perhaps. Lot had been reluctant to talk last time, too. Utu sat down and strained his ears to listen to the conversation.

"Are they staying with you?" Avraham gestured towards the cave.

Lot nodded. "Out looking for food."

They'd passed fig and olive trees on the way. Herbs and small edible plants also grew along the riverbanks.

Avraham laid a gentle hand on Lot's shoulder. "Come home with me. There's plenty for you still to do."

Lot shook off Avraham's hand. "Too late. You wouldn't want those girls if you knew."

"Knew what?"

Lot burped long and loud. "Took advantage."

"Took advantage of what?"

No matter how reluctant Lot was to talk, Avraham never gave up. Lot finally answered but too softly for Utu to hear.

"Of you?" Avraham said.

"Both of them. Got me drunk."

"And?"

Lot shook his head violently and sat head hanging down. Whatever had happened, he was keeping his mouth sealed.

"Two boys," Lot mumbled lifting his head. "Ben-Ammi and Moab."

Utu's eyes widened and the sourness of vomit filled his mouth. He glanced across at Eliezer, who also looked pale and shaken. Was Lot saying he was the father of Ben-Ammi and Moab? Utu shuddered. He wanted to spring to his feet and go and smash the man's face in. How could any relative of Avraham's fall so low?

* * *

That night after Avraham had gone to sleep, Utu finally asked Eliezer the question that had been niggling at him. "Why does Avraham bother with Lot? It's obvious Lot doesn't want help."

Eliezer chuckled. "I asked him the same thing after we found Lot in Zoar."

Utu waited. Eliezer would speak as long as he felt he wasn't betraying Avraham's confidence. It used to irritate Utu, but now he appreciated Eliezer's discretion. It was an essential skill for a steward.

"Avraham said God had shown him much mercy and patience, so he needed to extend the same to Lot."

"Avraham is nothing like Lot."

"I agree, but Avraham sees things differently. He is deeply ashamed of his failures in Egypt, and with Abimelech, and for giving in to Sara in the Hagar situation. He feels he was a poor example to all of us."

"He's human," Utu said. "I don't know what I'd do in the same situation. Of course, I hope I'd fight for Jemimah, but would I?"

"I think you would."

It was tempting to bask in Eliezer's good opinion, but it wouldn't be honest. "It's hard to know what we'd do if we feared for our lives."

"Yes, but Avraham rebukes himself, because he feels he'd known God long enough to trust him to have protected both him and Sara."

"I have never heard of any god like Avraham's," Utu said. "What were the gods like where you were from?"

"No different to any in Canaan." Eliezer poked the fire with a stick, sending a spray of sparks upwards. "I'd always doubted that the gods cared, but I was even more doubtful after my wife and parents died. All I saw was the priests getting richer from our offerings while the rest of us got poorer."

It didn't seem to matter which gods were worshiped or what country it was in, the gods and priests were almost identical in their demands.

"And when I went into the temples, the images of the gods were ugly and evil. I didn't want to give such gods my worship, yet I knew of no alternative."

The fire cracked and a coal leapt out onto the grass. Job grabbed a stick and knocked it back into the fire.

"When Avraham told me about the promises God made to him, something happened in my heart. I can't really explain it." Eliezer smoothed his beard. "A sort of thirst. A longing to follow this God who communicated with ordinary people."

"Especially one who didn't first demand a big offering," Job said.

"Yes, that was what intrigued me. A God who simply gave."

"And have you regretted your decision?" Utu asked.

"Not at all. There was nothing left for me in Damascus. The more I've learned of El Shaddai, the more I've known he is worthy of worship."

"But how do you worship someone you can't see?" Utu asked.

"That has been hard, but once I realized he created the heavens and earth, I have learned much about him from looking at what he has created." Eliezer swept his hands towards the heavens, where an uncountable number of stars glittered. Towards the horizon, a crescent moon slid between dark clouds lanced by lightning bolts. "Don't you see his power and creativity?"

Job nodded. "And his sense of humor." He chuckled. "Only a god who had a sense of humor could create a camel."

"Or a human," Utu added.

"I look at what God has made. From tiny ants to the camel, from the driest desert to the highest mountains, and I praise him. Each part of creation teaches me more of who he is."

Utu had seen all these things and other things he couldn't explain. Deep down, Utu knew this god was not only powerful but good. Good, but on his own terms. Avraham and Sara would have preferred to have had Yitzchak so much earlier, but maybe there was a reason for his late arrival.

CHAPTER TWENTY-FIVE

A few years later

*I*nanna wiped her forehead with her sleeve. It was hot stirring the pots on the fire, and it took strength to push the paddle through the gluggy mass of boiling dates. Tomorrow was a rare feast day, a day when they would celebrate the weaning of young Yitzchak.

She dipped the paddle in and did a complete stir. The first cooking of the date honey was nearly done. She mustn't burn it at this stage. She stirred it a few more times, then doused the flames with a bucket of water.

"Yishmael, come and help me for a minute," she called.

He looked over his shoulder at her and then sprinted away to tag someone before loping over panting. "If I help, can I have some of the date pulp?"

She smiled. "I want you to help whether I give you anything or not."

He grinned, knowing that she'd give him some anyway to share with his friends.

"Take one end of this." She handed him the filtering cloth.

Together they laid the cloth over the top of the pot. Cords hung down the sides of the pot, and they added a rock to each cord to weigh down the cover. No flies or wasps were going to get into the honey while it cooled.

"I'll call you when it's cooled, and you can help your mother and I with the filtering," Inanna said.

Yishmael nodded and dashed off.

Inanna stretched her back a few times. The date honey was going to be used for the seldom-eaten sweet cakes and breads. Then Inanna could leave the leftovers to candy for the family to enjoy as a treat later.

Sara was supervising a great crowd of women. Some were chopping onions, leeks, and garlic, and Inanna's eyes ran from the pungent scents. Others were kneading dough made from the finest wheat flour, flour that had taken two days to grind.

Inanna squeezed in next to Hagar.

"Are the dates done?" Hagar asked.

"They're cooling before the next stage. I've got plenty of time to help."

"I hope Yishmael was helpful."

Inanna chuckled. "Any boy will work for the promise of food. He's so excited that he'll be going with the men to hunt for ducks and geese this afternoon."

"I just hope he doesn't hurt himself," Hagar muttered.

"You know Job will look after him."

"Job should be looking after his own children by now," Hagar said. "You know he only has eyes for you."

And that knowledge made Inanna feel guilty. If only he would look elsewhere, she'd feel better. She was happy as she was, with two—soon to be three—nephews and nieces, and Yishmael. Her love shielded Yishmael from the fact that the father he adored seemed so distant. And now that Sara had to keep up with her own energetic child, she was too busy to notice Yishmael.

Inanna kneaded the bread while she watched the last tent being readied for the expected guests—Abimelech, Mamre, and other local chieftains and their retinues. People would come from far and wide to see the miracle baby born to such elderly parents. Utu had told her that Avraham was going to tell the whole story himself rather than allow rumor and speculation.

After lunch, Hagar and Yishmael came to assist with the date honey. A new pot was prepared, and Inanna transferred the filtering cloth then ladled the mixture from one pot to the other, scoop by scoop. They let the liquid drain through, then she squeezed the residue and transferred it into another pot. The children of the camp would devour the pulp.

When they were finished, Inanna lit a fire under the second pot. One more boil, and the syrup would thicken, ready for use the next morning.

"Yishmael, you're in charge of the pulp, but I want you to make sure each child gets some. Wait until the end to serve yourself."

"Yes, Aunt Inanna."

She ruffled his hair, and he ducked his head to escape. She sighed. He was growing up too fast.

"Come on, Hagar. Time to eat, before the men and Yishmael go out hunting."

"I look forward to a peaceful afternoon," Hagar said, yawning. "Pity we didn't save any of the pulp."

Inanna laughed. "You don't think I gave all of it to the children, do you?"

* * *

*I*nanna sniffed appreciatively. The smell of roasting meat from numerous spits filled the air: calf, lamb, goose, and duck. Somehow the boys had managed to shoot their share of the feast. They'd arrived back muddy but triumphant with only one minor injury.

Mamre and his retinue had arrived last night, and Inanna's mother had made herself scarce. Attar had no desire to return to Kiriath Arba, although Inanna intended to send a message to her uncle to let him know she was alive and well. She'd keep her eye open for a suitable messenger.

Inanna had put on a veil so she could watch Mamre without being obvious. In her mind, she could say "He is my father," but there was no connection between them except a vague disappointment that she meant nothing to him. She mattered to Utu and her mother and to Hagar and Yishmael, but not to the one who had caused her to be born. Utu had Mamre's nose and chin, and she had his eyes and confidence. Random bits of a person passed onto another without their choice.

"Inanna," Sara's voice broke into her reverie. "The cake makers are waiting for the date honey."

Inanna hurried to deliver the honey and didn't have a chance to consider such matters again until the meal was underway.

Groups of guests were seated on an array of carpets under every patch of shade. It would be a long afternoon of eating and talking. Trade alliances would likely be made, and Sara had warned all the women to wear veils so they didn't become part of any deal. Shapeless robes hid any hints of age or form. If Inanna had to be married, she did not intend it to be outside this household. Avraham and Sara had their faults, but this situation was much happier than most.

Avraham stood up to start the meal. Yitzchak stood by his side on a large rock so he was more visible.

"Welcome, friends, to the weaning feast for my son, Yitzchak. I know you are all curious to know how a child could be born to Sara and myself, but that story will have to wait until after we eat. For I know your mouths are watering like mine, and it would be cruel to make you wait." He symbolically raised a loaf of bread and broke it. "So break bread with me and enjoy the bounty the Creator of heaven and earth has given."

Sara signaled Inanna from her place at the main carpet where both Mamre and Abimelech were seated. A long line of servers went towards their assigned groups, bearing the food. Since Inanna had been put in charge, Sara had requested that she and Job serve the main group. Job carried the platter of meat, and Inanna distributed the curds, chopped onions, leeks, garlic, and herbs. The plentiful loaves of bread were already scattered over the serving mat.

"We miss you at Kiriath Arba," Mamre said to Avraham in his booming voice. "Planting and harvest go a lot more slowly without your help."

Inanna had thought Avraham might have stayed near Kiriath Arba, but maybe the constant reminder of what had happened at Sodom was too difficult for him.

"We're happy to have Avraham here with us for the moment," Abimelech said with a chuckle. "Some of my herdsmen are serving an apprenticeship with him and some of his are with mine."

The meal meandered along. Celebrations were rare and much-anticipated events.

After everyone had finished, Inanna and the other servers brought out raisins, dried figs, and pistachios.

Avraham waited until they were served before standing. "I know you are all curious to hear the story of our Yitzchak. No one, not even myself and Sara, could have believed it was possible to have a baby at ninety. And I tell you, sleepless nights at our age are no joke."

The guests laughed politely although most of them had little hands-on parenting experience. They had servants to do most of the work.

Inanna had been impressed by Sara. She hadn't passed off parenting to a wet nurse but did the job herself, no matter how little sleep she had. She'd cheered Yitzchak on as he took his first steps and been there to dry his tears when he fell.

"I originally came from Ur, beyond the river. Our family worshiped the moon god, Nannar, and my ancestors had a story of an ancestor, Noach. In his generation, the world had become so evil that the Creator sent a flood that covered the whole earth."

Some of the guests nudged their neighbors.

"Yes, some of your ancestral stories also speak of a great flood. My ancestor Noach followed the one true God. This God warned Noach about the coming flood and told him to make an enormous boat. Noach obeyed God, and he and his entire family were saved. The story didn't impact my life until years later, when the same God spoke to me."

He looked around at the group. "By then, Sara and I were living in Harran, well to the north of here. Noach's God told me to leave my country and my father, and to follow him."

"Did he not tell you where you were going?" Abimelech asked.

Avraham shook his head. "I was just told to follow. I did not know I would end up here, talking to you all."

"But this God I did not know promised me that I would become a great nation, and many would be blessed." Avraham cupped his ear, and the jangle of a goat's bell could be heard. "You can hear some of the blessings that I received, but all the animals in the world could not disguise the fact that I was never going to be a father of a nation without sons and sadly, there were none."

Yitzchak chose that exact moment to run towards his father with arms raised. Avraham strode forward and scooped him up, and Yitzchak amused himself tugging on his father's beard and beaming around the company as though he knew all this fuss was just for him.

"As you know, God waited until it was well past impossible for us to have a son, before he gave us this treasure beyond price to brighten our old age."

Yitzchak gave an enthusiastic tug on Avraham's beard. "Ouch, young man." He put Yitzchak down and pushed him gently towards his mother.

"The long wait was very hard, especially on my wife, and along the way we sometimes gave up trusting in God's word." He shook his head. "I was unfaithful, but God was always faithful. I used to be disappointed at the Lord's slowness to fulfill his word, but I've come to see that by waiting, he has done a far greater miracle. A miracle that will be remembered much longer than the length of our lives. If we'd had a child at forty or fifty, it would have been wonderful but not a miracle. But a child at ninety is most definitely a miracle. A miracle that can only be achieved by a great and powerful God."

He smiled broadly and looked around his guests. "Back when we lived in Ur, I never saw Nannar give gifts generously. I only saw him take and take and take again. But El Shaddai gives and gives, and he has now given us Yitzchak." He gestured towards his son. "I present him to you all. Yitzchak, our son who brings laughter to our old age."

The crowd roared and cheered, and Inanna hurried out to serve the sweet cakes and refill the bowls with the best of Avraham's produce.

CHAPTER TWENTY-SIX

*I*t happened soon after Avraham's speech. Most of the adults were taking a break from the endless eating, while Avraham and Sara had just finished moving from group to group to speak to their guests.

The only ones with any energy were the children, who were running around. Little Yitzchak ran around in his celebratory finery, trying to keep up with the bigger kids. Yishmael stopped and leaned down towards his younger brother and said something. Yitzchak stuck out his lip and wailed.

What had Yishmael said? Inanna switched direction to intercept Yishmael and nearly bumped into Avraham and Sara. Sara gripped Avraham's arm. "Get rid of that slave woman and her son, for that woman's son will never share in the inheritance with Yitzchak."

Heart pounding, Inanna ducked out of sight around the corner of a tent.

"Sara, Sara," Avraham's voice was tinged with sadness. "That is not fair. Both boys are my sons. Yitzchak will be my heir, but Yishmael deserves something too."

"I don't care what he deserves. I can't stand to have them here. You must get rid of him and his mother."

"We'll talk about this later. Right now, we have guests to look after."

Avraham and Sara moved off, and Inanna let out the breath she'd been holding. Her stomach ached with tension. Would Avraham be able to reason with Sara, or would Sara win, as she always had before? Avraham backed down too often.

Inanna watched Avraham as she served the fruit and sweet cakes. His expression would drop and become sad, then he'd sit up straight and engage Mamre or Abimelech in conversation.

Inanna kept her eye on Avraham the entire time, but by evening, she was no closer to knowing what would happen. Would Sara finally succeed in driving Hagar away?

* * *

"*L*et's go for a walk," Hagar said to Inanna the next morning after they'd finished the bread-making for the day.

Inanna looked at her friend, trying to gauge if this would be good news or bad. Hagar's expression gave no clues. Inanna stood up and dusted the flour off her hands. Walking away from the river was the best place for a private conversation.

"You'll be hearing soon enough, but I wanted to tell you myself. Yishmael and myself are leaving tomorrow," Hagar said once they were out of everyone's hearing.

The words struck Inanna like fists. "L-leaving?"

"Ever since Yitzchak was born, Sara has watched us closely."

Looking for an excuse to get rid of them both.

"She accused Yishmael of taunting Yitzchak. Yishmael says he didn't mean anything by it, but Sara won't accept it." Hagar sighed. "It was always going to happen. Having us around makes her uncomfortable. She's worried people will expect Yishmael to be the heir, because he is the oldest."

"It's not fair." The words burst out of Inanna. "You have only ever done what Sara wanted."

176

"Life has never been fair," Hagar said. "As a slave, you ought to know that."

"Of course I do, but it never makes it any easier to bear," Inanna said.

Hagar laid her hand on Inanna's arm. "You long to soar free, so you'll always feel imprisoned. I've learned to accept what can't be changed."

"But how do you learn that?"

"I don't know. Maybe it's the difference between us. It's been a huge help to know God sees me."

It was nice that Avraham's god worked for Hagar, but following him wasn't a solution Inanna was prepared to accept. The last thing she wanted was to submit to yet another male, divine or not, who felt he had the right to tell her what to do.

"But where will you go?" Inanna asked, picturing the vast wildernesses they'd walked through on their way from Egypt. Places where there were dangers not only from the environment but from wild animals and men too.

Hagar shrugged. "Further south, I guess."

Towards less populated areas and towards the far horizon that led back towards Egypt. Hagar had lived most of her life in Canaan, but where did she feel most at home? Probably right here. With the very people who were casting her out.

"I don't know how I will bear it without you," Inanna said. The closeness she'd once felt with Utu had diminished once he married, and Hagar had long since become her confidant.

"You've been a good friend," Hagar said.

They didn't talk of Yishmael, couldn't talk of Yishmael. For all these years, Inanna had been an extra parent to him. He'd run to her just as often as to Hagar when he scraped his knee or when the other children had picked on him. She'd dried his tears more times than she could remember. He was a passionate child, always asserting his rights. Perhaps it was because the rights he ought to have had were denied him, something he'd sensed even as a child. He sensed that Avraham didn't treat him as a father ought to.

"Avraham came to tell me himself." Hagar gnawed her lip. "He was very kind and apologized for all the pain he'd caused me. Apologized for not asking God when Sara first suggested the idea of my having a child."

"I'm glad someone apologized," Inanna snapped. It wasn't likely that Sara ever would. Indeed Sara probably thought she'd given Hagar a privilege rather than seeing that she'd stolen Hagar's future. It wasn't as if Hagar could marry and find happiness with someone else.

"Inanna, Inanna." Hagar patted Inanna's arm. "I appreciate you getting worked up on my behalf, but there is no need. I'm committing myself into the care of El Shaddai. He sees and knows what is happening and he will look after me."

Inanna hoped Hagar's trust wouldn't be misplaced. Hagar had only had one encounter with this god's messenger. Even Avraham had only had three or four encounters. Not much to build trust upon.

* * *

The sun hadn't yet risen when Inanna heard Hagar rise from her bed. Inanna got up and rolled her sleeping mat against the tent wall, out of the way.

Inanna headed across to Utu's tent where Yishmael was staying a final night. Peleg had run around after Yishmael from the day he could walk and thought of him as an older brother. At the tent entrance, she called softly. Footsteps padded across the ground, then her brother poked his head out. "I'll get him up."

Before long, Yishmael appeared with his bow, his most precious possession, slung across his chest. Avraham had given him this bow as a recent gift to replace the child's version that he'd had while learning to shoot. Yishmael carried it everywhere, only taking it off for sleep. Even then, it lay alongside him.

"Come on. Your mother is preparing something for you to eat." Inanna put her hand on his shoulder. He began to pull away, then stopped as if he realized it would be the last time and he wouldn't need to insist she treat him as an adult ever again. Her chest grew tight. He might be sad at leaving her now, but he'd soon forget her in the flood of new experiences. Things would be different for her.

She sat on a rock while Hagar and Yishmael ate. Before they finished, Avraham came out of the tent with a waterskin and another bag, presumably containing food.

"I'm sorry that it has had to be this way, but the Lord has reassured me that he will look after you and make you into a great nation also." Avraham handed the waterskin and bag to Hagar.

"Thank you, Avraham," Hagar said quietly. "I know you have not wished me harm."

Her friend was much more forgiving than Inanna would have been.

"But I did not fight to protect you either, and that was wrong," he said, face flushed. "Would you be willing for me to bless you before you leave?"

Hagar nodded and raised her hands to receive the blessing. Avraham placed his hand on Yishmael's head. "Almighty Lord, you are the God who sees all and judges rightly. You have seen the many injustices Hagar and Yishmael have suffered. Oh Lord, bless them. Fill them to overflowing with your grace and mercy. Protect them in their travels, and bring them to a place where they can rest and feel at home. Fulfill your promises to them and make them into a great nation." His voice shook. "And help them to know you are forever faithful."

Hagar lowered her hands. "Thank you."

Avraham turned to Inanna. "You and Utu will accompany them a little way?"

Inanna nodded. "Yes, and watch until they are out of sight."

The flap of Utu's tent lifted, and he came to join them. "Ready?"

Hagar slung the strap of the waterskin across her body, and the four of them set off. Hagar had wanted to leave before most people were up to avoid gossip.

There was sure to be plenty of gossip, but the gossipers would get nothing from herself or Utu.

At the top of a little rise, Hagar turned to Inanna. "This is far enough. Thank you."

Inanna threw her arms around Hagar and hugged her tightly, squeezing her eyelids together to prevent tears.

"I go with the God who sees," Hagar murmured in her ear.

Inanna hoped so. Yishmael wasn't yet responsible enough to bear his mother's burdens.

Seeing their hug, Yishmael joined in. He was still thin and wiry, but looked like he'd soon be filling out. A lump filled her throat and the first tears spilled. The thought of never seeing these two again filled her chest with an enormous rock of sorrow.

"Don't cry, Aunt Inanna. I'll look after Mama."

"Good boy." She patted his cheek. "You make sure you shoot lots of hares and birds along the way."

He puffed out his chest and grinned. "I will." He turned to his mother. "Come on."

Hagar gave Inanna's hand one last squeeze and followed Yishmael.

Utu stood with his arm around Inanna's shoulder, and they watched Hagar and Yishmael until they disappeared into the shimmer to the south.

CHAPTER TWENTY-SEVEN

Six months later

"Inanna, don't look so apprehensive," Avraham said. "I haven't sent for you and Utu because you've done something wrong."

With a whoosh, Inanna let out the breath she'd been holding. She had been afraid that she'd somehow offended Avraham ... or more likely, Sara. After all, she'd been a close friend of Hagar.

"I couldn't help noticing that giving Utu his freedom when he married was something he appreciated," Avraham said.

A smile lit up Utu's face. "It was a gift beyond measure."

"I confess I hadn't really thought of its significance, because I don't see any of you as slaves. To me, you're just part of the family."

Inanna clamped her teeth shut. Thus spoke a man who had never been a slave. Never known the indignity of having to ask permission to do anything, to go anywhere, to rest, to marry. Never known the sting of the whip or been separated from family against his will by the whim of a master who moved people around like they were flocks of sheep.

It had been hard not to be envious of Utu's freedom. It was wasted on him, for he hadn't taken advantage of his liberty to do what he wanted or go where he pleased. She'd often daydreamed about what she'd do with her freedom. Maybe she'd go and find Hagar. Or have her own home. Or just get out of bed when she wanted. And she'd climb trees and spend hours watching eagles.

"I wanted to thank you for your care of Hagar," Avraham said.

"She was my friend. It wasn't a chore," Inanna said, tears threatening to break through her eyelashes. Were Hagar and Yishmael safe? Yishmael liked to pretend he was a man, but he'd be little use if real danger threatened.

Avraham opened his hand and held it towards her. In his palm was a disc of clay. It looked fairly ordinary, but was it the precious disc of clay that occupied her dreams? The disc that would proclaim her freedom?

"For me?" she said, voice quavering.

"For you. In thanks for how you've cared faithfully for my family."

A lump blocked her throat, and Avraham's outstretched hand blurred in the shimmer of tears pooling in her eyes.

Utu cleared his throat.

"Thank you so very much," Inanna stammered before reaching for the disc. It was much lighter than it ought to be for an object of such significance. She stroked its surface with a tentative finger. Free. She was free at last. She wanted to shout it from the top of her tree. If she had had wings to swoop and dive with the eagles, she'd do it.

At last she had the thing she had wanted more than anything since she was snatched out of the tree and carried off to Egypt. Freedom. There was nothing better.

* * *

*I*nanna threw the stick she'd been swinging into the stream. "How come I feel no different from yesterday?"

"How did you expect to feel?" Job asked, dropping onto the nearest rock.

"Euphoric, like I did yesterday after Avraham gave me my freedom."

She'd woken in the morning with a headache and a mood as gray as the day. She should have been dancing and celebrating her first day of freedom, yet all she felt was a heaviness, a feeling that nothing had changed.

"What you want—freedom—is a mirage," Job said, rubbing his eyebrow. "No one is free. Look at your brother. It's wonderful to be a father. But he isn't free to do anything he wants, because he needs to look after the needs and demands of his family." Job's tone was wistful. "Not that he begrudges it."

He stood and paced in a circle, the gravel crunching under his feet. "And Mamre. He might be the leader of his people, but he has to provide for them. Every failed harvest means he must somehow find food. Every child who is kidnapped by slavers worries him. He is burdened by a host of responsibilities. It's the same for Avraham and Sara."

"You're free," she said.

"Am I?"

"Well, you have to look after the camels, but you've been free as a bird since Avraham freed you."

"Have I?" He colored and took a deep breath. "I haven't been free since soon after we met. I am bound to you whether or not you ever look on me favorably."

She felt her face heat. "I'm sorry."

He looked steadily towards the horizon. Probably embarrassed he'd said so much.

"I am not sorry to have met you."

The problem was that he was unable to escape her. The camp was big, but it wasn't that big. They might not see each other every day, but often enough to mean that they talked regularly. She regarded Job as a friend … no, he was more than a friend. More like a brother, but he didn't want to be merely her brother. It bothered her to know that her presence must hurt him, but he never treated her with anything other than respect and kindness. Was that enough? It was more than most marriages started with. Her mother hadn't even met her father before they were married, and she was only one wife among the many he'd wed. If Inanna married Job, she need not fear that she'd have a rival. Job had shown himself faithful over the years.

"Job, why don't you find someone else? There are plenty who would be delighted to marry you."

"I can't," he said gently, looking at her. "I've tried, but it seems that I'm bound to you no matter what I do."

She bit her lip. Was she a fool? Any other woman would be glad of such total devotion, but to her, Job's devotion felt like she was a bird enclosed in a cage. Her desire for the elusive thing called freedom had her slipping through the gap in the closing door before it imprisoned her within. Yet every time she thought she was soaring free, she plummeted back to earth.

She'd always thought she'd be free if she was no longer a slave, but being given her freedom had made little difference to everyday life. Now she could have chosen to lie in bed, she hadn't bothered to do so. She'd gotten up at the same time as usual this morning and done her usual daily tasks. Now she could go anywhere, she had no desire to leave the security of Avraham's camp.

As a child Inanna had found no freedom among the Amorites of Kiriath Arba despite being a chieftain's daughter. There'd been no freedom in Egypt, and there was no freedom here, even with the disc signifying her release from slavery around her neck.

Would freedom always be just beyond the horizon, disappearing even as she closed her hand upon it, like water disappearing into the thirsty sands of the desert? If all these things had not brought freedom, where was true freedom to be found?

CHAPTER TWENTY-EIGHT

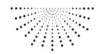

"*E*liezer, we have a problem," Utu said.

"A problem?" Eliezer looked up from counting the storage jars in the cave they used to keep stores cool.

"You know that well we dug a few weeks ago?"

Eliezer nodded. He'd sent Utu to supervise the digging, and Utu still had the calluses on his hands to prove it.

"Abimelech's herdsmen have seized it." And they'd been rough about it, beating two of Avraham's shepherds.

"Does Avraham know?"

Utu shook his head. "I came to you first."

"Why don't you go and talk to Avraham. Be ready to accompany him if he goes to talk to Abimelech."

Eliezer was letting Utu do more and more tasks on his own.

Utu hurried off to find Avraham and eventually found him talking to Sara. She'd been much more relaxed since Hagar and Yishmael had left. No one had heard a word from them since. Inanna worried about them but only shared her concerns with Utu.

He waited until Avraham had finished talking to Sara before telling Avraham what had happened.

"Thank you for letting me know," Avraham said. "I just received an invitation from Abimelech to meet him near the second well we dug. Maybe this is what he wants to talk about."

* * *

*A*bimelech and the commander of his forces, Phicol, were waiting in the shade of a tree near the well. Abimelech came forward and kissed Avraham on both cheeks. "You are looking well, my friend. You never seem to get any older."

"Yitzchak keeps me young. He's clamoring for me to teach him to ride a camel."

Abimelech laughed. "A real little champion."

Abimelech was a sociable man who loved to be around family and friends. What was he up to?

"I know you are a busy man, so I do not want to take up too much of your time." Abimelech cleared his throat. "It is obvious that your god is with you in everything you do. Now swear to me that you will not deal falsely with me, my children, or my descendants. Show to me and this country where you now reside as a foreigner the same kindness I have shown you."

Avraham opened his arms wide. "It would be my privilege to make this covenant with you. You have shown yourself to be a man among men. An honorable man in a time of many dishonorable ones. A forgiving man in a time of men who hold grudges. And a generous man in times of greed. You have taught me much about what it is to be a leader. But before we make a covenant there is a little matter which you may be unaware of." Avraham paused. "The well that we recently dug was seized by some of your servants, and they have blocked us from collecting water there."

Abimelech frowned. "Phicol, did you know of this?"

"No, my lord."

Phicol had more than enough responsibility keeping the town and fields safe from marauders.

"I did not know of this, my brother, but will immediately sort it out," Abimelech said.

"Thank you," Avraham said. "Why don't I give that well to you, and we will move closer to this one?"

Abimelech stroked his beard. "That sounds like a possible solution."

"I will remain here while I send Utu back to camp to alert them about the upcoming move. He will also bring the animals to make our covenant."

Avraham talked privately to Utu, and then Utu set off. Moving here should take the pressure off their relationship with Abimelech's herdsmen. Crowding often led to conflict, as Utu well remembered from the difficulties they'd had with Lot.

* * *

*T*he sun was well past its high point when Utu returned. Behind him were strung Avraham's gifts to Abimelech. Avraham was a generous man, and there were many animals—more than necessary to seal a treaty.

The flocks arrived first, because Utu made sure the cattle were a reasonable distance behind to allow the dust to partially settle.

Utu separated seven ewe lambs from the rest and put Peleg in charge. Like Eliezer had done in his own case, Utu was now rotating Peleg among the different tasks in the camp to find where he fit best. He was a thoughtful boy who seemed to enjoy the isolation of shepherding.

"What is this?" Abimelech asked Avraham, gesturing towards the extra animals.

"A gift for you to thank you for all your hospitality and the favor you have shown us."

"You've given much more than you've taken. Sharing your skills and working alongside us. Ever since you've been here, we've prospered."

Utu had often heard Abimelech's workers commenting on the bumper harvests, and the unusual number of animals having multiple offspring.

"El Shaddai promised me that he would bless whoever blessed me."

"Yes," Abimelech said. "I'd like to know more about your god."

"I would be happy to talk with you further."

Abimelech gestured towards Peleg's group of seven lambs. "Why have you separated off those seven?"

"Please accept those seven as a witness that we dug this well."

"Gladly," Abimelech said.

Both men stood, and Abimelech turned to Phicol. "Would you choose three more of our men to serve as witnesses?"

Utu did the same among the herdsmen.

Avraham and Abimelech faced each other, with each group of witnesses standing behind them.

Avraham raised his right hand. "I make this oath in the presence of El Shaddai, maker of heaven and earth, that I and my descendants will deal with favor towards Abimelech and his descendants as he has dealt with favor towards me, a foreigner and stranger in his lands. This oath is binding and is sealed with the gifts of flocks and herds you see behind me."

Abimelech cleared his throat and raised his right hand too. "I accept the generous gift of these animals, and I too make this oath in the presence of Avraham's god. Myself and my descendants will continue to show favor to Avraham and his descendants, but if we do not, then this oath is null and void. I also acknowledge that this well was dug by and belongs to Avraham and his descendants. Anyone who tries to take it does so at their own peril."

They bowed towards each other, then turned to their witnesses and said together, "You are the witnesses of this solemn oath and promise."

"We are the witnesses," Utu and the others said.

"And we shall name this well Beersheba, for it is both the well of our oath and the well of seven."

Avraham and Abimelech grasped each other's shoulders and formally kissed each other on the cheek.

"Go in peace, my brother," Avraham said.

"And may peace go with you too, my brother," Abimelech replied. Then he turned to Phicol. "Let us be on our way."

Some of Avraham's household escorted the sheep towards Gerar, and the air was full of lows and bleats and the calming voice of the herders.

Once they were gone, Avraham turned to Utu and Peleg and the remaining men. "Let's plant this tamarisk tree we brought along as a memorial. Then you can help me build an altar."

Utu assigned someone to dig the hole for the tree and left Avraham to choose the correct spot and water it in.

"Peleg, come here."

Utu looked around the site and spotted several flattish stones. He handed Peleg the digging tool. "Dig around the stone with this." Once he'd successfully done that, Utu inserted the other end of the tool under the rock and showed Peleg how to lever it out.

It wouldn't budge.

"We'll have to dig a little more underneath the rock," Utu said. Peleg burrowed away some more. On their second attempt to lever it out, they succeeded.

"Well done, son," Utu said. His heart filled with the warmth of accomplishment and the satisfaction of working with his son.

Together they carried their rock over and added it to the second layer of rocks.

When the altar was waist height, Avraham had them gather wood from under the nearby trees and laid it on top of the stones.

Someone had the lamb ready. They added some dry leaves and a little moss to a burning coal that Utu had brought from the main camp, and it only took a few minutes to produce a flame. Avraham waited a little longer and then he led them in prayer.

"Great God, King, and Father of All. Thank you for your care for all of us. You give us breath and you supply our daily food. We praise and honor you for the rain in season and the sunshine when it is needed to make everything grow. We praise you for protecting us from locusts, drought, and famine. We thank you for the blessings of fruitfulness, not only among our people and livestock but also on our crops and the fruit trees you have planted around us …"

The poetry of the praise caressed Utu's ears. The prayers of his childhood had involved begging the gods for blessing and were accompanied by elaborate rituals. Over and over Avraham's prayers had shown him that the creator wanted respect and praise more than precise ritual.

Yet how had Avraham worked these things out without any priest to teach him?

CHAPTER TWENTY-NINE

*I*nanna waded into the women's pool in the river. The cool water was refreshing after the three stifling days in the women's tent where she had to go into seclusion every month. She always insisted that one side of the tent be raised so she could look out on the trees and the river directly behind. The tent was the one space where women were allowed to rest, and they spent the time weaving and making clothes. The rest of the month, they had too many necessary daily duties.

Jemimah waded in beside her. "Oh, this feels wonderful."

"It's my favorite time of the month," Inanna said before ducking under the water. She'd unbraided her long hair and it floated around her. She scrubbed her scalp vigorously.

Then she stood on the pebbly bottom of the river. Soon she felt a tickle and then another. Peering down at her feet, she could see the tiny fish nibbling her skin. She reached down and picked up a handful of finer sand and rubbed it over the skin of her arms, legs, and feet. Her mother had shown her how to do this when she'd been a small child.

Jemimah giggled. "The sand always tickles, but you're right. It feels great afterwards."

"Keziah, don't go in too deep," Jemimah said to her youngest daughter. The other children were with Eliezer and Attar.

Her niece's curls were plastered around her face. She'd removed all her clothes and was bobbing under the surface of the water to pick up rocks. She examined each with concentration and threw back the ones that didn't meet her approval.

"Let's try to swim again," Inanna said. She'd seen the sheep swim through the deeper water recently and had been trying to imitate them.

"You go first," Jemimah said.

Inanna launched off into the deeper water. Water splashed and surged as she kicked her legs. It worked better if she curved her arms a little and made a scoop with her hands.

"Keep going," Jemimah yelled. "You're nearly there."

Inanna kept kicking until her knee scraped the bottom and she turned to look back at Jemimah. She'd gone far further than last time. She caught her breath then swam back to Jemimah.

"You'll be teaching the rest of us soon," Jemimah said. "I want all the children to learn as soon as possible."

One of the small children from Kiriath Arba had drowned recently. His mother had been chatting with her neighbor and hadn't noticed that her toddler had disappeared until it was too late. The woman had been inconsolable, and Inanna had been determined to make sure it didn't happen to anyone else's child.

They sat in the shallows, letting the water lap around them. Keziah put her selected stones on the water's edge, then found a stick and dug a hole.

"It is lovely to actually talk with you, Jemimah."

Jemimah laughed. "For me, too. I love the children, but they don't give me much time to talk to other adults."

Inanna still missed having Hagar around. Maybe Jemimah could become a friend if they spent more time together. What use was freedom if she continued to work as hard as ever? Now that her mother spent so much time with Sara, Inanna could take time for things other than work.

"I want to spend more time with you and the children," Inanna said.

Jemimah grinned at her. "That would be great, but beware—the more time you invest, the more it will cost you."

Inanna squinted at her. "What do you mean?"

"You've always valued your freedom, but the more time you spend with us, the less free you'll be."

Had Jemimah been talking to Job?

"It's a choice, really. The closer you are to people, the more you will feel their hurts and be burdened by the things that burden them." She let some water trickle through her fingers. "But it's worth it, because we love them."

"So you think we miss out if we hold ourselves back?"

Jemimah put her head to one side. "Pain and loss are the cost of love. That's why it hurt Abba to lose my mother. I asked him once if it would have been better if he'd not known her, and he told me firmly that grief is the price of love, but it is always better to love."

"He loves you."

"And it is a huge risk, as it is for your brother. Life is uncertain. Look at that death in the town last week. That poor man couldn't have expected a stone would fall off the wall just as he passed by."

The suddenness of the young man's death had shaken them all, and what Jemimah was saying made sense. Inanna had loved Hagar and Yishmael, and their leaving had torn a hole in her heart. It hurt so badly that she'd held herself back from loving Yitzchak. Not that Sara had given her much of a chance to spend time with her precious son.

"Holding ourselves back from others might protect us from pain, but it also deprives us of great joys," Jemimah said. "It's not worth it in the end."

Keziah came over to her mother and held out her dirty hands.

"Into the water with you." Jemimah laughed, and helped Keziah wash her hands. Little Keziah giggled as she splashed more than the job required.

Inanna's heart clenched. Yishmael had run to her for help as much as he'd run to his mother.

Jemimah's words held wisdom. It was time to make some changes.

A breeze rippled across the water.

"Brr," Inanna said. "Time to get out and return to normal life again."

"Or you could swim the river once more," Jemimah said. "I'll try after you. You've inspired me."

CHAPTER THIRTY

Six months later

*I*t was going to be a long, hot day. Avraham and Yitzchak had left Utu and Job with the donkey and told them to wait until he and Yitzchak returned.

Three days before, Eliezer had woken Utu early and told him he needed to go with Avraham and not ask any questions. By the time Utu had hurried out to where Avraham was waiting, the donkey had already been loaded with wood and Avraham was pacing up and down. He barely greeted Utu before striding forward, Yitzchak followed after him.

The only clue to the purpose of the sudden trip was the cut wood, which suggested a burnt offering. If so, Avraham had forgotten the sacrifice. Maybe he'd intended to buy one on the way. Yet during the three days they hadn't passed any towns but had simply walked steadily in a direction only Avraham seemed clear about.

The whole situation was odd. Yitzchak had been running ahead and hunting for grasshoppers and bugs as usual, but Avraham hadn't laughed at all. Avraham, who hadn't stopped laughing since the day Yitzchak had been born.

They'd stopped at mid-afternoon, and Avraham called Yitzchak over and loaded the wood on Yitzchak's back. That had quieted Yitzchak down, but as Avraham picked up the knife and fire, he'd looked haggard and gray.

Job had offered to carry the wood instead of Yitzchak, but Avraham had refused Job's assistance.

"Stay here with the donkey while I and the boy go over there." Avraham had gestured towards the nearest hill. "We will worship. Then we will come back to you."

Had there been a quaver in Avraham's voice? If so, he'd quickly covered it.

"Abba, the fire and the wood are here, but where is the lamb for the burnt offering?" Yitzchak asked in his piercing voice after he and Avraham had only walked a short distance.

Job had been about to say something to Utu, but Utu held up his hand. He wanted to hear whatever Avraham might answer.

"My son, God himself will provide the lamb for the burnt offering."

Utu swallowed. What did that mean? That Avraham expected god to send him an animal out of nowhere? Avraham was not carrying any means to bring down an animal. No spear, no bow and arrows and no animal was going to leap onto Avraham's knife.

Utu closed his eyes and pictured the tension that crackled like lightning in the dry air of summer. His eyes blinked open. That was it. The way Avraham laid the wood on Yitzchak's back, as though Yitzchak himself was the sacrifice. Utu's heart sped up to a gallop. Surely not.

"You've gone quite pale," Job said. "Are you alright?"

"Just having horrible thoughts."

"What about?"

Utu shook his head and sat down in the shade with his back against a tree. "I don't know if I can bring myself to say them out loud."

"You're concerned about where Avraham and Yitzchak have gone and what they're doing?"

Utu nodded, fear making his limbs heavy.

"Avraham won't harm Yitzchak, if that's what's bothering you," Job said, squatting in the shade from a second tree.

"What if his god asks him to?" Utu said, confusion whirling inside him.

Job looked across. "I think you're getting confused. Some of the gods around us might demand child sacrifice, but have you ever known Avraham's god to be vindictive or cruel?"

"N-no."

"But?" Job raised an eyebrow.

"But he doesn't always do things the way that Avraham expected."

"Oh, I agree that El Shaddai is not predictable, but I think you would agree that he is good?" Job swatted a fly.

Utu scrolled back in his mind to all he knew of El Shaddai. A god who made extravagant promises and who had kept them. A god who moved in light and spoke with a voice that awed him but had never made him afraid. A god who rescued an undeserving man like Lot from terrible judgment. A god who could give old people a child and then give them the energy to keep up.

"Good? Yes, I do think he is good."

"Then what do you have to worry about? If you can't calm down, why don't you try praying like Avraham and Eliezer do." Job covered his eyes and lay down for a sleep. "Keep an eye on that donkey," he mumbled. "He likes to wander."

There wasn't much grass around, but Utu tied the donkey close to a few tufts and next to bushes it could graze on.

He'd heard Avraham praying many times and lately Eliezer had prayed out loud several times when they ate together. Maybe he'd give prayer a go.

Utu checked that Job was deeply asleep and then he opened his mouth and murmured. "Avraham's god, it's me, Utu." He laughed to himself. He shouldn't need to tell this god who he was as he'd had to do for the gods of his childhood. For those gods, he'd had to recite not only his own name but the names of his parents and grandparents and where he lived.

"I don't know how to pray to you. I don't even know if I'm

allowed to. Maybe you only permit special people like Avraham to pray to you." It felt foolish talking to someone he couldn't see. "Look after Avraham and Yitzchak and bring them back safely to us. We—I mean, I—feel quite helpless here." His voice trailed off. He didn't know how to end his prayer or even if what he'd said was acceptable. If Avraham ever came back, he'd ask him how to pray. Avraham's prayers were increasingly eloquent, but maybe he'd struggled in the beginning too.

* * *

"*I*s that them?" Job leapt to his feet.

The wait had seemed long, and the long shadows of late afternoon streaked the ground.

"Them?" Hope trembled in Utu's voice. He peered towards where he'd seen Avraham and Yitzchak disappear around a fold on the hill. He could see Avraham, but no sign of anyone with him. Avraham strode along energetically as though he'd been for a refreshing bathe in cool water rather than hiking up a hill after three long days of walking.

Job punched Utu's shoulder. "Look. Yitzchak's with him."

Yitzchak came from behind Avraham. Usually he'd run ahead of his father, but this time he stuck close.

"Come on," Job said, untying the donkey. "Let's meet them."

Utu followed. As they drew close to the pair, Avraham waved, a grin of pure joy making his face young.

Something had happened while they waited, and he hoped Avraham would tell them.

* * *

*T*hey started walking back towards Beersheba early the next morning.

"Sorry I couldn't talk last night," Avraham said. "I was too exhausted and overwhelmed to communicate."

In fact, he'd only eaten a few mouthfuls of bread before going straight to sleep.

"The Lord asked me to do something I didn't have the strength to do. I didn't know he was testing me or that he planned to give me the strength I needed."

"Testing you?" Utu asked, leading the donkey on which they'd loaded their few supplies.

"You know I haven't always trusted God. There have been times when I've relied on my own plans and forgotten to ask God for help." Avraham looked at each of them from under his bushy eyebrows. "I hope you've learned from my mistakes."

Utu nodded. It would have felt rude to deny it. He admired Avraham for admitting his failings.

"This time, the Lord asked me to do the impossible." Avraham lowered his voice. "God called out to me and said, 'Take your son, your only son, whom you love—Yitzchak—and go to the region of Moriah. Sacrifice him there as a burnt offering on a mountain I will show you.'"

It was exactly as Utu had feared. He looked ahead of them to where Yitzchak trotted along, swinging a stick and humming to himself.

"When El Shaddai asked this of me, I was devastated." Avraham shook his head. "I couldn't say anything to Sara, but I knew I had to obey as too often in the past, I'd failed."

"But didn't you question this command?" Utu asked.

"Of course I questioned it. Since the very first time El Shaddai spoke to me in Harran, I have trusted that he was both good and powerful, but this request confused me. Suddenly this good God sounded like the worst Canaanite gods."

"Then why did you get up and go to Mount Moriah? I don't think I would have." Utu shuddered at the thought of having to sacrifice any of his children.

"I didn't sleep for most of the night after God spoke to me. Instead I went round and round in my mind trying to decide if I was going to trust God or not."

"And what made your mind up?" Job asked.

"I went over every single encounter I'd had with God. He'd never failed me. Not once. For a long time, I doubted he could fulfill the promises about descendants but look." He pointed at Yitzchak. "Even that was fulfilled. Every time I tried to solve my own problems, God protected me from the consequences of my choices. I didn't protect Sara, but God did."

They all stopped for a drink.

"It was the memory of God's faithfulness that got me up that first morning," Avraham said once they were walking again. "I didn't know how he intended to save Yitzchak, but I trusted him to do so. I chose to obey and trust him to either stop me at the last moment or raise Yitzchak back to life."

Utu blew out a gusty breath. He didn't think he could have done what Avraham had done.

"Every step during the three days, I kept telling God I'd take the next step and he'd have to give me courage to take the following one. Finally I seemed to have learned to trust God for every bit of strength." Avraham chuckled. "It's taken me long enough."

"So what happened up there?" Utu pointed towards Mount Moriah.

"I just kept walking until the Lord told me to stop. Then I asked Yitzchak to help me build an altar, and we arranged all the wood on top of it."

"But didn't Yitzchak ask you where the animal was?"

Avraham shook his head. "He'd asked as we left you. Of course, I told him God would provide, even though I couldn't see how it would happen."

It was puzzling. Yitzchak was an intelligent boy. Why didn't he keep asking?

"As we got closer and closer to the sacrifice, it became harder and harder to obey." Avraham wiped his eyes. "It nearly destroyed me to tie Yitzchak and place him on the wood." He swallowed. "He just stared at me. Th-there was such trust in his eyes, yet he must have known what was happening."

What had Yitzchak felt at that moment? Had he been afraid? Or had God given him a miraculous faith even greater than his father's?

"That last moment was the worst of all. It took all my courage to bring the knife near his throat. In the end, I think I closed my eyes."

Utu's chest was tight. He didn't want to imagine this scene. All he saw was his own children.

"And just at that moment, God called from heaven, 'Avraham! Avraham!' and I said, 'Here I am.' These were exactly the words I'd replied when God had called me the three days before."

"And what did your god say?" Job asked, giving the donkey a slap on its behind. It hee-hawed in shock and trotted forward.

Once the donkey had settled down, Avraham continued, "The Lord said, 'Do not lay a hand on the boy. Do not do anything to him. Now I know you fear God, because you have not withheld from me your son, your only son.'"

It didn't seem the right moment to ask why Avraham's god kept calling Yitzchak Avraham's only son. El Shaddai knew of Yishmael's existence, yet kept repeating the phrase "only son." What was the significance of the phrase?

"Then I heard a bleat behind me," Avraham said. "I turned and saw a ram caught by its horns in the thicket."

Job rubbed his forehead. "But surely if there had been a ram there, you would have seen or heard it before."

"Exactly," Avraham said. "The God who had arranged the precise timing of every step must have divinely put it there at exactly the right moment."

An awe filled Utu's belly despite his still-lingering questions. What kind of god was this who put each piece of his plan together as precisely as the path of each star in the sky?

"I untied Yitzchak, and I don't think El Shaddai minded that we had a long hug before we took that ram and sacrificed it in Yitzchak's place. As the smoke of the burning went up to heaven, we stood there and praised God."

Yitzchak came running back to them, as though he sensed which part of the story Avraham had been telling. His hands were closed around something. Carefully opening his hand a crack, he let Avraham see whatever creature was inside.

"Beautiful, son," Avraham said as he ruffled Yitzchak's hair. "Let it go free."

Yitzchak opened his hand. The blue butterfly lay on his palm, opening and closing its wings before fluttering towards the nearest bushes.

"We called that place, 'The Lord will provide' for we had seen that on his mountain, the Lord provides."

As Avraham spoke the words, his voice trembled with awe and joy, as though he was saying something of eternal significance, although Utu had no clue what it might be. Maybe this whole test from god had some greater significance than any of them now understood.

"Again the angel of the Lord spoke to me and said, 'I swear by myself, declares the Lord, that because you have done this and have not withheld your son, your only son, I will surely bless you and make your descendants as numerous as the stars in the sky and as the sand on the seashore. Your descendants will take possession of the cities of their enemies, and through your offspring all nations on earth will be blessed, because you have obeyed me.'"

They walked on in silence, their steps crunching over the dry ground and accompanied by the occasional whirr of a grasshopper. What did it all mean? Avraham trusted this god, as did Eliezer, and Utu suspected Jemimah did as well. But what was this god asking of him? How did one follow such a god? So unknown, so different?

CHAPTER THIRTY-ONE

*I*t had been an emotional week for Utu. Jemimah had presented him with a fourth son. As he'd held this gift in his arms, Utu had blinked back far more than the usual tears. He'd been choking up all week whenever he saw Yitzchak or any of his own children.

Jemimah touched his foot from where she lay on her sleeping mat, resting from her labors. The warmth of her understanding comforted him. He'd told her all about what Avraham had been asked to do.

He tightened his arms around his new son, and the baby opened its eyes and squirmed. "Alright," he muttered. "I won't squeeze you."

If he could protect his children by the depth of his love, he would, but it wasn't that easy. No matter how much they'd planned and prepared, it hadn't been enough for four of their unborn children. They had died before birth, and they didn't even know whether they'd been girls or boys. Each time, Jemimah had wept through many days and nights. No matter that they now had six healthy children, it didn't wipe out the loss of the others. And Avraham had only had two sons, and one had gone no one knew where. Was that why the Lord had called Yitzchak "your only son" so many times, or was there some other meaning?

If this god asked Utu to sacrifice any of his children or Jemimah, could he do it? Once again, he held his newborn close. Never. How could he give up what was most precious?

* * *

*L*ate one afternoon, a messenger arrived in Beersheba and was taken straight to Avraham. Utu arrived at Avraham's favorite seat at the entrance of his tent as the messenger introduced himself.

"I've come from Mamre. He has been struck down by a paralysis and asks if you can return to Kiriath Arba."

Utu froze, awash with different emotions. He hadn't expected to feel sadness, but it was there, mixed in with regret and guilt and disappointment.

"How serious is his condition?" Avraham asked.

"He can talk, though his words are slurred, but he cannot move any of this side." The messenger indicated his right arm and leg. "He's preparing his affairs just in case."

Utu's head pounded. Neither he nor Inanna had ever revealed their identity to Mamre. They'd seen him and their half brothers occasionally, but they'd never felt any real connection to most of their blood relatives. Eliezer and Jemimah were much more family to them.

"Rest now, and we will discuss our plans." Avraham waited until someone had taken the messenger off to a cool spot, then turned to Eliezer. "I will go immediately. Mamre has been a friend all these years. I have spoken to him about El Shaddai, but I don't think he really understands who God is."

Could any of them really understand? How did a man worship a god who had no visible image and who only turned up every so often? And yet, Eliezer followed this god. Maybe it was easier because he'd had a dream and seen it fulfilled. Yet Utu had also seen and heard this god. Was that why he was more willing to consider the possibility of following this god than Inanna? She was totally closed to all conversation on the subject.

"Utu, will you come with us?" Eliezer asked.

Would he? He hesitated, then nodded. If he went, he still had time on the trip to make up his mind about seeing Mamre or staying outside.

* * *

*M*amre's steward was waiting outside the gate of Kiriath Arba. He bowed towards Avraham.

Avraham looked at his downcast face. "Are we too late?"

The steward nodded. "He had another visitation by the gods last night and was gone almost immediately."

Utu turned his head away and took a shaky breath, not sure if he was upset at being too late or relieved the decision had been taken away from him. Eliezer moved closer. Utu would have welcomed a hand on his shoulder, but Eliezer couldn't do that here. Jemimah and Eliezer were the only two people who knew Mamre was his father, and they'd understand his conflicted emotions. It was now too late to change his mind about revealing the relationship.

Time would tell if Avraham would be able to maintain a friendship with Mamre's heir. Utu certainly wouldn't be foolish enough to declare himself now. Heirs were often insecure and new rulers had been wiping out their opposition since the beginning of time.

"As Lord Mamre cannot deliver his message, I will deliver it in his place," the steward said. "Lord Mamre could sense his time drawing near and wanted to ask you to return to Kiriath Arba to be here if our new lord needed assistance."

And probably because surrounding lords would soon know there was a new ruler and that he was vulnerable. Having Avraham's large household with their fighting men camped outside the walls was an extra layer of protection. If his half brother was wise enough, he'd ally himself with Avraham rather than depending on himself. Mamre might not have been the best of fathers to his younger children, but he had been a wise ruler. He had looked after his people, and they were strong and prosperous.

Avraham looked at Eliezer, who nodded. "We will send messengers back to ask the household to pack up and return, but Eliezer and his assistant and I will stay," Avraham said.

"Let me show you to your accommodation," the steward said.

* * *

*T*omorrow Mamre would be buried. Utu sighed, turned over on his back, and put his hands behind his head.

"Can't sleep?" Eliezer asked through the darkness.

"No."

"Not surprising. Are you pondering the might-have-beens?"

"Yes." Utu said. "And no. I never really knew him."

"How old were you when you were kidnapped?"

"I was discussing that with Inanna the other night. We think we were about eight or nine summers."

"You were still fairly young when the Lord brought you to us," Eliezer said.

"Do you think this god arranges things like that?"

"He certainly did for me. I like to think I wouldn't have killed myself but I was very low in spirit when the Lord's messenger appeared in my dreams. And Avraham worshiped the moon-god like everyone else around him. Yet God spoke to him and sent him not only on a physical journey, but on a spiritual journey of discovery."

Eliezer turned over, and Utu could see the blur of his face in the light from the crescent moon.

"And through Avraham, Sara was introduced to El Shaddai, then Jemimah, and finally yourself."

The list was growing longer, and he remembered another. "Inanna said the Lord spoke to Hagar in the wilderness."

"Yes, and she will likely teach Yishmael and any children he may have."

And then Abimelech and Mamre. It was like sparks from the fire. If it was too dry and windy, they didn't risk lighting a fire because they couldn't extinguish all the sparks being blown about. Maybe the spread of El Shaddai's name was slow at the moment, but one day this god might bring about the right conditions for a faster spread.

"This God pursues all people, so that they might come to know him," Eliezer said.

"All people?" Utu asked.

"I believe so."

Utu hadn't talked much about the deeper questions of life and faith with his father-in-law. He valued their relationship too much to risk ruining it, but maybe no relationship could really mean very much unless deeper things could be discussed. Discussing their pain after the deaths of their babies had deepened the roots of his and Jemimah's marriage. He'd assumed the pain was his alone until she'd shared hers.

"I don't understand ..."

"You don't understand what?" Eliezer said with the skill of a healer probing a wound to dig out the grit and stones.

"I don't understand why El Shaddai asked Avraham to give up Yitzchak, the most precious person in his and Sara's lives."

"I've struggled with that as well," Eliezer said. "Do you think it might be because El Shaddai was asking Avraham to consider who was the most precious in his life? Was it Yitzchak, or was it the God who miraculously gave him a son?"

Utu had never thought of the question in that way.

"When God asked Avraham to sacrifice Yitzchak, he already knew he'd provide the ram. He was asking Avraham to trust him."

As Avraham had failed to do with Pharaoh and Abimelech. Was the test also an opportunity for Avraham to put the shame of his failures behind him? Certainly he'd gained a quiet assurance since they'd returned from Mount Moriah, and Utu had heard Avraham use a new name for God in his prayers, Jehovah Jireh, the provider.

"There comes a point in everyone's life when we all face the same question. Will we put our life in God's hands and trust him for everything?"

Utu propped himself up on his elbow. "And you've done that?"

"Yes, son. It wasn't anything dramatic for me but a gradual growing in trust. The night before I asked if you'd marry Jemimah, I struggled, because I didn't know if I trusted any man to love and care for her more than I do. That night, I realized it wasn't you I was called to rely on. You might fail, but if we were trusting her Creator, then there was nothing to fear."

Utu released a long breath. It sounded so simple but also so unfamiliar. The gods of his father's ancestors had frightened him. Rather than serve them, he'd relied on himself. But relying on self was like relying on the twigs at the top of the oak tree to support his weight.

"What do I need to do to follow El Shaddai?"

Eliezer chuckled. "He already knows your every thought and what you want, even before you do. Perhaps you could just talk to him and tell him what's in your heart."

"I'm not sure I know how."

"And I might not be the best teacher," Eliezer said, sitting up. "But if he's the Creator and the ruler and sustainer of the heavens and earth, perhaps we'd better approach him with honor and respect."

Utu sat up and knelt by his mat with his head bowed and his hands raised. If what Eliezer said was correct, there was no need for a magic incantation. No words that could manipulate such a God. He must simply speak in honest sincerity.

"El Shaddai, you are the Creator, the great and mighty one. Thank you for looking down from your throne and noticing me." His skin tingled at the thought. "Thank you for bringing me into Avraham's household and for allowing me to know you. I don't know much, but I place my life and my family into your hands. We are yours. Please accept us and help us to introduce you to others."

He lowered his arms. "Do you think that was alright?" he whispered to Eliezer.

Eliezer reached over and put his hands on Utu's shoulders. "Son. I think he is as happy to have you as a son as I am."

Utu's eyes stung and he awkwardly raised his hand and touched Eliezer's hand. "Thank you, Abba."

He got back into bed and lay down. He'd made his decision, and it was the right one. Jemimah would be thrilled, but Inanna? She might have an altogether stronger reaction and it wasn't likely to be positive.

CHAPTER THIRTY-TWO

"What are you doing up there?" Inanna called up to Utu. He looked down at her from their favorite tree. "Enjoying the breeze." And reveling in the joy of his decision to follow Avraham's God. Not that he could say that anymore. Avraham's God was now his God. He'd woken this morning ready to shout his joy, but the next best thing was being up here, swinging his legs, and pondering.

"I'm coming up," Inanna said.

Of course she was. He watched her as she climbed, still lithe, and so at home in the tree that she moved without hesitation from branch to branch. She drew level with him and settled herself in the fork of a branch.

"Family gets too much for you?" she said with a wink.

"Jemimah said she had things under control and sent me to enjoy a moment of quiet."

"Which I've now interrupted."

He chuckled. "I never object to talking with you." But he would have preferred a little more time to enjoy his new status as Utu, follower and worshiper of El Shaddai, Creator of heaven and earth. And a lot more time to prepare what he might say to Inanna.

"Are you glad to be back?" he asked.

Inanna put her head to one side. "Mostly. This is the place I feel most at home."

She didn't need to explain herself. She meant this grove of oak trees and this tree in particular, not the town of Kiriath Arba.

"But it is always a little unsettling moving again."

They'd lived near Abimelech and his people for over a dozen harvests, almost all of Yitzchak's life.

"It is." She touched his arm. "I'm sorry you were too late to see father."

Grief pierced him. "I don't know if I'm sorry or not. It's not as though I could have said, 'Do you recognize me? I'm your son.'"

"I can't believe that after all these years, Father simply chose our oldest brother to be chief."

"It was wise. People expect the oldest to be the heir. He'd only have chosen another brother if the first was unsuitable."

"We'll soon know if he made the right decision."

"Mmm."

She narrowed her eyes. "You've always seemed content, but today you're positively brimming with something. Is Jemimah having another child?"

She'd always known what he was feeling. Would she keep digging until she forced him to reveal his latest decision? His stomach churned. She was not likely to be pleased.

"Not that I know of," he said.

"Then what is it?" She fixed her gaze on him. "You look different somehow. I don't know how to describe it. Excited. No, that's not right. Less placid." She pursed her lips. "No, still not quite right. More alive. Yes, I think that's right."

More alive? Yes, that was a good description. As he'd sat here, it seemed as though the colors around him were brighter. He was more aware of things he'd mostly ignored before, like the way the oak leaves danced in the breeze, and the chirping of birds, each with a different song to praise their Creator. It was like his ears and eyes and nose were more sensitive to the world around him. Maybe when someone started worshiping the Creator, they became more attuned to his world.

He gripped the branch in front of him. "I made a decision yesterday. An important decision."

She frowned. "You wouldn't leave, would you?"

"You don't need to worry about that."

"Good. So what decision have you made?"

His stomach churned. "I made the decision to follow El Shaddai."

She gasped, and there was a long silence.

El Shaddai, help.

"Why would you do something like that?"

"Umm." The words caught in his throat. "It's been a long, slow journey—"

"How could you even think about following Avraham's god?" Scorn sizzled across her words. "Look how Avraham treated Hagar and Yishmael. Look at how he lied about Sara."

"I'm not sure El Shaddai can be blamed for how Avraham has behaved."

"Why not? Avraham claims to be his follower. His life should reflect it."

She had a point. One he'd do well to remember as he took his first faltering steps on this journey.

"And look at what you told me about Yitzchak. What kind of god would tell a father to sacrifice his own son?"

"Avraham didn't actually have to do it." He knew she'd pounce on him before he finished.

"But Avraham didn't know that. He and Yitzchak had to endure the suffering of thinking it had to be done."

"Avraham said it was agony, but he isn't bitter about it."

She snorted.

"I still don't fully understand why God asked Avraham to do it," Utu said. Doubts filled his mind at her accusations. He closed his eyes and forced himself to remember why he'd made his decision.

"And I'm hurt that you didn't speak to me first."

He opened his eyes. Her cheeks were flushed, and even the curls of her hair looked indignant.

"You would have tried to convince me not to."

"Of course I would. I don't want you to make major decisions you'll regret."

He smiled sadly at her. "I won't regret it." He straightened. No matter what she said, he'd made the right decision. He hated her to feel left out, a feeling she must have had but never voiced when he and Jemimah had married, and a feeling she must have now. His life was now filled with Jemimah and the children, but she had much less to focus on.

"I'm sorry you are upset by my decision, but—"

"No, don't say anything else." She held her hand up. "I've heard enough."

She turned away from him and without saying anything more, descended the tree. He watched her go, heart in his throat.

El Shaddai, is this what it means to follow you? Must I walk this path without her?

* * *

Utu found Eliezer in the storage cave checking the supplies and ensuring no creatures had entered and damaged anything.

"Eliezer, I made a mess of things with Inanna," he said, sadness punching him in the belly.

"Tell me." Eliezer stopped what he was doing and sat on a convenient rock.

"I hadn't intended telling her anything yet about my decision, but she noticed that something was different and dragged the news out of me."

"And why do you think you messed up?"

"Because she got angry, refused to let me speak anymore, and left as fast as she could."

"Give her time. It is hard to accept change and hard to respect other people's freedom to choose a different road."

Inanna had always followed her own way. Might she eventually allow him the same privilege? Not that he wanted to walk it without her.

He told Eliezer all that had happened, the words tumbling out of him until he had nothing left to say.

Eliezer stroked his beard. "You're being too hard on yourself. You spoke up and you left her ideas to consider."

"It was horrible watching her turn her back on me."

"Of course it was," Eliezer said. "Sometimes love must give people the freedom to walk away."

If only it didn't hurt so much.

Eliezer shifted on the rock. "Why don't we pray for her now?"

"What? Right here?"

"Why not? El Shaddai must be glad for us to speak to him anywhere and anytime. I know I love it when any of the children come and speak to me."

Utu hadn't thought of it like that.

Eliezer raised his hands, and Utu copied him.

"Great Creator and Lord of all. You see Utu's pain and you know the pain in Inanna's heart."

Yes, he wasn't the only one who was hurting.

"Your ways are far above our ways. We don't understand why some accept you easily, like a child, and others take much longer. Thank you for your patience with us. Give us the perseverance to keep praying and bring all our family to know and love you. Soften Inanna's heart as you are softening Attar's heart."

It had been wonderful to see Mama change from indifference to actively asking questions.

Eliezer lowered his hands. "Never give up, Utu, for the Lord never gives up on us."

Utu had seen that in Avraham's perseverance with Lot. He was not alone. Jemimah and Eliezer would stand with him. So would Job. Job had been praying for Inanna and the rest of them for years.

CHAPTER THIRTY-THREE

About fifteen years later
Kiriath Arba

*I*nanna stood under the olive tree with the other women, each holding one side of the cloth while the menfolk used long poles to shake the tree branches. The ripe olives fell like rain and rolled into the center of the cloth. They'd picked the olives one at a time until Utu had seen how easily they shook free from the tree and came up with this more efficient method.

One voice started singing, and others joined in. A song of praise to Avraham's god that one of the older men had written. A song of praise for the harvest and all the creator's good gifts. The tune was catchy, and Inanna couldn't help humming along, but she wasn't going to sing the words even if Utu did.

"Someone's coming," Utu said to Inanna, gesturing towards the ridge behind them.

She looked to where he indicated. "More than one someone." It was too dangerous to travel alone through these lands. There were always raiders or outlaws willing to take the opportunity to steal from the unwary.

The group were on camelback. Before long, Utu could pick out five men traveling together. Whether they came from the same place or had simply gathered for mutual protection they'd have to ask, because it looked like they were heading straight for the harvesters.

Utu went to meet them, and Inanna jumped up to follow. Visitors were few and far between.

The man on the leading camel raised his hand in greeting. "I'm looking for Avram and Sarai."

She hadn't heard those names in a long time.

"Who is looking?" Utu asked before Inanna could welcome them.

"We bring news of Avram's brother, Nahor, far to the north."

Avraham's brother! In all the years Inanna had been with the family, there'd never been a single visitor from Avraham's relatives.

"Then welcome," Utu said warmly. "They will be delighted to see you."

Sara had often said that the hardest part of coming to Canaan was separation from their family. The messengers would be welcomed, even if they brought bad news.

Utu gave some instructions to the harvesters and then turned to Inanna. "I'll accompany the visitors. Please go ahead and find Sara and send someone to find Avraham and Yitzchak."

Utu would bring the camels the roundabout, less steep route, but Inanna should beat them if she picked up her skirts and took the shortcut between the trees. At this time of day, Sara would be down at the river, where it was cooler.

Sara was on the riverbank, combing out her long, white hair. It reached to her waist, and she'd obviously washed it that morning and dried it in the sun.

Inanna slowed to a walk. When she reached Sara, Inanna bobbed her head. "Mistress, some visitors have arrived bringing news of Nahor and his family."

Sara's mouth rounded in an O and her face shone with joy, making her look much younger than her nearly six-score years.

"Good thing we made some of the fine wheat-flour bread this

morning." She scrambled up the riverbank and stood next to Inanna, puffing. "Please get the women together to prepare the food."

Inanna headed for the main tent, instructing four older boys on the way to get the carpets and lay them under the shadiest tree. She dropped in on Eliezer so he could get a guest tent set up, and made it back to the main food preparation area by the time Utu arrived with the guests.

After all these years of hosting guests, they worked together like a team of well-matched oxen. They had the guests seated, with their hands and feet washed, and plied them with dried fruit, fresh bread, and curds, before Avraham, Sara, and Yitzchak arrived and exchanged greetings and introductions.

Greeting those guests was only the second time that Inanna could remember Sara with tears of joy in her eyes. Following their god had been a sacrifice of all she had found familiar.

"Is Father still alive?" Sara asked.

"That's what prompted us to come and find you," the leader of the delegation said. "He has only died recently, but he had always longed to know where your God had taken you."

Terah had been Sara's father too. Avraham's lies to Pharaoh and Abimelech had been a half truth. Inanna could see how he'd justified them, but his motivation had been fear, which Inanna despised. Despised that a man would protect himself rather than the woman he'd promised to shield.

"How old was grandfather?" Yitzchak asked.

"Two hundred and five summers, by his reckoning," the spokesman said.

Inanna choked back an exclamation. She'd thought Avraham was old, as he approached one hundred and forty. Sara was ten years younger, but lately she'd been looking her age. She took longer to get going in the morning and often asked for them to speak more loudly.

"And is my brother, Nahor, still alive?"

The man nodded. "He and Milkah have eight sons, and their children also have children. He has been much blessed ..."

Sara winced at the same time as Inanna did. Was blessing only to be measured in the numbers of sons? Surely there were other ways to measure blessing. Unmarried and childless as Inanna was, did others consider her cursed?

"His concubine, Reumah, also has four sons." The man rattled off their names.

"You'll have to slow down," Sara said. "Inanna, could you pick up a pile of little rocks and some of those pods."

What was Sara up to now?

Once Inanna had collected the rocks and pods, Sara arranged them on the ground. "I'll use the rocks to represent sons and the pods for the daughters. Now, can you go slowly and tell me about each one?"

Inanna stifled a yawn. All this might be fascinating to Sara, but it was going to be a tedious few days for everyone else.

As the visitors shared about each one of Nahor and Milkah's sons, starting with Uz, the firstborn, Sara would place a rock or pod to represent them. It must have helped her memory because by the time she'd added Buz, Kemuel, Kesed, Hazo, Pildash, Jidlaph, and Bethuel, she could recite their names and details. Uz the confident hunter and joker, Buz trying to keep up. Kemuel who loved growing different plants and seeking to increase the productivity of each. Sara soaked in the details, but Yitzchak was soon tapping his forefinger on his knee. Avraham's responsibilities were increasingly on his shoulders, allowing Avraham more time to sit in the sun.

By now, the olives would be back and ready for sorting, and the donkeys would be harnessed to the olive press to turn the upper stone and crush the fruit for their precious oil. Inanna would prefer to be harvesting, but serving guests was now her role, and she'd be here for days yet. Every piece of information would be stored in their memories and repeated to family members desperate for news.

Sara gave the signal for more drinks, and Inanna went back into the storage area next to a stream to collect more wine and fresh goat's milk from the morning's milking. It was satisfying to see all the produce stored in the cool of the cave. The sight reminded her that she was lucky to have been part of this household for so long.

CHAPTER THIRTY-FOUR

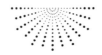

About nine years later

"*I*nanna. Inanna."

The urgent whisper intruded into Inanna's dreams, and she woke with a start. It was still dark.

"Inanna," the hoarse voice said again.

Inanna turned over and sat up. "Yes, mistress."

"You used to call me Sara."

She had, all those years ago in Egypt.

"Yes, mis-Sara."

"I can't sleep," Sara murmured.

Now Inanna wouldn't sleep either, but she didn't grudge it. Last week, Sara had supervised the making of date honey. That evening, she'd taken to her bed and hadn't been up since. Inanna and Attar were taking turns sleeping near Sara in case she needed anything during the night. Avraham had moved in with Yitzchak, so he could have the benefit of unbroken sleep.

"I wronged Hagar—and Yishmael," Sara whispered.

What was Inanna supposed to say? She couldn't deny it, for it was true.

"I was jealous and angry."

Inanna kept quiet. There was something about the darkness that inspired confidences, and perhaps Sara could not go peacefully to her death with a guilt-ridden conscience.

"And instead of dealing with the root causes of my jealousy, I took it out on Hagar." There was silence. "Inanna, if you see Hagar and Yishmael again, will you tell them I'm sorry?"

"I will." Easy words to say, but what were the chances that she'd ever see either of them again? She had no idea where to look, except to the south. It would take years to search every valley and town. Maybe one of the reasons Avraham had stayed near Kiriath Arba or Beersheba all these years had been so he could be found easily should anyone come looking. According to Utu, Avraham had never fully given up on Lot and his daughters, but they had never come.

"Come here," Sara said urgently.

Inanna moved quickly over to Sara's side, and Sara grasped her hand. "Swear to me, by El Shaddai, that you will tell them I am sorry."

Inanna shivered in the pre-dawn chill. She'd prefer to simply make a promise. She might not have chosen to follow El Shaddai, but she couldn't avoid knowing that he existed and was powerful. Utu regularly prayed with Jemimah and Eliezer, and all of them were seeking to follow this god's instructions, what they knew of them.

"Swear to me," Sara insisted again.

"I swear," Inanna said.

"On El Shaddai's name."

Inanna shivered again. She hoped she wasn't doing something that would get her struck down if she said it. "I swear it, on El Shaddai himself."

Sara's grip relaxed. "Good. I know you won't let me down."

But the promise could only be fulfilled if Inanna could somehow see Hagar and Yishmael again.

"Would you like me to massage your feet?" Inanna asked. Avraham had asked her if she remembered anything about the oils from Egypt, and Inanna had managed to create one with olive oil and herbs. It probably had no healing powers, but it comforted Sara and reminded

Inanna how they'd met and all that had followed. Sometimes she tried to imagine what would have happened if she'd remained in Egypt. She'd probably still be serving in the depths of Pharaoh's palace, cut off from the cycle of seasons and any family. She would never have found her mother.

Inanna smoothed on the scented oil and massaged it gently into Sara's cracked and calloused feet. Feet that had spent 127 years carrying their mistress from Babylon, through Mesopotamia, south to Canaan, and across deserts to Egypt and back. Feet that had walked further than most people walked in many lifetimes.

Sara began to relax, then drifted into sleep with a gentle sigh. *Sleep, Sara. Rest so you can be with us a little longer.* The thought of losing her was surprisingly sharp in Inanna's throat. Like the sun and moon, Sara was one of the constants in Inanna's life.

* * *

Sara's condition had deteriorated steadily since the night that Inanna massaged her feet, as though confessing her guilt had loosened her grip on life.

"Don't talk, my love," Avraham said as he sat hunched by his wife's bed. "Don't talk."

"I still have things to say," Sara murmured.

Inanna had arranged the bed on a platform, so Avraham could sit with her rather than having to kneel. His knees couldn't handle kneeling anymore.

They'd half-opened one of the tent flaps, so it wasn't so stifling in the tent and to blow away the smell of old age and death. It wouldn't be long now. Sara slept most of the time and Inanna was beside Sara constantly. She slept beside her so she could attend to Sara's every need. In the morning, she turned her and washed her body to keep it clean. While awake, she quietly prepared the grave clothes.

"You have been a good wife to me, much better than I deserved." Avraham sucked his teeth. "I was so wrong to keep making you say you were my sister."

Sara raised a weak hand to his lips. "Shh. That is past. I was wrong to hold onto bitterness for so long. To punish you for it."

"It was understandable."

"Understandable, but still wrong." Sara reached up and smoothed Avraham's eyebrows.

Sara had spent the last few days dealing with some unresolved issues. Perhaps death did that. It focused a person's thinking and showed them the importance of making peace with those one was going to have to leave.

"I worried about dragging you along with me all these years," Avraham said. "Taking you away from our family."

"I would not have allowed you to leave me behind."

He leaned over and kissed her tenderly on the lips. Inanna averted her eyes. Avraham would be so alone when Sara departed. They had been together since the day Sara had been born.

"But now you're leaving me behind," he said gently. "Going on an adventure, where I can't accompany you."

"What do you think happens?" Sara asked.

He squeezed her hand. "I don't know, my love."

"Do you think I'll meet El Shaddai?" she asked, looking up at him.

"Perhaps. Why would he make the effort to know us here if it was just for this life?"

"Life with El Shaddai," Sara whispered. "I wonder if I'll like it."

"You have loved his world," Avraham said. "His kingdom must be even better. Like Eden at the beginning of time."

"Eden," she breathed. "I'm sure I will like that." She closed her eyes and lay there with a smile tweaking the corner of her mouth.

Inanna left them and went out to prepare food. Later, as she carried it back, she heard the sound of Avraham's broken-hearted weeping. A bubble of emptiness expanded in her chest. Sara was gone.

Inanna left Avraham to weep and went numbly to heat some water. Sara would no longer care if the water was cold, but Inanna wanted to give the best she could. Once the water was heating on the fire, she headed for Utu's tent where her mother was resting. The two of them would wash Sara's body.

Avraham took a long time over his goodbyes before taking Eliezer and Utu to the town to find the town elders.

Inanna's mother touched Sara's hand and then covered her eyes.

"Mama, don't weep. She died peacefully." Inanna crouched down to hug her mother.

"I never had a friend like her." Mama sniffed.

From the first moment her mother had arrived, Sara and she had bonded like sisters. Sisters who understood each other because of similar life circumstances and hardships, even though her mother was much the younger of the two. Inanna had often caught them giggling together at some shared joke. Sara's friendship with Inanna's mother had completed the softening process that had begun with the birth of Yitzchak.

"Come on, Mama," Inanna said. Together they undressed Sara and washed her whole body. Then Inanna massaged scented oils into her skin. It seemed appropriate to be finishing her service to Sara as she had begun. The ravages wrought by time and death on Sara's body would one day be hers as well. And for what? What was the purpose of all the years Sara had lived? Were she and Avraham right, that life continued beyond the grave? And if so, in what form?

Inanna's mother picked up the newly made robe, and together they worked to slip it over Sara's head. They sprinkled spices between the robe and the body, and the tent was full of the sweet scent. Finally they filled the sleeves with spices and tied them gently closed so Sara's hands no longer showed.

As Inanna sat beside Sara's body, it struck her that Sara was free. Free from old age and sickness. Free from other people's expectations that somehow she could solve every household problem. And if Avraham was right, free to go on to the next adventure. An adventure along a new way to a new world. An adventure that Utu and Jemimah would one day set out upon, but she'd be barred from. A tightness filled Inanna's chest. Did she want to be left behind?

* * *

liezer and Utu followed Avraham towards Kiriath Arba. They'd spent yesterday scouting for a possible burial site for Sara, and now they were looking for the site's owner.

They pushed their way through the throng at the market outside the gate. Those with something to exchange laid their selection of goods on a cloth on the ground in the shade cast by the wall. The air was full of the smell of sweat and the babble of voices fighting for bargains.

"These eggs were laid today. I'd like two handfuls of onions in exchange."

"Two handfuls!" The man snorted. "My onions are the tastiest in the area. If you're willing to take one less, then I'll agree."

They left the two men haggling and passed another two bargaining as they squatted near some figs and honeycomb. The owner of the honey picked up the figs and sniffed them before agreeing to the exchange with a curt nod.

It was a rare day when Jemimah sent Utu to exchange items, as they had most things they needed. They ate whatever was in season and only stored oil, grain, and dried fruit.

They continued past the market towards the city gate. Here the older men of Kiriath Arba sat and talked business. They stood and bowed when Avraham approached them and dusted off a place for him to sit.

"We're sorry for your loss," the oldest said.

"Thank you. Sara was a queen among women," Avraham said.

There were murmurs of agreement.

"I am a foreigner and stranger among you. Sell me some property for a burial site here, so I can bury my dead," Avraham said.

"Sir, listen to us," the elder spokesman said. "You are a mighty prince among us. Bury your dead in the choicest of our tombs. None of us will refuse you his tomb for burying your dead."

Avraham rose from his seat and bowed. "If you are willing to let me bury my dead, then intercede with Ephron son of Zohar on my behalf so he will sell me the cave of Machpelah, which belongs to him and is at the end of his field. Ask him to sell it to me for the full price as a burial site among you."

Ephron now also stood and spoke in a loud, clear voice. "No, my lord. Listen to me. I give you the field and the cave that is in it. I give it to you in the presence of all the people here. Bury your dead."

Utu had never seen such a transaction, but Eliezer had explained how this back and forth was the usual way things were done.

Avraham bowed again before the elders. "Listen to me, if you will. I will pay the price of the field. Accept it from me, so I can bury my dead there."

How did Avraham feel? He who owned no piece of land yet had received promises that one day all this land would be his. And his first field and trees would be for a burial site instead of land for growing crops or building a home.

"The land is worth four hundred shekels of silver, but what is that between you and me?" Ephron said. "Bury your dead."

Avraham gestured to Eliezer, who carried the leather sack which contained their silver. In the presence of all the elders, they weighed out the full amount, and then Ephron and Avraham talked quietly together before Ephron raised his hand for attention.

He stepped into the middle of the elders and raised his voice. "Today, you have witnessed that Avraham, son of Terah, son of Nahor, has paid the full price of four hundred shekels of silver for the field of Machpelah including its cave, its field, and all trees within its boundaries. He will use this ground as a burial ground for his family and their descendants. Are you witnesses?"

"We are," the elders said.

A man came towards Ephron.

"This man will now write out the deed on leather to be given to Avraham and you will be witnesses."

"Yes, we will be witnesses," the elders repeated.

Avraham sat again, and they all waited until the land was described and recorded on the leather. Once it was done, they returned to camp. Inanna and the other women would have Sara's body washed and ready for immediate burial.

CHAPTER THIRTY-FIVE

Three years later

*U*tu turned in the saddle of his camel and waved back at Jemimah and their grandchildren. He'd be gone for several moons, and the thought of being away from his loved ones tugged at his heart. *El Shaddai, keep them safe until I return.*

A few days ago, Avraham had called out to him and Eliezer from where they sat in the sun at the front of his tent. "I need one of you to return to Aram Naharaim."

Utu knew nothing about Aram Naharaim except that Avraham's brother Nahor and his descendants lived there, and it was a long, long way north.

"Sara made me promise not to find Yitzchak a Canaanite wife but to find him one from among our relatives."

Eliezer bowed. "I am glad you will find Yitzchak a wife, but I am too old to go on such a journey."

"My friend, it must be someone who follows El Shaddai as you do," Avraham said.

"I would trust no one but Utu," Eliezer said. "In all ways, he can represent me."

A warmth filled Utu's chest. He still felt like a mere child in following El Shaddai, but he and Eliezer started each day with praise to El Shaddai, thanksgiving for the previous day, and their requests for the coming day. In the evenings, before sleep, he and Jemimah prayed for each member of their family.

"After I am gone, Utu will be senior steward," Eliezer said. "He has more than proved himself."

"With you to train him, he wouldn't dare to be anything but the best." Avraham chuckled and turned to Utu. "Come and put your hand under my thigh and swear to the Lord, the God of heaven and the God of earth, that you will go to my country and my relatives and get a wife from there for Yitzchak."

"But what if the woman is unwilling to come back with me to this land? Shall I then take Yitzchak back to the country where you are from?"

Avraham shook his head. "Make sure you don't take my son back there. The Lord, the God of heaven, who brought me out of my father's household and my native land and who spoke to me and promised me on oath saying, 'To your offspring I will give this land,' he will send his angel ahead of you so you can get a wife for my son. If the woman is unwilling to come back with you, then you will be released from this oath." Avraham fixed a piercing look at Utu. "Only do not take my son back there."

Responsibility heavy on his shoulders, Utu put his hand under Avraham's thigh. "I swear to our Lord that I will go and look for a wife for Yitzchak among your own relatives."

"And may the Lord, Creator of all, be with you in your quest," Avraham said. Then he turned to Eliezer. "Would it help if Inanna went to stay with Jemimah?"

"Jemimah would be grateful," Utu said, trying not to think of how long he'd be away. Jemimah was still pretty spry for her sixty-something years, but an extra pair of hands would be appreciated for their growing number of grandchildren and great grand-children. Job would promise to keep an eye on the family too.

It was times like this that Utu missed his mother most. She had died peacefully in her sleep during the barley harvest. They missed her, but the Lord had answered his prayers, and she too had chosen to follow El Shaddai shortly before she died. Those last weeks had been weeks of an irrepressible joy and remembering them brought him comfort. If only Inanna would make the same choice.

Utu gave a last wave as his camel topped the rise and then began to jog towards the north. Utu forced himself to think about his immediate route, not the vast distance to his destination. His heart sank when thinking about how far he and his men had to travel. As Eliezer had reminded him in his parting prayer, the Lord was with him and would guide him.

* * *

"How far to Harran?" Utu called to the shepherd. He'd thought they were close, but there was no sign of the town.

"Just behind that rise. You'll be there before sunset," the man said, leaning on his staff.

Utu waved his thanks and clicked his tongue to move his camel forward. The other camels followed. In his prayer at their parting, Eliezer had asked the Lord to guide and protect him, and they'd covered the distance far more quickly than Utu expected, taking less than one full moon to arrive.

His camel grumbled a little as they went up the last hill. As they topped the rise, Utu gasped. The city was larger than any he'd ever seen. A huge wall wound around it, at least twice the height of his camels. A high platform stood in the center of the city. Was that the temple of the moon god, the god Avraham's family used to worship? His gaze shifted away from the temple and towards the curious domed structures. Were they used to store food?

The other men clustered around him, whispering in awe at the sight of so large a city. How would they ever find Nahor or Bethuel in such a place? There were several entrances to the city, and Utu looked towards what seemed to be the main gate. Shading his eyes, he stared at the structure in front.

"Men," he said. "We will head for that well."

They set off down the slope. On the plain, the camels broke into a trot as they smelled water. The sun was sinking in the sky. They reached the well as the shadows lengthened and Utu had his camel kneel. Flocks converged on the well from all sides.

"Lord, God of my master Avraham, make me successful today, and show kindness to my master Avraham," Utu prayed. "See, I am standing beside this spring, and the daughters of the town are coming out to draw water. May it be that when I say to a young woman, 'Please let down your jar that I may have a drink,' and she says, 'Drink, and I'll water your camels too,' let her be the one you have chosen for your servant Yitzchak. By this I will know you have shown kindness to my master."

Utu slid off his camel and staked its lead in the ground before walking towards the spring. A young woman approached the spring with a water jar on her shoulder. She went down the steps to the well and filled her jar with water.

Is this the one, Lord?

As the woman climbed the last step, Utu hurried towards her. "Please, could you give me a drink from your water jar?"

"Drink, my lord." She took the jar off her shoulder and tilted it towards him.

He allowed the refreshing coolness to pour into his palm and slurped up every drop. The next palmful he sluiced over his face and beard and sighed out his contentment.

"You look like you have come a long way," she said.

"Many, many days of travel from the south."

"Let me draw water for your camels." She said as she ran back down the steps.

Excitement coursed through him. *Lord, is this the one?*

She was back before he could pray again. She poured the water in a stone trough and was gone before he could thank her. He whistled to the other men, and they brought the first of the camels forward.

"Form a line, men," Utu called.

Two of the men went down the steps and positioned themselves to take the jar from the woman. Watering ten thirsty camels was no small task. The jar was passed up the line, and Utu took it and poured it into the trough before passing it back down the line.

Other women came with their water jars and detoured around them to fetch their water. There were a number of other watering troughs, and no one paid them much attention. Avraham had said Harran was a major trading crossroads. Strangers probably weren't unusual.

The woman switched places with one of the other men and took her place on the top step. Her forehead above her veil was flushed from the activity, but she did not pause in her promise to water the camels. The first few drank their fill and were fast followed by the other thirsty animals. The shadows continued to lengthen until the last camel drew back from the trough. Only then did the woman put the full water jar on the ground and stretch.

Lord, I believe she is the one.

Utu went to the saddlebags and undid the leather strap. He took out a gold nose ring weighing a beka, and two ten-shekel gold bracelets. He secreted the objects in the pouch at his waist and walked back to the well.

"Whose daughter are you?" he asked. "We are strangers here. Is there any room in your father's house for us to spend the night?"

"I am Rivka, the daughter of Bethuel, the son of Milkah and Nahor."

Awe flooded through Utu. *Yes Lord, she is the one you prepared.*

He drew the nose ring and the bracelets out of his pocket and placed them in Rivka's hands. "These are for you. Gifts from Avraham."

He heard the intake of breath as her eyes widened. "They're beautiful, and yes, we have plenty of straw and fodder, as well as room for you to spend the night. I will go and speak to my father." She left her water jar and turned to run back towards the city's main gate.

Utu fell to his knees with his face to the ground. *Praise be to you, the*

God of Avraham, who has not abandoned his kindness and faithfulness to my master. For you have led me on a journey to the very home of my master's relatives.

Eliezer had told him El Shaddai answered prayer, but it was hard to prove his prayers were answered if he simply prayed for health for his family. Was their continued health an answer to prayer or would they have been healthy without any prayer at all? Yet today he'd made a specific request, and God had answered. He must learn how to pray more specifically. Each answer would build his trust in this God he'd chosen to follow. Tonight he would begin a concentrated prayer for Inanna, that she would come to trust El Shaddai too. He'd also pray that each of his children and grandchildren would conquer their greatest weakness, be it worry, or fear, or outbursts of anger.

"Utu, someone is coming," one of the men said.

Utu looked up. A man about the same age as Rivka was hurrying towards them. As he approached them, he called, "Come, you who are blessed by the Lord. Why are you standing out here? I am Laban, brother of Rivka, and I have already prepared the house and a place for you all."

After initial greetings, they set off towards the city. Laban led them through wide streets lined with stones, towards a complex of buildings next to the city wall. Up close, the domed roofs were like a tall hat. They seemed to be made of hardened brick and had no windows. Instead, there was a hole with a cap on it, right at the highest point.

Laban led them to a partially covered area where the camels could be unloaded. He clapped his hands, and a stream of servants took their saddlebags into one of the pointy-topped buildings. Servants brought straw and fodder for the camels, then brought out water and washed the men's feet.

"Come inside," Laban said. "Food has been prepared."

They passed through a doorway, and Utu paused to look at the thick mud and straw walls. The coolness of the interior enveloped him, reminding him of the temperature near a desert oasis. They took off their footwear and padded over carpets into an inner area where several people were standing and waiting near an array of food.

"Welcome to our home," Laban said. "This is my father, Bethuel, and my mother."

Bethuel came and kissed Utu on both cheeks, and gestured for them to sit. Rivka and her mother sat quietly in one corner.

"Before we eat, I want to tell you why we've come," Utu said as he sat down.

"Tell us," Bethuel said.

"I am Avraham's servant," Utu said. "The Lord has blessed my master abundantly, and he has become wealthy. He has given him sheep and cattle, silver and gold, male and female servants, and camels and donkeys."

"This we know," Laban said. "The men who went to find you and tell you of my great-grandfather's death came and told us what they had found. They also told us of the miracle of Yitzchak's birth."

"We are glad your messengers made it safely back here. Yitzchak is Avraham's heir, and Avraham made me swear an oath, 'You must not get a wife for my son from the daughters of the Canaanites, but go to my father's family and to my own clan, and get a wife for my son.' I agreed to that oath but asked Avraham, 'What if the woman refuses to return with me?'"

"And what did Avraham say?" Bethuel asked.

Utu laughed. "Avraham was not worried about such a situation. He replied, 'The Lord, before whom I have walked faithfully, will send his angel with you and make your journey a success, but you will be released from my oath if, when you go to my clan, they refuse to give her to you.' So when I came to the spring today, I prayed and asked the Lord for a miracle, that when I asked for a drink, the one who would be Yitzchak's wife would offer to water our camels. Before I had even finished praying in my heart, Rivka arrived and answered my prayer."

"Go on," Laban said.

Again awe filled him. "When I discovered the Lord had brought me to Avraham's own family, I gave her jewelry and praised God who had led me on the right road to find the granddaughter of my master's brother for his son."

Utu looked around the room at Bethuel, Laban, and the other men of their household. "Now if you will show kindness and faithfulness to my master, tell me. If not, tell me that also, so I may know which way to turn."

"This is from the Lord," Bethuel said. "We can say nothing to you one way or the other. Here is Rivka; take her and go, and let her become the wife of your master's son, as the Lord has directed."

Utu bowed down to the ground, his heart overflowing with praise to the Lord. Then he went over to the saddlebags which were leaning against the wall and brought out gold and silver jewelry and articles of clothing and gave them to Rivka. Gifts that Sara had labored over for several years before her death. Gifts for her future daughter-in-law, whom she would never meet. He also brought out other costly gifts for Laban, Bethuel, and Rivka's mother.

"Eat with us on this glad day," Bethuel said. They sat on the floor, and he tore the fresh loaves apart with his hands and passed them around the room. "I am sorry we did not have better food for you."

"When you've been eating around a campfire every evening, this is beyond luxury," Utu said, inclining his head towards Rivka and her mother. Having seen how much work it was for Inanna and Jemimah to prepare for unexpected guests, he was more than content with what was laid on the cloth in front of them. Fresh herbs and fruit, onions, curds, bread, and some foodstuffs he'd never seen.

They ate until late, then slept.

Utu rose early the next morning, ready to head for home as soon as possible. He found Laban and his parents out in the yard, supervising the washing of Avraham's camels.

Utu greeted them. "Please allow me to return to Avraham as soon as possible."

Rivka's mother laid a hand on her husband's arm.

"Please let Rivka stay with us for another ten days or so," Bethuel said "Then you may go."

"I understand it will be hard to say goodbye to your daughter." Utu caught his breath at the thought that he might one day have to say goodbye to any of his own family. "Do not detain me now the Lord has granted success to my journey. Send me on my way, so I may go to my master."

They held a whispered consultation with Laban. "Let's call Rivka and ask her opinion," Bethuel said.

When Rivka arrived, they asked, "Will you go with this man immediately, rather than waiting?"

She looked around at her family and nodded. "I will go."

"We will need today to get ready," Bethuel said "Rivka's nurse and several attendants will accompany her."

Early the next morning, Laban and his other siblings accompanied Utu, Rivka, and the rest of their group to the city gates. The sky was flushed with delicate pink.

The family put their hands on Rivka's head. "Our sister, may you increase to thousands upon thousands, may your offspring possess the cities of their enemies."

Utu blinked. Avraham had told him and Eliezer that God had promised his descendants would take possession of the cities of their enemies and they would be as many as stars in the sky and the sand of the seashore. If that promise was to be fulfilled, this woman would be part of it.

CHAPTER THIRTY-SIX

*U*tu was consumed with excitement. They were nearly home to Kiriath Arba, and he would see Jemimah soon. He'd never been away from her for so long before, and he wasn't planning on ever being apart again. All he wanted was to taste her cooking and be in her arms again.

"Saba," yelled a voice.

Utu looked up. There he was! Shem, the youngest of his grandchildren, was up a tree and waving wildly. Utu waved back. He was home and Jemimah would be waiting for him. Shem was already scrambling down the tree. *Don't fall.*

Shem jumped nimbly to the ground and ran to find his grandmother. There was no need to worry, because Shem was as agile as his great-aunt had once been. Not that Inanna wasn't still agile. It hadn't been that long since he'd found her up her favorite tree. He'd opened his mouth to tell her to be careful, but Job had grinned.

"That's why I love her. You never know what she's going to do next."

Behind him, Rivka asked, "Who is that man in the field coming to meet us?"

Utu turned and shaded his eyes. "It is my master, Yitzchak."

Rivka got off her camel and veiled her face once again. She'd traveled unveiled during their journey unless they'd met strangers. Her beauty reminded him of Sara and how she must have looked in her younger days. Rivka would not be unveiled again until after the wedding.

Everyone dismounted from their camels and they walked together towards the camp.

Job came out to meet them, and Utu gladly handed Job the lead rope of his camel. The camels clustered around Job as he patted them and welcomed them each with a treat.

Shem threw his arms around Utu, and Utu breathed in the familiar scent of the fields and sheep his grandson loved to work with. Oh, it was good to be home.

"Come on, Saba," Shem said pulling him along.

Utu ruffled Shem's hair. "I need to look after our guests first. But run ahead and tell your grandmother we're back and I'll be there as soon as possible."

If Rivka hadn't been a stranger and a guest of honor, nothing would have stopped him dashing home and hugging Jemimah until she was breathless.

Avraham was waiting at the entrance to the main tent, and he bowed to Rivka. "Welcome home, daughter."

"Thank you, Abba. I am pleased to be here."

Utu had told Rivka much about her new home and family on the way. She'd shown a keen interest in everything he said and the lands they passed through. Best of all, there'd been no word of complaint from her although some of the attendants hadn't held back.

"Come and rest," Avraham said. He spoke to a woman Utu had never seen before, and she scurried towards the main tent.

Utu raised an eyebrow towards Eliezer.

"Later," Eliezer mouthed.

Utu waited until he was sure Rivka and her nurse and attendants were looked after before he headed home.

Jemimah was waiting at the entrance of their tent. She took his arm, and once inside he kissed her soundly.

She broke out of his embrace and wrinkled her nose. "You smell of camel."

He grinned. "What do you expect?"

"Come and get washed. Then your meal will be ready."

He hoped Yitzchak would be as happy with his Rivka as he'd been with Jemimah. Even if he was half as happy, Yitzchak could consider himself blessed.

After dinner, Utu sighed with contentment. "No one makes bread like you do, my dear."

She flushed with pleasure, and he kissed her nose and murmured against her lips. "What happened to Shem?"

"I encouraged him to go home and promised him I'd take him fishing in the morning."

Utu smiled. She thought of everything.

* * *

*I*n the morning, Jemimah lay in the crook of his arm, and he remembered his question from the night before.

"Who was the woman with Avraham?"

"Ah," Jemimah said. "That was Keturah, from the town. Avraham married her not long after you left."

"Married her?" Utu's voice rose. He'd assumed she was a new slave.

She nodded. "Maybe it was all the talk about finding a wife for Yitzchak. Anyway, she is married to him and settling in well."

What had Eliezer thought of the idea, or hadn't he been consulted?

"And what does Yitzchak think of his father's marriage?"

"We don't really know. He didn't say anything. He headed south for the Negev desert as soon as his father married, and only returned a few days ago."

Utu rubbed an itch on his nose. "He could have left to give them space, or simply because he wanted to stretch his wings and have some independence. Avraham might be one hundred and forty, but he's still very much the one in charge."

Jemimah murmured her agreement, and he kissed her on the

cheek. "I'm sorry my love, but I have to get up. There's a wedding to prepare for."

Jemimah clambered to her feet. Now their children were grown, Jemimah often worked with Inanna when extra hands were needed to prepare for guests.

* * *

*T*he beat of drums went right through Inanna's head. Her back and feet ached after the two days of wedding preparations. She'd been feeling stiff first thing in the morning lately, which wasn't surprising when she considered she was over seventy.

She missed her mother with a fierce longing. Once Sara had died, her mother had spent nearly all her time with her own grandchildren and great-grandchildren. They'd been sweet days. During the last weeks of Attar's life, she'd become so tender towards Inanna, giving many hugs and telling Inanna how much she loved her. Inanna blinked back tears.

Aging and death were a curse. The only person who never seemed to age was Avraham, and he'd seemed even younger since his marriage. Keturah might be an outsider, but she was eager to learn. She'd worked hard the first day of the wedding preparations, but they'd heard her retching on the second and told her to go and rest. It didn't seem possible at Avraham's age, but it looked as though Yitzchak was going to have another brother or sister.

Under Inanna's direction, the wedding feast had gone smoothly. Towards the end, Avraham had seen her exhaustion and asked her to come and sit with Eliezer, Utu, and their multiplying family. She'd gladly appointed a deputy and left the younger legs to do the actual work.

The drums were followed by a flute of some sort made out of a tough reed. It made a pleasant sound, and she relaxed to listen. Yitzchak and Rivka were talking quietly under the wedding canopy decorated with all sorts of greenery and flowers. Only Rivka's eyes could be seen, and it made the possibility of becoming friends hard work. She had seemed pleasant enough, but there was probably no point in making friends with her, because Yitzchak planned to leave after the wedding and move south to Beer Lahai Roi again.

Inanna chuckled under her breath. He probably didn't know the significance of the place. Beer Lahai Roi was the place Hagar had named "The One who sees me" when the heavenly messenger had found her running from Sara's ill-treatment. Had Avraham's god continued to see and care for Hagar? Was she even still alive? Inanna liked to think Yishmael would let her know if Hagar died, but there had been no news in all the intervening years. Nothing to say whether Yishmael or Hagar were alive, let alone prospering. The only thing that gave her comfort was that Avraham and Utu's god had promised blessing to Yishmael too. So far, much as she hated to admit it, El Shaddai had never failed to fulfill his promises.

The music ended, and Utu stood with Peleg to help Avraham to his feet. There was no unsteadiness once Avraham stood, but it was a long way up from the ground. She'd have to ask Job if he could make some sort of raised platform for Avraham to sit on. Job was clever with his hands. She sighed. Thinking of Job always made her feel sad and guilty. He would have made an excellent husband ... for someone else.

Avraham coughed and waited for everyone to stop talking. "Friends and honored guests, today is a special day of great joy." He swallowed. "Sara longed for this day and insisted we find Yitzchak a bride from among our relatives. We praise God that he has brought Rivka to us." He looked across all the guests. "Let me pray a prayer of blessing over them."

He gestured to Yitzchak and Rivka. Yitzchak assisted Rivka to her feet and they both knelt in front of Avraham. Avraham placed his right hand on Yitzchak's head and his left on Rivka's, and raised his voice. "Great and sovereign Lord. You who brought the stars into being by your command and provide all the good things we enjoy every day. We thank you for the fruit trees, vegetables, and abundant flocks and herds. Thank you that although your power is beyond imagining, you care for us. You have showered your blessing onto this family as you promised."

The poetry of the language swirled around Inanna. She was surrounded by these things and couldn't deny this god's power, but she did doubt his care. She'd never seen it for herself. And what about Hagar and Yishmael? They'd been cast out of this family through no fault of their own.

"... bless this union, and may Yitzchak and Rivka be the parents and grandparents of a multitude."

Typical man. Praying for a huge family but with no idea how much it drained a woman's body. No idea how much work it was to raise a large family. No idea how many sleepless nights and worries children caused. Jemimah had loved her brood of eight, but she'd lost others before birth and it had taken a toll. She might tell Inanna it had all been worth it, but Inanna was glad it hadn't been her lot in life.

CHAPTER THIRTY-SEVEN

Twenty-five years later
Beer Lahai Roi

"*G*ive that back," Yaakov yelled, rage mottling his face with fury. He pounded after Esaw with his five-year-old legs.

Inanna didn't know why he bothered. Esaw may only have been a few breaths older, but he was bigger and stronger and always won. And when he won, he trumpeted his victory with his ruddy head held high and his eyes flashing. There were right royal battles brewing for the future and it wasn't helped by their parents playing favorites. Yitzchak championed Esaw as Yitzchak himself had once been championed, and Rivka championed Yaakov.

Esaw had scrambled up onto a pile of rocks. "Can't get me. Can't get me," he chanted.

Yaakov vainly looked for a way to get up on the tall rock. His legs were a fraction too short, and Esaw knew it.

Yitzchak was off shearing the sheep, so Inanna scanned the area to check that Rivka was out of sight and couldn't interfere, then she walked over to the rock.

"Esaw, come down this instant. Yaakov, stop wailing. That's not the way to solve problems."

Esaw looked sullen, but he knew better than to disobey. Yaakov closed his mouth with a snap and switched to ingratiating mode. "Can you get my stick back for me, ple-ease?"

Inanna said nothing but held her hand out for the stick which Esaw reluctantly gave her.

"Thank you, boys. I will look after this stick for now."

Esaw winked at her, recognizing he'd lost, but Yaakov screwed his face up and wailed.

Rivka poked her head out of the main tent entrance. "Oh, there you are boys." She looked at Yaakov. "Why are you crying?" Yaakov ran towards her, knowing he'd get sympathy.

Inanna sighed. She much preferred hanging around with Utu and Jemimah's grandchildren, and the generation after that.

Rivka and Yitzchak had been married for twenty years before the arrival of the twins, and there'd been no pregnancies since. It was sometimes hard for parents to look past the value of a child to see their weaknesses and faults. Faults that needed to be trained out of them. Rivka had told her that the babies had jostled in her womb, and she'd cried out to the Lord asking what was happening. He'd told her, "Two nations are in your womb, and two peoples from within you will be separated, one people will be stronger than the other and the older will serve the younger."

Maybe that was the reason for Rivka's preference for Yaakov, but the way things were going wasn't healthy. Avraham seemed aware of the problems with his grandsons, but he was too old to have the energy to curb such wild spirits. Their recent move to Beer Lahai-Roi to join Yitzchak had made sense in some ways but created problems in others.

* * *

*I*nanna stood next to her brother and pretended not to watch the scene before them. Not that the scene could be ignored by anyone within earshot. Donkeys brayed in excitement and several flocks of sheep milled around. Shepherds waved their arms as they struggled to keep them separate.

Avraham was probably giving last-minute instructions to the oldest three of his and Keturah's sons before they set off to the east to establish their own families. Poor Keturah was weeping. Inanna's heart clenched with pity. This was Hagar and Yishmael all over again. Once again, children were being sent away so Yitzchak could take all the sunlight in the oak grove. Poor Keturah would eventually have to go through this again with her three younger children. Keturah had fought Avraham to wait until the second and third sons were older so the first three could leave at the same time, and he'd given in.

Inanna turned to Utu. "Why is it that women always have to pay the price?"

He was silent. Was it because he didn't know the answer or because he didn't understand her pain? Instead, he tucked her arm in his. Just having him there made her world a little less stark. He'd been an excellent father and grandfather, and Jemimah reported he was an excellent husband as well. Inanna was proud of him, and she was equally proud of Utu's children, grandchildren, and great-grandchildren. Their mother and Eliezer, who'd died during the last olive harvest, would have beamed with pleasure to see the ever-expanding family.

Above the cacophony came the indignant rumbling of camels. She turned her head to see Job leading the camels. No, he wouldn't, would he? Chest tight and her heart pounding, Inanna turned towards Utu.

"Don't look at me like that, Inanna. Go and ask him what he's doing."

Inanna broke away from her brother and headed down the path towards the camels. Avraham had called for volunteers to leave his household and go with his sons to wherever they ended up. Many of the younger shepherds and servants had been enthusiastic, but surely Job wouldn't leave. The urgency of her panic was unsettling.

She wove her way around the milling sheep and kept an eye on the ground to avoid stepping in the dung scattered everywhere.

"Whoa," Job said as he came around one of the camels. "Where are you going in such a hurry?"

"You're not going, are you?" Inanna said with an embarrassing quaver in her voice. "You love your camels, and these are some of your best."

"I didn't think you paid any attention to camels."

"Well, I know you hand-reared that one with the star when its mother died, and that one there with the brown blotch on its face."

"I'm impressed," he said with a grin.

"I don't have to like them to notice them," she snapped. "And you haven't answered my question."

"I'm not sure I remember the question."

"There's nothing wrong with your memory. You're just being irritating. I asked you if you were going with them."

"What do you mean, going?"

He was teasing her. Already she regretted embarrassing herself.

"Of course I'm not going," he said. "I'm too old for traveling." His expression turned serious. "Besides which, everything I love is right here."

"But you love your camels."

He cocked an eyebrow. "There are many kinds of love, and I can differentiate between the importance of animals and people. People win every time. My place is here."

She smiled tremulously. She'd made a fool of herself. She should have known Job would never leave Utu and Jemimah and their family. Without a family of his own, he'd become a general favorite among all the generations. Always ready to listen. Always ready to offer wise advice. Always ready to pray for someone. She didn't know when he'd committed his life to El Shaddai, but Utu said it was some time before he had. Yet another person journeying away from her. Journeying where she could not follow.

CHAPTER THIRTY-EIGHT

Ten years later
Kiriath Arba

"*U*tu—" Avraham coughed, leaning over as the cough rattled through his body.

Utu moved over next to where Avraham lay.

"Utu." Avraham clutched his arm. "Please send messengers to search for Yishmael."

Avraham had been sick for days, and he wasn't bouncing back as he had in the past. Not surprising for a man who was 175. Utu had seen Avraham's deterioration and had already discussed with Peleg how they'd go about finding Yishmael. Utu was almost certain he'd be somewhere to the south in the Negev region or its borders, maybe even towards Egypt.

"They'll leave tomorrow."

"Good man." Avraham fell back to his position on his side. "Hope you aren't planning to go." He coughed again, drawing up his legs.

Utu waited until Avraham had caught his breath. "I'm too old for gallivanting around. I'll send some of my grandsons."

"Eliezer did a wonderful thing when he apprenticed you."

Utu's throat narrowed and he blinked. Eliezer's death had hit him hard, but the man he'd long considered his father had been happy to go. Eliezer had been doubled over with pain and unable to speak for the last months of his life. Watching him deteriorate had been heart-wrenching, but they'd looked after him as best they could. They'd all been around him holding his hands when he slipped away with a smile on his lips.

Soon it would be his and Jemimah's turn. As his body stiffened and began to fail him, he found himself beginning to look forward to the new adventures he and Jemimah had become more and more convinced awaited them on the other side of death. But he didn't want to leave this earth until he'd seen Inanna choose to follow El Shaddai.

"I'll return once all the preparations are made," Utu said. "Meanwhile, here are Keturah and Inanna with your food."

"Not sure I'd call it food," Avraham muttered.

He only had a few teeth left in his mouth and all he could manage were soups, porridges, or bread soaked in milk. Inanna did her best to make it interesting by adding herbs and the wild honey which two of Utu's great-grandsons were skilled at collecting.

* * *

*U*tu had positioned a watchman to alert him as soon as the messengers returned. Already four pairs had returned but one pair had sent messages saying they were headed further south, towards the Desert of Paran. They had found people who had seen Yishmael further south.

Avraham was no worse, but he wasn't better either. Yitzchak had moved back into the area while his father needed him and visited twice a day. Yaakov also spent much time with his grandfather. He said it was because he wanted to learn Avraham's story, but Utu suspected it was an excuse to escape work. Yaakov was much more of a home-body than his brother. Esaw loved nothing better than to go out hunting with the older men. Inanna predicted that there'd be trouble between them in the not too distant future.

One of Utu's great-grandsons came running towards him. "Dust on the horizon," he panted.

Utu handed him a water bag and let him take a mouthful. "Do you think they are coming this way?"

He nodded. "And the watchman said it's a big group."

They were prepared for a group. Yishmael, if he was still alive, wouldn't come alone. They'd already erected a complex of tents and made space for twenty if needed. Utu would alert the cooks.

He set off to find Inanna. She was outside Avraham's tent, under a shady tree, stirring something over the fire.

"Someone's coming."

Inanna looked up at him, eyes shining. "Do you think it might be Yishmael?"

"Patience, sister, patience. We'll know soon enough."

She smiled wryly. "You know patience has never been one of my strengths."

He hoped she wasn't going to be disappointed, but Yishmael would be an old man himself now.

He left her stirring Avraham's meal and walked to the lookout post. The dust was much closer, and the figures within were now visible. One of the figures raised his hand in greeting.

Soon after, the camels and their riders approached. The leading rider commanded his heavily ornamented camel to kneel, and he slid to the ground. The man was wiry, and his face was creased like desert canyons.

"Yishmael?" Utu asked.

"Not the little runt I once was, eh Utu?" the man laughed.

"I see you still love your bow." Utu pointed. The bow and the air of command had alerted him to Yishmael's identity. That, and Avraham's eyes. Eyes that were constantly alert and ready for action.

"Don't go anywhere without it."

"Welcome," Utu said. "We've prepared a tent and food for you."

"First, I will take the camels down to the water and have a good swim. I don't want to appear at a disadvantage to my little brother. He is still around, I presume?"

"He is," Utu said. The meeting would be an interesting. Yitzchak had only been a small child when Yishmael had left.

* * *

"*A*unt Inanna." Yishmael bowed.

"Don't go all formal on me," she said, standing on tiptoes to kiss him warmly on both cheeks. "It is wonderful to see you."

"And it's wonderful for me too." Ishmael held her away from himself and looked at her. "You have aged better than I have. There is much to talk about, but first I must see my father."

"He has been waiting eagerly for you."

Inanna led him to the entrance of Avraham's tent. "He's weak, but still able to talk."

"Is that Yishmael?" A quavering voice called. "Is that my son?"

Yishmael squared his shoulders, placed his sandals next to his bow, and smoothed down his beard and hair before going into the inner room.

He crossed the room in two strides and dropped to his knees next to Avraham. "Abba."

"My son," Avraham's voice cracked. "Oh, my son."

He struggled to sit.

Inanna moved forward. "Yishmael, help me get these pillows behind him."

Together they positioned Avraham as comfortably as possible. He stared at Yishmael as though trying to memorize every wrinkle and gray hair. Yishmael was dressed in supple leather with metal bands around his arms. He looked fit and battle ready. She drew in a quick breath. He'd always had a quick temper. Perhaps battle had been a big part of his life.

"Thank you for coming," Avraham said.

"Of course," Yishmael said, looking uncomfortable.

Would he have come earlier if they'd asked him? This man she'd known as a boy was now a stranger. They didn't know anything about him except that he was a skillful hunter. Was he still an outsider striving to prove himself? Or had he found peace?

"Did your mother come with you?"

Yishmael shook his head. "She's too old to travel. Soon she will depart this earth."

Tears pricked Inanna's eyes. It hurt to know they would never meet again. Jemimah was now a good friend, but Inanna had connected deeply with Hagar. They had both been outsiders. Inanna wiped her eyes. She would send a message back with Yishmael.

"And your family?" Avraham asked.

Yishmael straightened. "I have twelve sons." He indicated over his shoulder. "I brought them as they all wanted to meet their grandfather."

Avraham laughed, then began to cough. Inanna darted forward as the coughs shook Avraham's whole body. "Sometimes it helps to lie him on his side."

They positioned him together. Once he was comfortable, she moistened his mouth with honey water. Avraham smiled his thanks but hadn't the strength to speak. He closed his eyes and drifted off to sleep. Once he was snoring, they got to their feet and left the tent.

"It won't be long now. He's been holding on for your arrival." She took his arm. "Come and introduce me to your sons."

* * *

*I*nanna sat quietly in the corner. Avraham's labored breaths filled the tent. He'd been drifting in and out of sleep since Yishmael arrived. He'd woken for long enough to meet Yishmael's twelve sons, but they were now out hunting with Esaw and some of her nephews.

Avraham had surprised her by insisting that she be here with Utu, Yitzchak, and Yishmael. She'd want the same when her time came. To be surrounded by the people she'd known the longest, Utu and Jemimah. And Job. She would not forget Job. He'd remained a friend. Whenever she had need, he'd appear at her elbow.

Avraham opened his eyes and squinted to focus on their faces. "Ah, you are here. Good."

He hesitated as though to sort out which of the things on his mind to say first.

He looked first at Yishmael. "I am sorry your mother cannot be here. I would have liked to apologize again for the wrongs she suffered."

Yishmael knelt down next to his father. "She forgave those things long ago."

If she had, then she was a better woman than Inanna. The burn of bitterness still filled Inanna's gut when she thought of Hagar and Yishmael.

"She was a fine woman, your mother," Avraham murmured. "A fine woman." He gripped Yishmael's hand. "And you. You I wronged also."

"Mother helped me work through my anger," Yishmael said.

"But I caused that anger, and for that I am sorry," Avraham said, wheezing.

Yishmael leaned down and kissed his father on the forehead and each cheek. "All things are right between us. El Shaddai has blessed me too, as he promised. My sons are already the leaders of twelve clans who must spread out because the land cannot support all our people and their flocks and herds."

Pride welled up in Inanna's heart. The young boy she'd known had railed against the injustices done to him. Some must still rankle, but he was choosing to let his father depart in peace.

Yishmael drew back from the bed.

"Come closer, all of you," Avraham said,

They clustered around where he lay, kneeling or sitting so they did not loom over him. This close, even his skin smelled musty.

"Utu, do you remember the flaming fire pot?"

Utu had told her he would never forget it.

"When God made his covenant with you?" Utu said.

"You did not hear everything God said." Avraham took several raspy breaths. "I did not want to tell you the details sooner, because it concerned your people, and you were still young."

"I left my people long ago. Your people have become my people."

Avraham smiled. "Yes, you have been faithful … like Eliezer." Avraham pointed to his mouth, and Inanna gave him a few sips of the water she had ready to hand.

"The Lord said to me that I would not receive this land of the Lord's promise during my lifetime, because the sins of the Amorites had not yet reached their full measure."

In that case, Sodom and Gomorrah's sins must have reached the limit, because they'd been wiped out. Jemimah reported that Utu still sometimes woke up shouting in terror when he dreamed of what he'd seen.

"And Yitzchak," Avraham said, turning his head to look to the other side. "Your children will not own the land either, for God told me our descendants will be strangers and slaves in a country not their own."

"Abba, there is no need to speak of these things," Yitzchak said, leaning forward. "Don't tire yourself."

"I will soon have more than enough time to rest," Avraham said. "The Lord said he will punish the nation our descendants serve, and that I would be buried at a good old age and die in peace." He gave a toothless grin. "And as you can see, I've reached a good age. Not as good as my father, but still good …"

His eyelids drooped and he slid into sleep.

"He keeps doing that," Inanna whispered. "He'll wake up again soon."

* * *

Someone was shaking her. Inanna pushed the hand away and then sat up, rubbing her eyes. The morning bird chorus was just warming up. "Yitzchak, are you alright?"

He'd insisted on staying with his father overnight.

"He's gone," Yitzchak said, dropping down to sit on the carpet. "Not long ago."

Although she'd expected it, a feeling of great tiredness swept over her. Serving this family had been her life's work. What would she do now? Keturah and the new concubines weren't likely to stay around. They'd never felt part of the family, so Keturah would go to live with her sons. And Rivka had younger women to help her.

He yawned. "I fell asleep and couldn't work out what woke me, but it was the quietness. Abba had stopped breathing."

Together they went over to Avraham and gently covered him with the sheep's wool covering.

"Last night, when Rivka was here, he urged us to follow El Shaddai. To never give up pursuing him."

Inanna looked away from the intensity of his gaze. If she'd been there, would Avraham have urged her to trust his god? Probably. He'd been urging quite a few people in the last few days, including Keturah. Keturah had been heartbroken when Avraham had sent off each of her six sons. Each had received an inheritance, but Keturah thought it unfair that Yitzchak's rights trumped every other son's right to live with the family.

Every time Inanna thought about Keturah and Hagar, anger welled up from somewhere deep inside her. Yet Yishmael said Hagar had forgiven Avraham and Sara. Where had she found the strength?

CHAPTER THIRTY-NINE

$\mathcal{W}$hen Avraham had first been sick, he'd begged them to return from the south to the oaks of Mamre. He'd said he wanted to die near Sara and in the place that felt most like home. Most of the household had stayed at Beer Lahai Roi, which Yitzchak had claimed as his home area, but the family and Avraham's closest servants had traveled back to the oaks.

It had comforted Avraham to know his body would soon rest beside Sara's in the one piece of land he owned, the field and cave he'd bought from Ephron the Hittite.

Inanna had washed, bound, and dressed Avraham's body with Rivka and Keturah. Now Yitzchak, Yishmael, Yaakov, Esaw, and two of Yishmael's sons bore the body on a richly woven carpet towards the cave. They walked in a silence only broken by the rattle of the weapons Yishmael's family wore. Yitzchak had objected, but Yishmael said it was their way to honor such a great man and Yishmael had won. Inanna smiled grimly. Yishmael was due a win or two.

As the procession passed the gates of Kiriath Arba, the walls of the town were lined with people who bowed their heads as they passed. Inanna's breath caught in her throat, and she took Jemimah's hand.

Job and Utu walked close by. Job walked with the aid of a hefty stick after a fall from one of his beloved camels.

Canaanite funerals were noisy affairs of much wailing and cutting of flesh, but Avraham had been clear he did not want such scenes. She had never experienced a silence like this, but it suited the man. Dignified. Instead of being a threat, Avraham had made friends with all those who could so easily have been his enemies. This was a silence to honor a man they respected.

She hadn't always understood or agreed with Avraham's choices, but she had come to respect him as someone who had followed his god as well as he knew how. When he made the wrong decisions, he had a heart big enough to recognize his faults and learned to apologize. Only great men had that kind of courage.

They crossed the field of Machpelah and approached the cave. With a wave of his arm, Yishmael summoned two of his sons, who came forward and put their brawny shoulders to the rock across the cave mouth. When it didn't move, they found some branches, dug the debris away from the bottom of the rock, and prepared a channel for it to roll along.

They put the branches down, pushed again, and this time the rock rumbled aside, leaving a gap wide enough for the burial party to pass through.

Yishmael and his sons emerged quickly, as did Esaw. Esaw had far more in common with his cousins than his father and brother, and he had stayed close to his cousins from the moment they met.

Finally Yaakov and Yitzchak emerged. Yitzchak was pale, with tears on his cheeks. All the responsibilities that had been on Avraham's shoulders were now on his. He would have to learn who to trust and how to reconcile his fifteen-year-old sons.

Yishmael's sons pushed the stone at the tomb entrance, and it dropped into place with a thump of finality.

* * *

I thought I'd find you here, Aunt Inanna," Yishmael said. "You always loved this grove of trees."

Inanna placed her hand on the trunk of the nearest tree. "They comfort me. They were here before I was born, and they'll be here long after."

"I still climb trees," Yishmael said. "You taught me that. A sturdy branch is the best place to think or watch for desert creatures." He sat on an exposed root and patted it. "Sit with me. Mother wanted me to talk to you."

She'd hoped Hagar had sent a message, but it had not been appropriate to ask while Avraham was so sick. She found a less knobbly root and sat.

"We will leave at first light tomorrow, but Mother would never forgive me if I didn't say all she wanted me to."

Inanna laughed. "She always was feisty."

"Which is why you got along so well," Yishmael said with a wink. "Now let me remember what she wanted me to say." He leaned back against the trunk of the tree and stared through the branches to the blue sky above.

"First, she wanted to tell you she has never forgotten your kindness and she has prayed for you every day."

Inanna squeezed her eyes shut. She hadn't been as faithful in remembering her friend. Not that she would have prayed, but she understood that Hagar considered prayer as a way to care. She'd known Utu and Jemimah prayed for her every day and now Hagar. It put her under pressure. She didn't want to follow El Shaddai to please the people who loved her. If she was to follow El Shaddai, it must be because she fully trusted this god, with nothing held back. If he was who they said he was, he deserved that.

"Mama wanted me to tell you what happened after we left here. She said you'd remember the story of how God sent his messenger to her at Beer Lahai Roi."

Inanna nodded.

"Abba sent us off with some supplies and even some gold. The journey was easy at first—there was plenty of water and food we could forage along the way." He shook his head. "But then we wandered into the desert of Beersheba. It was a particularly dry year and soon our water bag was close to empty." He looked across at Inanna. "Of course Mama denied herself so I could drink, but eventually there was nothing left."

She imagined the desert. Endless pale sand and pebbles. Unending, burning heat during the day, and bone-chilling cold at night. She shivered. She'd had recurring nightmares of Hagar and Yishmael's bones being picked by vultures and lying bleached in the sun. She reached out her hand and touched his arm, reassuringly warm and solid.

"She told me later that she couldn't bear to watch me die, so she put me under some thorn bushes and went a bowshot away to sit with her back towards me and wept."

"This is what I feared had happened all these years, but you obviously survived."

"The Lord sent his angel."

Inanna's skin prickled and her heart raced. Another angel. Another proof that El Shaddai was watching out for Hagar.

"The angel said, 'What's the matter, Hagar? Don't be afraid. God has heard the boy crying as he lies there. Lift the boy up and take him by the hand, for I will make him into a great nation.'"

Inanna leaned towards him, eyes wide. "Did you hear the voice too?"

"I don't remember any voice. Maybe I was already unconscious, but I remember Mama coming and raising my head, and I remember that we both heard the trickle of water at the same time."

"How had you missed that before?"

"Oh, I don't think we missed it. I'm sure it wasn't there."

"Do you mean—?"

"I mean that God brought water out of the ground just when we needed it and saved our lives."

Inanna stood and walked forward a few paces, staring between the trees back towards the camp. The hairs on her arms stood up, and she hugged her arms around herself. Who was this god who opened up the earth to save two people? Two people others despised. A god who cared for the slaves and the unloved.

She turned back to where Yishmael was still sitting under the tree.

"Mama always said she could never reject such a God. Twice he had rescued her, but it wasn't the miracles that touched her most."

Inanna returned to her seat. "What touched her?"

"He called her by name." Yishmael's voice shook with emotion. "Both times the Lord's messengers called her by name."

Tears stung Inanna's eyes. To call someone by name was to acknowledge that they were important. That they were human, and not merely a slave at everyone's beck and call.

"And it wasn't just the messengers using her name, but the way they said it. They spoke as if she was the most important person in the whole world. As if they knew her and loved her."

And to a woman who'd been used for others' purposes and married off against her will, that would touch her innermost being. It touched Inanna, and she was only hearing the story.

"That's why Mama didn't hold a grudge against Avraham or even Sara. Knowing God sees her and cares for her erases everything else."

Erases everything else. Inanna turned the words over in her mind. Erased like snake tracks in the sand obliterated by a gust of wind.

"She said she can't hold a grudge when she has seen that God's plans always prevail."

And that was something Inanna couldn't deny. When they were in the midst of events, things were messy, similar to the underside of a carpet. But looking back, this god's plans had been revealed like the stunning design on the front of the carpet. Over and over, this god had protected them. He'd protected Hagar from dying of thirst. He'd protected Sara from Pharaoh, from Abimelech, and even from the mess of her own schemes. He'd protected Avraham from all the dangers that had threatened them in Canaan. And he had protected Utu and herself when they'd come into Avraham's household. How had she missed this truth for so long?

There was much to ponder, but first she had to fulfill a promise.

"Yishmael, on Sara's deathbed she made me promise to tell you and your mother how sorry she was." Inanna returned to the moment in her thoughts. "She said she was sorry for all the pain she caused. And she admitted she was the one at fault."

Yishmael swallowed. "Even though Mama forgave Sara, she will be pleased to hear these words." He turned to Inanna and looked her in the eyes. "Mama prays you will not only come to know the Lord's power but also to trust his goodness."

And that was the burr under her saddle. She'd used Hagar's misfortunes as an excuse to not trust this god, but what excuses did she have now? Avraham's god had seen Hagar and raised her up and kept all his promises to her. Hagar trusted god with her whole heart. After all these years, could Inanna do the same?

CHAPTER FORTY

*I*nanna watched Yishmael leave the oak grove. In the morning he'd be gone, breaking her final link with Hagar. He wouldn't be returning. Yitzchak had shown little interest in his older brother, and maybe Yishmael being older was the problem. An older brother was a threat. If Yishmael was around, people would always be asking why Yitzchak was the heir, not the outgoing older brother who could fight and hunt and charm those around him.

The new spring leaves rustled above Inanna's head. She looked longingly up at the tree, but there was no way she could reach the lowest branch anymore. Even if she could have climbed into its branches and dreamed of flying with the eagles, she was just as likely to fall to earth with a thump. Her body was no longer lithe, and her arms would not hold her up if she slipped.

She put her arms around the tree and rested her head against the trunk. The bark was rough against her cheek. She'd spent her whole life longing to be free. To be free from her mother's ideas of what was appropriate for her only daughter. To be free from being a slave and subject to others' wishes and commands. To be free to make her own decisions, in her own way. But each time freedom seemed within her grasp, she had discovered it was as if she'd been trying to grab water. Once she opened her hand, there was nothing there.

And even when she gained her freedom from slavery, this longed-for liberty had turned to dust. What if freedom wasn't the golden treasure she'd imagined? Or what if she'd always been trying to find the wrong sort of freedom?

Those in her life who had seemed to have the most freedom hadn't necessarily been free. They'd seemed to be, and she had envied them. Her father and elder brothers had seemed to have freedom, because they were men in a men's world and ruled by the strength of their hands, but they'd still been bound by responsibilities, traditions, and expectations.

Avraham and Sara had been blessed with wealth in every area but the one they most wanted. They'd struggled to trust El Shaddai in that one area and bound themselves in tangles of their own making.

Inanna sagged against the tree. She was tired. Tired of struggling to be free. Tired of bursting through into what she thought was freedom, only to discover she was still bound. Yet, Utu and Jemimah, Eliezer and Job, and even Hagar were free. Free in ways she'd never experienced. Maybe she'd been running away from the very thing she most needed.

No, not a thing. A being. She'd rejected El Shaddai because she didn't trust him. Had she allowed her warped ideas about freedom to keep her from the very one who gave freedom?

El Shaddai had given freedom to Eliezer, who'd been burdened with grief and could see no light. El Shaddai had brought life and hope. El Shaddai had brought Avraham and Sara from beyond the great river and given abundant blessing and purpose to their lives. And El Shaddai had brought blessing to so many of the lives around her as well.

But it was Hagar's story that spoke most clearly to her. A story she couldn't escape. Jehovah Jireh, the provider, had given status and love to an Egyptian slave. Best of all, he'd given her the strength to forgive and to keep living in light of that choice. God had even changed Avraham and helped him see his faults.

Inanna had clung to the injustice done to Hagar, using it as a barrier between her and El Shaddai. Using it as her excuse not to trust. But the barrier had always been dust and now it had blown away.

It was time, more than time, to talk to the one she'd run from for so long.

She lowered herself stiffly to her knees and bowed her head. It seemed an appropriate posture. "Creator God, you who made all things ..." Inside she still sensed her desire to flee. She struggled against her desire to have freedom on her own terms, her pride, her self-sufficiency. But what had her pride and self-sufficiency ever achieved?

She plowed on with her prayer. "Forgive me for my stubborn pride and my continual running. I have not trusted you because I have not wanted to trust you. Yet when I look back, you have shown your trustworthiness over and over to our whole family. You brought me and Utu into this family. You reunited us with our dear mother. You've given me opportunity after opportunity to hear of your great-ness and love. Thank you for the faithfulness of Utu and Jemimah and Hagar and Job, and Mama and Eliezer as well."

She pictured each of them in her mind. Each one, precious and faithfully following this God. Even when she'd rejected El Shaddai, deep down she'd envied them for their quiet confidence. The confi-dence and gratitude that came from the God in whom they trusted.

"Thank you that they have never stopped praying and hoping. They have shown me your heart which longs for us, your creatures. Thank you. Thank you for the beauty of this world you have made for us to enjoy, and thank you that you want to be my Jehovah Jireh, my provider. Please help me to trust you from this day forward, all the way until you take me through the gateway of death into whatever you have prepared beyond."

She rested her head on the tree and listened to the sounds around her: a bird singing from a high branch; the creak of the branches; the breeze ruffling the grasses between the trees. Sounds she'd heard all her life. Sounds she'd loved, but never allowed to drive her praise to their Creator. "Thank you, Creator of all."

Far above, she heard the calls of the eagles. They'd be soaring up above where she'd always longed to join them. She laughed. They belonged in the heavens, but she belonged right here. Right here where she'd been born. Right here where she'd found the peace of true freedom at last.

She lingered, smelling the scent of the dry grass and the damp earth, and reveling in the freedom she'd yearned for for so long. Freedom that could have been hers years ago. Freedom that would have made her free, even while she was a slave.

Using her hands, she clambered upright. She'd better hurry. She had another message for Hagar. The sort of message Hagar would greet with joy. They might never see each other again on this earth, but she'd hold onto hope that they might meet again one day if Avraham had been right about the afterlife.

Utu and Jemimah would be excited too, but first she was going to tell Job. He'd once said his heart was not free, that he was bound to her. Could two old people adapt to each other? She laughed out loud at the thought. She'd always loved adventures, and it looked like there were still more to come.

Adventures El Shaddai had known about and planned from all eternity.

ENJOYED WELLS AND WANDERERS?

One of the best ways readers can thank authors is to write a review.

This book is independently published which means the only way it will be discovered is if readers tell others. Online reviews are a concrete way of doing this.

How to write a review – easy as 1-2-3

1. A few sentences about why you liked the book or what kind of readers might enjoy this book. Even one word turns a mere star rating into a review.
2. Upload your review - the same review can be copied and pasted to each site. https://www.storytellerchristine.com/blog/reviews-the-how-and-where/ tells you where and how, for the priority sites.
3. If you loved the book please also share your review on social media. Anywhere you can spread the word is appreciated.

A book can never have too many reviews.

HISTORICAL NOTES

The first stage in the research for this novel was to read and reread Genesis 11-25. I took extensive notes and was left with many questions. One big question was why Avraham settled temporarily and later returned to the 'oaks of Mamre' outside Kiriath Arba? When I did some research on the Amorites, there was the suggestion that the Amorites might have originally come from the region of Ur. Thus, the reason may have been as simple as that they spoke a similar language and/or felt culturally similar to Avraham. Of course, it might also have been that Mamre and Avraham got along or that Mamre was the first to make Avraham feel welcome and so he stayed in the area.

Names of the characters

One of the difficulties about writing a story where many of the incidents are well known is figuring out how to make the story fresh. I decided to call the biblical characters by less familiar names to make us enter their world with new eyes. I consulted several places for how to better anglicize the Old Testament names.

Names of God

You might have noticed that I used both capitals and non-capitals when referring to God. If it is written as 'god' then the character is not a believer (yet).

This was easy for some characters but harder for others. For example, when did Sara come to trust God for herself? There is no mention in the Bible of her having personal experiences of God (unlike Hagar who saw an angel twice). Sara also went through several traumatic experiences due to her husband's fear of death, and also faced years of shame for not producing children. I have therefore changed to a capital at the birth of Yitzchak.

Yishmael too was hard as the Bible does not make it clear if he was a follower of El Shaddai. I do hope to meet him one day as I hope to meet all those with whom Avraham had contact.

STORYTELLER FRIENDS

Becoming a **storyteller friend** (https://subscribe. storytellerchristine.com/) will ensure you don't miss out on new books, deals, and behind the scenes book news. Once you're signed up, check your junk mail or the promotions folder (gmail addresses) for the confirmation email. This two-stage process ensures only true friends can join.

Facebook: As well as a public author page, I also have a VIP group (https://www.facebook.com/groups/242910632748639) which you need to ask permission to join.

BookBub - allows you to see my top book recommendations and be alerted to any new releases and special deals. It is free to join.

DISCUSSION QUESTIONS

- Who is your favourite character? Why?
- What were significant steps in their spiritual journeys?
- What were significant barriers?
- Why might it have been harder for Inanna to trust God than Utu?
- Did you learn any new things about the biblical stories? Or ancient cultures?
- Would you have found it easy to live in those times? Why or why not?
- How much did Avraham actually know about God? What did Avraham know about God's character?
- What were God's purposes for Avraham? (Genesis 12:1-3)
- When and why did Avraham fail?
- How did God work through Avraham's failures?
- What were Sara's failures?
- What were Hagar's failures?
- Which of the biblical characters do you relate to most? Why?
- Which people did Avraham have the opportunity to introduce to the Creator?

- Who might those people have influenced?
- Why might God have allowed Avraham to wander?
- How did this story encourage or inspire you?

Please feel free to write your own discussion questions. I would love to see them and am happy to include them for others if you give permission.

FICTION BY CHRISTINE DILLON

Prior to writing Biblical-era fiction, I wrote a 6-book contemporary Australian set of novels.

I prefer you to buy the ebooks/audio directly from my online store (https://payhip.com/ChristineDillon#). It uses PayPal or Stripe (Visa/Mastercard).

Book 1 is also available in Dutch.

Of course the books are available from a wide range of other stores.

The *Light of Nations* series will likely be at least nine books. The best way to hear about upcoming books is to subscribe and become a storyteller friend.

ACKNOWLEDGMENTS

In 2004, I began a journey that would profoundly influence my life and work. I was introduced to Bible storytelling. I had no idea that I'd soon tell many stories each week and regularly train others. When God first gave me the ideas for the novel that became *Grace in Strange Disguise,* I wrote two practice novels based on biblical characters. As my stand-alone contemporary novel turned into a series of six, I began to think about a series of biblical-era fiction. I knew I wanted to concentrate on the *Light of Nations* idea. That is, God reaching out to the nations, not just the Israelites. It started as another six-book series but is likely to become a nine-book series because one of my readers requested a book on the Gibeonites (Joshua 9-10) and it is best to write in multiples of three.

Launching out into a new genre is never easy and a lot of research is necessary. It is really spiritually stimulating to write biblical-era fiction. Special thanks to two Old Testament lecturers, Dr Janson Condren and Dr Geoff Harper at *Sydney Missionary and Bible College* who read the manuscript and freely shared their expertise. Thanks also to Sarah P who brought her expertise to the story too.

Thank you to the other early readers: Claire U., Laura T., Lizzie R., Kate B., and Julie I. Your comments always push me to write better books.

Thank you also to my proofreading team: Elizabeth W., Lizzie R., Stephanie M., Suzanne R., Kim W., and Anne M. You've done well managing a switch from Australian grammar and punctuation to U.S. conventions.

I continue to be blessed by Iola Goulton's editing and Joy Lankshear's cover design. Designing the first cover in a series is always the hardest, because it will be the template for all the following books.

Thank you too to friends and family who have to cope with me partially existing in a long-ago time and place. It can sometimes be hard to switch back and forth.

And thank you to you, my readers. Your words of encouragement through emails, messages, and online reviews, keep me going through the tough parts of the process. A special thank you to those who pray for this part of my ministry. I am not a full-time author (no where near it) and your prayers help me juggle the different parts of my life. Thank you for letting me know you're praying.

NON-FICTION BY CHRISTINE DILLON

1-2-1 Discipleship: Helping One Another Grow Spiritually (Christian Focus, Ross-shire, Scotland, 2009).

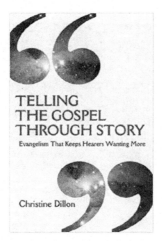

Telling the Gospel Through Story: Evangelism That Keeps Hearers Wanting More (IVP, Downer's Grove, Illinois, 2012).

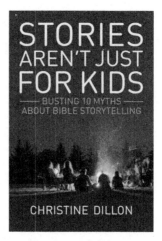

Stories Aren't Just For Kids: Busting 10 Myths About Bible Storytelling
(2017).

This book is free for subscribers (http://subscribe.storytellerchristine.com/). It's a 'taster' book and includes many testimonies to get you excited about the potential of Bible storying. All these books have also been translated into Chinese.

Sword Fighting: Applying God's word to win the battle for our mind
(July, 2020).

This book is also now available in German under the title: *Siegreich Sein: mit Gottes Wort.*

ABOUT THE AUTHOR

Christine writes both fiction and non-fiction. Her non-fiction concentrates in the areas of evangelism, discipleship, and spiritual growth/warfare.

Christine worked in Taiwan, with OMF International, from 1999 to 2021 and is now based out of Australia.

It's best not to ask Christine, "Where are you from?" She's a missionary kid who isn't sure if she should say her passport country (Australia) or her Dad's country (New Zealand) or where she's spent most of her life (Asia - Taiwan, Malaysia and the Philippines).

Christine used to be a physiotherapist, but now writes 'storyteller' on airport forms. She spends most of her time either telling Bible stories or training others to do so.

In her spare time, Christine loves all things active – hiking, cycling, swimming, snorkelling. But she also likes reading and genealogical research.

Connect with Christine
www.storytellerchristine.com/

facebook.com/storytellerchristine
pinterest.com/storytellerchristine

Printed in Great Britain
by Amazon

55764118R00155